8th
confession

Also by James Patterson

For more information about James Patterson's novels, visit
www.jamespatterson.co.uk

8th confession

James Patterson

WITH MAXINE PAETRO

Century · London

Published by Century 2009

2 4 6 8 10 9 7 5 3 1

Copyright © James Patterson 2009

James Patterson has asserted his right under the Copyright, Designs
and Patents Act 1988 to be identified as the author of this work

First published in Great Britain in 2009 by
Century
Random House, 20 Vauxhall Bridge Road,
London SW1V 2SA

www.randomhouse.co.uk

Addresses for companies within The Random House Group Limited can be found at:
www.randomhouse.co.uk/offices.htm

The Random House Group Limited Reg. No. 954009

A CIP catalogue record for this book
is available from the British Library

HB ISBN 9781846052583
TPB ISBN 9781846052590

The Random House Group Limited supports The Forest Stewardship
Council (FSC), the leading international forest certification organisation. All our
titles that are printed on Greenpeace approved FSC certified paper carry the FSC logo.
Our paper procurement policy can be found at
www.rbooks.co.uk/environment

Mixed Sources
Product group from well-managed
forests and other controlled sources
www.fsc.org   Cert no. TT-COC-2139
© 1996 Forest Stewardship Council
FSC

Printed and bound in Great Britain by
Clays Ltd, St Ives Plc

To Suzie and Jack
And to John, Brendan, and Alex

Acknowledgments

OUR GREAT THANKS to these top professionals who shared with us their valuable time and expertise during the writing of this book: Captain Richard Conklin, Dr. Humphrey Germaniuk, Chuck Hanni, Mickey Sherman, Philip R. Hoffman, Dr. Michelle Koo, Dr. Maria Paige, Tim Hettrich, and Rebecca DiLiberto.

Our special thanks to Maryellen Dankenbrink for her bus rap, to Chris Cooper, to Narayan Radhakrishnan, and to two first-class team players, Lynn Colomello and Mary Jordan.

Prologue

BUS STOP

One

THE OLD CHROME-YELLOW school bus crawled south on Market Street at half past seven that May morning. Its side and back windows were blacked out, and a hip-hop hit throbbed into the low-lying mist that floated like a silk veil between the sun and San Francisco.

> Got my ice
> Got my smoke
> Got my ride
> Ain't got no hope
> Hold ya heads up high
> Don't know when
> Ya gonna die. . . .

The traffic light changed to yellow at the intersection of Fourth and Market. The stop-sign arm at the driver's side of the school bus swung out, the four-way hazard lights burned amber, and the vehicle came to a halt.

To the right of the bus was a shopping mall, a huge one: Bloomingdale's, Nordstrom, the windows papered with large Abercrombie posters of provocative half-naked teens in black and white.

To the left of the bus was a blue Ford van and then one of two islands splitting the road—a staging area for bus passengers and tourists.

Two cars behind the school bus, Louise Lindenmeyer, office manager, late for work, braked her old gray Volvo. She buzzed down her window and glared at that goddamned school bus.

She'd been stuck on its tailpipe since Buena Vista Park, then watched it pull away from her at the light at Fifth and Market as a stream of traffic took the turn and pulled in front of her.

And now that bus had stuck her at a light . . . again.

Louise heard a shout. *"Hey, asshole!"*

A man in his shirtsleeves, tie flapping, face bunched up, dried shaving cream under his left ear, walked past her car to give the bus driver *hell.*

A horn honked, and another, and then a cacophony of horns.

The light was green.

Louise took her foot off the brake and at that instant felt a concussive shock, her ears ringing as she saw the roof of the school bus explode violently upward.

Chunks of burning metal, steel-and-glass shrapnel, shot out in all directions faster than gunfire. A mushroom cloud like that of a small A-bomb formed above the bus, and the box-shaped vehicle became a fireball. Oily smoke colored the air.

Louise saw the blue van in the lane to the left of the bus bloom with flame, then blacken in front of her eyes.

No one got out of the van!

And now the blaze rushed at the silver Camry directly in front of her. The gas tank blew, and fire danced over the car, consuming it in vivid, leaping flames.

The bunch-faced man pulled himself up off the pavement to the hole where her passenger-side window had been. His shirt was gone. His hair was black frizz. The skin of his face was draped over his collarbone like tissue paper.

Louise recoiled in horror, grappled with her door handle as fire lapped at the hood of her Volvo. The car door opened and the heat rushed in.

That's when she saw the skin of her own arm still on the steering wheel, as if it were a *glove* turned inside out. Louise couldn't hear the businessman's horrified screams or her own. It was as though her ears had been plugged with wax. Her vision was all dancing spots and blurry shapes.

And then she was sucked down into a well of black.

Two

MY PARTNER, RICH CONKLIN, was at the wheel of our unmarked car and I was sugaring my coffee when I *felt* the concussion.

The dashboard shook. Hot coffee slopped over my hand. I shouted, "What the *hell?*" A few moments later the radio sputtered, the dispatcher calling out, *"Reports of an explosion at Market and Fourth. Nearby units identify and respond."*

I dumped my coffee out the window, grabbed the mic, and told Dispatch we were two blocks away as Conklin accelerated up the hill, then braked so that our car slewed across Fourth Street, blocking traffic.

We bolted from the car, Conklin yelling, *"Lindsay,* watch *out.* There could be secondary explosions!"

The air was opaque with roiling smoke, rank with burning rubber, plastic, and human flesh. I stopped running, wiped my sleeve across my stinging eyes, and fought against my gag reflex. I took in the hellish scene—and my hair literally lifted away from the back of my neck.

Market Street is a major artery. It should have been pulsing with commuter traffic, but instead it looked like Baghdad after a suicide bomb. People were screaming, running in circles, blinded by panic and a screen of smoky haze.

I called Chief Tracchio, reported that I was the first officer on the scene.

"What's happening, Sergeant?"

I told him what I saw: five dead on the street, two more at the bus stop. "Unknown number of victims alive or dead, still in their cars," I coughed into the phone.

"You okay, Boxer?"

"Yes, sir."

I signed off as cruisers, fire rigs, and EMS units, their sirens whooping, streamed onto Market and formed a perimeter at Third and at Fifth, blocking off oncoming traffic. Moments later, the command vehicle rolled up, and the bomb squad, covered top to toe in gray protective suits, poured onto the debris field.

A bloodied woman of indeterminate age and race staggered toward me. I caught her as her knees buckled, and Conklin and I helped her to a gurney.

"I saw it," the victim whispered. She pointed to a blackened hulk at the intersection. "That school bus was a bomb."

"A *school* bus? *Please, God, not kids!*"

I looked everywhere but saw no children.

Had they all been burned alive?

7

Three

WATER STREAMED from fire hoses, dousing flame. Metal sizzled and the air turned rancid.

I found Chuck Hanni, arson investigator and explosion expert, stooping outside the school bus's side door. He had his hair slicked back, and he wore khakis and a denim shirt, sleeves rolled up, showing the old burn scar that ran from the base of his right thumb to his elbow.

Hanni looked up, said, "God-awful disaster, Lindsay."

He walked me through what he called a "catastrophic explosion," showed me the two adult-size "crispy critters" curled between the double row of seats near the driver's side. Pointed out that the bus's front tires were full of air, the back tires, flat.

"The explosion started in the rear, not the engine compartment. And I found this."

Hanni indicated rounded pieces of glass, conduction

tubes, and blue plastic shards melted into a mass behind the bus door.

"Imagine the explosive force," he said, pointing to a metal projectile embedded in the wall. "That's a triple beam balance," he said, "and I'm guessing the blue plastic is from a cooler. Only took a few gallons of ether and a spark to do all this..."

A wave of his hand to indicate the three blocks of utter destruction.

I heard hacking coughs and boots crunching on glass. Conklin, his six-foot-two frame materializing out of the haze. "There's something you guys should see before the bomb squad throws us outta here."

Hanni and I followed Conklin across the intersection to where a man's body lay folded up against a lamppost.

Conklin said, "A witness saw this guy fly out of the bus's windshield when it blew."

The dead man was Hispanic, his face sliced up, his hair in dyed-red twists matted with blood, his body barely covered in the remnants of an electric-blue sweatshirt and jeans, his skull bashed in from his collision with the lamppost. From the age lines in his face, I guessed this man had lived a hard forty years. I dug his wallet out of his hip pocket, opened it to his driver's license.

"His name is Juan Gomez. According to this, he's only twenty-three."

Hanni bent down, peeled back the dead man's lips. I saw two broken rows of decayed stubs where his teeth had once been.

"A tweaker," Hanni said. "He was probably the cook. Lindsay, this case belongs to Narcotics, maybe the DEA."

Hanni punched buttons on his cell phone as I stared down at Juan Gomez's body. First visible sign of methamphetamine use is rotten teeth. It takes a couple of years of food- and sleep-deprivation to age a meth head twenty years. By then, the drug would have eaten away big hunks of his brain.

Gomez was on his way out *before* the explosion.

"So the bus was a mobile meth lab?" said Conklin.

Hanni was on hold for Narcotics.

"Yep," he said. "Until it blew all to hell."

Part One

BAGMAN JESUS

Chapter 1

CINDY THOMAS BUTTONED her lightweight Burberry trench coat, said, "Morning, Pinky," as the doorman held open the front doors of the Blakely Arms. He touched his hat brim and searched Cindy's eyes, saying, "Have a good day, Ms. Thomas. You take care."

Cindy couldn't say that she never looked for trouble. She worked the crime desk at the *Chronicle* and liked to say, "Bad news is good news to me."

But a year and a half ago a psycho with an illegal sublet and an anger-management problem, *living two floors above her,* had sneaked into apartments and gone on a brutal killing spree.

The killer had been caught and convicted, and was currently quarantined on death row at the "Q."

But still, there were aftershocks at the Blakely Arms. The residents triple-locked their doors every night, flinched at sudden noises, felt the loss of common, everyday security.

Cindy was determined not to live with this kind of fear.

She smiled at the doorman, said, "I'm a *badass*, Pinky. Thugs had better watch out for *me*."

Then she breezed outside into the early May morning.

Striding down Townsend from Third to Fifth—two very long blocks—Cindy traveled between the old and new San Francisco. She passed the liquor store next to her building, the drive-through McDonald's across the street, the Starbucks and the Borders on the ground floor of a new residential high-rise, using the time to return calls, book appointments, set up her day.

She paused near the recently rejuvenated Caltrain station that used to be a *hell pit* of homeless druggies, now much improved as the neighborhood gentrification took hold.

But behind the Caltrain station was a fenced-off and buckled stretch of sidewalk that ran along the train yard. Rusted junkers and vans from the Jimi Hendrix era parked on the street. The vehicles were crash pads for the homeless.

As Cindy mentally geared up for her power walk through that "no-fly zone," she noticed a clump of street people ahead—and some of them seemed to be crying.

Cindy hesitated.

Then she drew her laminated ID card out of her coat, held it in front of her like a badge, pushed her way into the crowd—and it parted for her.

The ailanthus trees shooting up through cracks in the pavement cast a netted shade on a pile of rags, old newspapers, and fast-food trash that was lying at the base of the chain-link fence.

8th Confession

Cindy felt a wave of nausea, sucked in her breath.

The pile of rags was, in fact, a dead man. His clothes were blood-soaked and his face so beaten to mush, Cindy couldn't make out his features.

She asked a bystander, "What *happened?* Who is this man?"

The bystander was a heavyset woman, toothless, wearing many layers and textures of clothes. Her legs were bandaged to the knees and her nose was pink from crying.

She gave Cindy a sidelong look.

"It's B-B-Bagman Jesus. Someone *killed* him!"

Cindy thumbed 911 on her Treo, reported what had clearly been a murder, and waited for the police to arrive.

As she waited, street people gathered around her.

These were the unwashed, the uncounted, the unnoticed, fringe people who slipped through the cracks, lived where the Census Bureau feared to tread.

They stank and they twitched, they stammered and scratched, and they jockeyed to get closer to Cindy. They reached out to touch her, talked over and corrected one another.

They wanted to be heard.

And although a half hour ago Cindy would have avoided all contact with them, she now wanted very much to hear them. As time passed and the police didn't come, Cindy felt a story budding, getting ready to bloom.

She used her cell again, called her friend Lindsay at home.

The phone rang six times before a masculine voice rasped,

15

"Hello?" Sounded to Cindy like maybe she'd interrupted Lindsay and Joe at an inopportune moment.

"Beautiful timing, Cindy," Joe panted.

"Sorry, Joe, really," said Cindy. "But I've got to speak to Lindsay."

Chapter 2

"DON'T BE MAD," I said, tucking the blanket under Joe's chin, patting his stubbly cheeks, planting a PG-13-rated kiss on his mouth, careful not to get him going again because I just didn't have enough time to get back in the mood.

"I'm not mad," he said, eyes closed. "But I am going to be seeking retribution tonight, so prepare yourself."

I laughed at my big, handsome guy, said, "Actually, I can't wait."

"Cindy's a bad influence."

I laughed some more.

Cindy is a pit bull in disguise. She's all girlie-girl on the outside but tenacious through and through, which is how she pushed her way into my gory crime scene six years back and wouldn't give up until she'd nailed her story and I'd solved my case. I wished all of my *cops* were like Cindy.

"Cindy's a peach," I said to my lover. "She grows on you."

"Yeah? I'll have to take your word for it." Joe smirked.

"Honey, would you mind—?"

"Will I walk Martha? Yes. Because *I* work at home and *you* have a real job."

"Thanks, Joe," I said. "Will you do it soon? Because I think she's got to go."

Joe looked at me deadpan, his big blue eyes giving me the business. I blew him a kiss, then I made a run for the shower.

Several months had blown by since my cozy apartment on Potrero Hill had burned out to the walls—and I was *still* getting used to living with Joe in his new crib in the high-rent district.

Not that I didn't enjoy his travertine shower stall with the dual heads and a gizmo that dispensed gel, shampoo, and moisturizer, plus the hotel-style bath sheets folded over a heated brass rack.

I mean, yeah. Things could be worse!

I turned the water up hot and high, soaked and lathered my hair, my mind going to Cindy's phone call, wondering what she was so charged up about.

Last I heard, dead bums didn't make headlines. But Cindy was telling me this was some kind of special bum with a special name. And she was asking me to check out the scene as a favor to her.

I dried my hair, padded down the carpeted hallway to my own walk-in closet, which was still mostly empty. I stepped into clean work pants, shrugged on an aqua-colored pullover, checked my gun, buckled my shoulder holster, and topped it all off with my second-best blue blazer.

8th Confession

I bent to ruffle the silky ears of my lovely border collie, Sweet Martha, and called out, "Bye, honey," to Joe.

Then I headed out to meet Cindy's newest passion: a dead bum with a certifiably crazy name.

Bagman Jesus.

Chapter 3

CINDY STOOD AT the dead man's side and filled her note-book, getting down the names, the descriptions, the exact quotes from Bagman Jesus's friends and mourners.

"He wore a really big *cross*," said a Mexican dishwasher who worked at a Thai restaurant. He sported an Adidas T-shirt and jeans under a dirty white apron. Had koi tattooed on his arms. "The cross was made of two, whatchamacallit, *nails*—"

"It was a *crucifix*, Tommy," said a bent white-haired woman leaning against her shopping cart at the edge of the crowd, sores on her legs, her filthy red coat dragging in the street.

"'Scuuuuse me, boss. What I meant was, a *crucifix*."

"And they weren't nails, they were *bolts*, about three inches long, tied together with copper wire. And don't forget that toy *baby* on that cross. A little pink baby." The old woman held a thumb and forefinger an inch apart to show Cindy how small that toy baby was.

8th Confession

"Why would someone take his crucifix?" the heavyset woman asked. "But his b-b-bag. That was a real leather bag! Lady, write this down! He was murdered for his *s-s-stuff*."

"We didden even know his real name," said Babe, a big girl from the Chinese massage parlor. "He give me ten dollah when I had no food. He didden want *nothing* for it."

"Bagman took care of me when I had pneumonia," said a gray-haired man, his chalk-striped suit pants cinched at the waist with twine. "My name is Bunker. Charles Bunker," he told Cindy.

He stuck out his hand, and Cindy shook it.

"I heard shots last night," Bunker said. "It was after midnight."

"Did you see who shot him?"

"I wish I had."

"Did he have any enemies?"

"Will you let me *through*?" said a black man with dreads, a gold nose stud, and a white turtleneck under an old tuxedo jacket who was threading his way through the crowd toward Cindy.

He slowly spelled out his name — Harry Bainbridge — so Cindy would get it right. Then Bainbridge held a long, bony finger above Bagman's body, traced the letters stitched to the back of Bagman's bloody coat.

"You can read that?" he asked her.

Cindy nodded.

"Tells you everything you want to know."

Cindy wrote it down in her book.

Jesus Saves.

Chapter 4

BY THE TIME Conklin and I got to Fourth and Townsend, uniforms had taped off the area, shunted the commuters the long way around to the station entrance, shooed bystanders behind the tape, and blocked off all but official traffic.

Cindy was standing in the street.

She flagged us down, opened my car door for me, started pitching her story before I put my feet on the ground.

"I feel a five-part human-interest series coming on," she said, "about the homeless of San Francisco. And I'm going to start with that man's life and death."

She pointed to a dead man lying stiff in his bloody rags.

"Thirty people were crying over his body, Lindsay. I don't know if that many people would cry if it was me lying there."

"Shut up," Conklin said, coming around the front of the

car. "You're crazy." He gently shook Cindy's shoulder, making her blond curls bounce.

"Okay, okay," Cindy said. She smiled up at Conklin, her slightly overlapping front teeth adding a vulnerable quality to her natural adorableness. "Just kidding. But I'm real serious about Bagman Jesus. You guys keep me in the loop, okay?"

"You betcha," I said, but I didn't get why Cindy regarded Bagman Jesus as a *celebrity,* and his death as a major deal.

I said, "Cindy, street people die every day—"

"And nobody gives a *damn.* Hell, people *want* them dead. That's my point!"

I left Cindy and Conklin in the street and went over to show my badge to K. J. Grealish, the CSI in charge. She was young, dark-haired, and skinny, and had nearly chewed her lips off from stress.

"I've been on my feet for the last twenty-seven hours straight," Grealish told me, "and this pointless dung heap of a crime scene could take another twenty-seven hours. Tell me again. Why are we here?"

As the trains rumbled into the yard, dust blew up, leaves fell from the trees, and newspapers flew into the air, further contaminating the crime scene.

A horn honked—the coroner's van clearing cops out of the way. It parked in the middle of the street. The door slid open, and Dr. Claire Washburn stepped out. She put her hands on her size-16 hips, beamed her Madonna smile at me—and I beamed back. Then I walked over and gave her a hug.

Claire is not only San Francisco's chief medical examiner but my closest friend. We'd bonded together a decade and a half back when she was a plump, black assistant medical examiner and I was a tall blonde with a 34D bra size, trying to survive my first savage year of on-the-job training in Homicide.

Those had been tough, bloody years for both of us, just trying to do our jobs in a man's world.

We still talked every day. I was her new baby's godmother, and I felt closer to Claire than I did to my own sister. But I hadn't seen her in more than a week.

When we turned each other loose from the hug, Claire asked the CSI, "K.J.? You got your photos of the victim?"

Grealish said she had, so Claire and I ducked under the tape and, no surprise, Cindy came along with us.

"It's okay," I said to Grealish. "She's with me."

"Actually," Cindy said under her breath, "you're with *me*."

We stepped around the blood trail, skirted the cones and markers, then Claire put down her bag and stooped beside the body. She turned Bagman's head from side to side with her gloved hand, gently palpated his scalp, probing for lacerations, fractures, or other injuries. After a long pause, she said, "Holy moly."

"That's enough of that medical jargon," I said to my friend. "Let's have it in English."

"As usual, Lindsay"—Claire sighed—"I'm not making any pronouncements until I do the post. But this much I'll tell you...and this is off the record, girl reporter," she said to Cindy. "You hear me?"

8th Confession

"Okay, okay. My lips are sealed. My mouth's a *safe*."

"Looks like your guy wasn't just given a vicious *beat-down*," Claire murmured. "This poor sucker took multiple gunshots to his head. I'm saying he was shot at close range, probably until the gun was *empty*."

Chapter 5

THE KILLING OF a street person has zero priority in Homicide. Sounds cold, but we just don't have the resources to work cases where the killer will never be found.

Conklin and I talked it over while sitting in the car.

"Bagman Jesus was robbed, right?" said Conklin. "Some other homeless dude beat the crap out of him and, when he fought back, blew him away."

"About those gunshots. I don't know. Sounds more like gangbangers. Or a bunch of kids rolling a bum for kicks, then capping him because they could get away with it. Just *look* at that," I said, indicating the crime scene: bloody footprints crisscrossing the pavement, tracking in nonevidentiary trace with every step.

And to add to that mess, there were no witnesses to the shooting, no handy video cam bolted to a streetlight, and no shell casings to be found.

8th Confession

We didn't even know the victim's real name.

Were it not for the drama Cindy was about to create in the *Chronicle*, this homeless man's case file would have gone to the bottom of the stack until he was forgotten.

Even by me.

But those multiple gunshots fired "at close range" nagged at me.

"Beating *and* shooting is crazy for a robbery, Rich. I'm sensing a hate crime. Or some kind of crime of passion."

Conklin flashed his lady-killer smile.

"So let's work it," he said.

He turned off the engine and we walked down to the end of the block, where Cindy's subjects still loitered outside the barrier tape.

We reinterviewed them all, then expanded our scope to include all of Townsend as well as Clyde Street and Lusk Alley. We talked to bodega cashiers, salesclerks at a gay men's novelty sex shop, hookers and druggies hanging out on the street.

Together we knocked on apartment doors in low-rent housing and spent the afternoon questioning forklift operators and laborers in the warehouses along Townsend, asking about the shooting last night outside the Caltrain yard, asking about Bagman Jesus.

Admittedly, many people scattered when they saw our badges. Others claimed to have no knowledge of Bagman or his death.

But the people who knew of Bagman Jesus had anecdotes to tell. How he'd broken up a liquor-store holdup, sometimes worked in a soup kitchen, said that he always had a few dollars for someone who needed it.

He was the elite, king of the street, we were told, a bum with a heart of gold. And his loss was tragic for those who counted him a friend.

By day's end, my attitude had shifted from skepticism to curiosity, and I realized that I'd caught Cindy's fever—or maybe the fever had caught me.

Bagman Jesus had been the good shepherd of a wounded flock.

So why had he been murdered?

Had he simply been in the wrong place at the wrong time?

Or had his death been specific and deliberate?

And that left us with two big questions no good cop could dodge with a clear conscience: Who had killed Bagman Jesus? And why?

Chapter 6

CONKLIN AND I got to the Hall around five, crossed the squad room to Lieutenant Warren Jacobi's small glassed-in office that once had been mine.

Jacobi once had been mine, too—that is, he used to be my partner. And although we'd swapped jobs and disagreed often, we'd put in so many years and miles together, he could read my thoughts like no one else—not Claire, not Conklin, not Cindy, not Joe.

Jacobi was sitting behind his junkyard of a desk when we walked in. My old friend and boss is a gray-haired, lumpy-featured, fifty-three-year-old cop with more than twenty-five years' experience in Homicide. His sharp gray eyes fixed on me, and I noted the laugh lines bracketing his mouth—because he wasn't laughing.

Not even a little.

"What the hell have you two been doing all day?" he asked

me. "Have I got this right? You've been working a homeless DOA?"

Inspector Hottie, as Conklin is known around the Hall, offered me the chair across from Jacobi's desk, then parked his cute butt on the credenza—and started to laugh.

"I say something funny, Conklin?" Jacobi snapped. "You've got twelve unsolveds on your desk. Want me to list them?"

Jacobi was touchy because San Francisco's homicide-solution rate was hovering at the bottom, somewhere below Detroit's.

"I'll tell him," I said to Conklin.

I put my feet up against the front edge of Jacobi's desk and said, "Time got away from us, Warren. This crime has a few odd angles, and the victim's death is going to be written up in great big type in the *Chronicle* tomorrow. I thought we should get out in front of the story."

"Keep talking," said Jacobi, as if I were a suspect and he had me in the box.

I filled him in on the reported good works and the varying theories: that Bagman Jesus was a missionary or a philanthropist, that the baby on his crucifix was a pro-life statement or that it symbolized how we'd all once been innocent and pure—like Baby Jesus.

"The guy had a way with people," I concluded. "Very charismatic, some kind of homeless person's saint."

Jacobi drummed his fingers. "You don't know this saint's name, do you, Boxer?"

"*No.*"

"And you have no clue as to who killed him or what the motive was?"

"Not a *hint* of a clue."

"That's it, then," Jacobi said, slapping the desk. "It's over. Finished. Unless someone walks in and confesses, you're done wasting department time. Get me?"

"Yes, sir," said Conklin.

"Boxer?"

"I hear you, Lieutenant."

We cleared out of Jacobi's office and punched out for the day. I said to Conklin, "You understood that, right?"

"What's not to understand about 'finished'?"

"Rich, Jacobi was clear as *day*. He told us to work Bagman Jesus *on our own time*. I'm going down to see Claire. You coming?"

Chapter 7

CLAIRE WAS WEARING a surgical gown with a butterfly pin at the neckline, apron stretched across her girth, flowered shower cap covering her hair. On the stainless autopsy table in front of her lay a naked Bagman Jesus, his terrible bashed-in features facing up at the lights.

A Y incision ran from clavicles to pubis and had been sewn up in baseball stitches with coarse white thread. He had bruises all over his body and overlapping lacerations and contusions.

Bagman Jesus had been worked over with a vengeance.

"I got back the X-rays," Claire said. As she talked, I looked over at where they were pinned to the light box on the wall.

"Broken right hand, probably took a swing at his attacker or it was stomped on when he was down. He's got a lot of fractures involving his facial bones, as well as multiple skull fractures. Broken ribs, of course, three of them.

"All this multiple blunt-force trauma might have killed him, but by the time someone took a bat to him, he was already dead."

"Cause of death? Give it to me, Butterfly. I'm ready."

"Jeez," she said. "Working as fast as I can and still not up to Lindsay time."

"Please?" I said.

Resigned, Claire reached behind her, held up a bunch of small glassine bags with what looked like distorted slugs inside.

"Those are twenty-twos?" Conklin asked her.

"Right you are, Rich. Four of the shots to the head did the old internal ricochet. Went in here, here, right here, and back here, whizzed around under the scalp, and laid there like bugs under a rug.

"But I suppose there's an outside chance Mr. Jesus could've survived *those* four slugs."

"And so?" I asked. "What killed him?"

"Soooo, baby girl, the shooter plugged Mr. Jesus through the temple, and that was likely your murder round. Shot him again at the back of his neck for good measure."

"And *then* his killer beat his face in? Broke his ribs?" I asked, incredulous. "Talk about crime of *passion*."

"Oh, someone hated him, all right," Claire told us. She called out to her assistant. "Put Mr. Jesus away for me, will you, Bunny? Get Joey to help you. And write 'John Doe number twenty-seven' and the date on his toe tag."

Conklin and I followed Claire to her office.

"Got something else to show you," Claire told us. She tore off her shower cap and peeled off her surgical gown. Underneath,

Claire wore blue scrubs and her favorite T-shirt, the one with the famous quote on the front: "I may be fat and I may be forty, but here I is."

That line cracked Claire up, but since she's now forty-five, I was thinking she might be getting a *new* favorite T-shirt one of these days.

Meanwhile, she offered us seats, sat down behind her desk, and unlocked the top drawer. She took out another glassine evidence bag, put it on the desk, and bent her gooseneck lamp down to throw light directly on it.

"That's Bagman's *crucifix*," I said, staring at a piece of tramp art that had the patina of an ancient and valuable artifact.

It was in fact as described: two bolts, copper wire, a toy baby lashed to the cross.

"Could be some prints on the plastic baby," I said. "Where did you find this?"

"In Bagman's gullet," Claire told me, taking a swig of water. "Someone tried to ram it down his throat."

Chapter 8

I WAS EAGER to hear Joe's thoughts on Bagman Jesus.

We were having dinner that night at Foreign Cinema. Although it is located on a crappy block in the city's dodgiest neighborhood, surrounded by bodegas and dollar stores, Foreign Cinema's marquis and fine design make it look as though a UFO picked it up in L.A. and dropped it down in the Mission by mistake.

But apart from the way it looks, what makes Foreign Cinema a real treat are the picnic tables in the back garden, where old films are projected on the blank wall of a neighboring building.

The sky was clear that early May night, the evening made even cozier by the heat lamps all around the yard. Sean Penn was at one of the tables with some of his pals, but the big draw for me was having a dinner date with Joe without either of us having to book a flight to do it.

After so many gut-wrenching speed bumps, the roller-coaster ride of our formerly long-distance relationship had smoothed out when Joe moved to San Francisco to be with me. Now we were finally living together.

Finally giving ourselves a real chance.

As *The Umbrellas of Cherbourg,* an old French film, flickered without sound against the wall, Joe listened intently as I told him about my astounding day: how Conklin and I had walked our feet off trying to find out who had murdered Bagman Jesus.

"Claire took five slugs out of his head, four of them just under the scalp," I told Joe. "The fifth shot was to the temple and was likely the money shot. Then Bagman took another slug to the back of the neck, postmortem. Kind of a personal act of violence, don't you think?"

"Those slugs. They were twenty-fives or twenty-twos?"

"Twenty-twos," I said.

"Figures. They had to be soft or they all would have gone through his skull. Were there any shell casings at the scene?"

"Not a one. Shooter probably used a revolver."

"Or he used a semiautomatic, picked up those casings. That kind of guy was evidence-conscious. Thinking ahead."

"So, okay, that's a good point." I turned Joe's thought around in my mind. "So maybe it was premeditated, you're saying?"

"It's not hopeless, Linds. That soft lead could have striations. See what the lab says. Too bad you won't be getting prints off the casings."

"There might be some prints on that plastic baby."

Joe nodded, but I could tell he didn't agree.

"No?" I asked him.

"If the shooter picked up the casings, maybe he was a pro. A contract killer or a military guy. Or a cop. Or a con. If he was a pro—"

"Then there won't be any prints on the crucifix either," I said. "But why would a pro kill a street dweller so viciously?"

"It's only *day one*, Linds. Give yourself some time."

I told him, "Sure," but Jacobi had already pulled the plug on this case. I put my head in my hands as Joe called the waiter over and ordered wine. Then he turned a big, unreadable smile on me.

I sat back and analyzed that smile, getting only that Joe looked like a kid with a secret.

I asked him what was going on, waited for him to sample the wine. Then, when he'd made me wait plenty long enough, he leaned across the table and took my hands in his.

"Well, Blondie, guess who got a call from the Pentagon today?"

Chapter 9

"OH MY GOD," I blurted. "*Don't* tell me."

I couldn't help myself. My first thought was that Joe was being recruited back to Washington—and I just couldn't stand even the *idea* of that.

"Lindsay, take it easy. The call was about an *assignment.* Could be the beginning of other assignments, all lucrative, a great boost for my consulting business."

When I met Joe while working a case, his business card read, DEPUTY DIRECTOR, HOMELAND SECURITY. He was the best anti-terrorism guy in Washington. And that was the job he'd given up when he'd moved out to the left coast to be with me.

His credentials and his reputation were first-rate, but the opportunities hadn't come to him in San Francisco as quickly as we'd expected.

I blamed that on the current administration being PO'ed that super-well-liked Joseph Molinari had walked off the job in an election year. Apparently they were getting over their pique.

That was good.

I relaxed. I smiled. I said, "Whew. Scared me, Joe." And I started to get excited for him.

"So tell me about the *assignment*," I said.

"Sure, but let's order first."

I don't remember what I picked from the menu because when the food came, Joe told me that he was leaving for a conference in the Middle East—in the morning.

And that he might be in Jordan for three weeks or more.

Joe put down his fork, said, "What's wrong, Lindsay? What's troubling you?"

He asked nicely. He really wanted to know, but my blood pressure had rocketed and I couldn't tell him *nicely* why.

"It's your birthday tomorrow, Joe. We were going to Cat's house for the weekend, remember?"

Catherine is my sister, six years younger than me, lives in the pretty coastal town of Half Moon Bay with her two girls. It was supposed to be a family weekend, quality time, kind of a big deal for me, bringing Joe home to pretty much the only family I have.

"We can stay with Cat some other time, hon. I have to go to this conference. Besides, Lindsay, all I want for my birthday is tonight and you."

"I can't talk to you right now," I said, tossing my napkin down on the table, standing up in front of the movie playing against the wall, hearing people shout at me to sit down.

I walked through the restaurant and out the thirty-foot-long corridor lined on each side with a waist-high niche of votive candles, pulled my cell phone out of my pocket, and called for a taxi before I got to the street.

I waited out there on Mission, smack in the middle of Dodge City, feeling outraged, then stupid, then really, really mad at myself.

I'd behaved like the dumb-blonde stereotype that I'd always despised.

Chapter 10

I SAID TO MYSELF, *You frickin' bimbo.* I leaned down, gave the cabbie a five, and waved him off.

Then I made that romantic, candlelit march all by myself down the thirty-foot corridor, through the restaurant, and out to the back garden.

I got there as the waiter was taking the plates away.

"Down in front!" the person who'd yelled before yelled again. "You. Yes, you."

I sat down across from Joe, said, "That was stupid of me and I'm sorry."

Joe's expression told me that he was really wounded. He said, "I'm sorry, too. I shouldn't have sprung that on you, but I didn't imagine you'd react like that."

"No, don't apologize. You were right and I was a complete idiot, Joe. Will you please forgive me?"

"I've already forgiven you. But Lindsay, every time we fight, the elephant in our relationship does what it does."

"Trumpets?" I asked, trying to be helpful.

Joe smiled, but it was a sad smile.

"You're going on forty."

"I know that. Thank you."

"I'll be forty-seven, as you pointed out, tomorrow. Last year I asked you to marry me. The ring I gave you is still in a box in a drawer, not on your finger. What I want for my birthday? I want you to decide, Lindsay."

With the precisely inconvenient timing waiters around the world have perfected, a trio of young men grouped around our table, a small cake in hand, candles burning, and began singing "Happy Birthday" to Joe. Just as I had planned.

The song was picked up by other diners, and a lot of eyes turned on us. Joe smiled, blew out the candles.

Then he looked at me, love written all over his face. He said, "Don't beg, Blondie. I'm not going to say what I wished for."

Did I feel the fool for blighting our evening?

I did.

Did I know what to do about Joe's wish and that diamond ring in its black velvet box?

I did not.

But I was pretty sure my indecision had nothing to do with Joe.

Chapter 11

WE WOKE UP before dawn and made urgent love without speaking. Hair was pulled, lips were bitten, pillows were thrown on the floor.

The fierce lovemaking was true, heartfelt acknowledgment that we were stuck. That there was nothing either one of us could say that the other didn't already know.

Our skin glistening in the afterglow, we lay together side by side, our hands gripped tightly together. The high-tech clock on the nightstand projected the time and outside temperature on the ceiling in large red digits.

Five fifteen a.m.

Fifty-two degrees.

Joe said, "I had a good dream. Everything is going to be okay."

Was he assuring me? Or reassuring himself?

"What was the dream?"

"We were swimming together, naked, under a waterfall. Water. That's sex, right?"

He released my hand. The mattress shifted. He shook out the blanket and covered my body.

I heard the shower running as I lay in the dark, feeling pent-up and tearful and unresolved. I dozed, waking to Joe's hand touching my hair.

"I'm going now, Lindsay."

I reached up and put my arms around his neck, and we kissed in the dark.

I said, "Have a good trip. Don't forget to write."

"I'll *call*."

It was all the wrong tone to let Joe leave on this cool note. The front door closed. The locks clicked into place.

I bolted out of bed.

I dressed in jeans and one of Joe's sweaters, ran barefoot out into the hallway. I pressed the *down* button at the elevator station, one long push until the car made the climb back up to the eleventh floor and jumped open.

I despaired as the elevator dropped me slowly down. In my mind's eye, Joe's bags were in the trunk, the car moving now along Lake Street, picking up speed as it headed toward the airport.

But when the elevator finally released me into the lobby, I saw Joe through the glass front doors, standing beside a Lincoln sedan. I blew past the doorman and ran out into the street, calling Joe's name.

He looked up and opened his arms, and I fell against him, pressed my face to his jacket, felt the tears slip out of my eyes.

"I love you so much, Joe."

"I love you, too, Blondie."

"Joe, when we were in that waterfall, was I wearing my ring?"

"Yeah. Big old sparkler. Could see it from the Moon."

I laughed into his shoulder. We kissed and hugged, did it again, until the driver joked, "Save a little for later, okay?"

"I'd better go," Joe said.

I stepped back reluctantly, and Joe got into the car.

I waved and Joe waved back as the black Lincoln took my lover away.

Chapter 12

YUKI WAS IN HER OFFICE, one of the dozens of window-less, grubby warrens for assistant district attorneys in the Hall of Justice. She was prepped, primed, and in full court dress: a gray Anne Klein suit, ice-pink silk shirt, three-hundred-dollar shoes she'd gotten half off at Neiman.

It was half past six in the morning.

In about three hours she would be making her closing argument in the bloody awful and complex murder trial of Stacey Glenn, a twenty-five-year-old former pageant queen who'd managed to be both a beauty *and* a beast.

What Stacey Glenn had done to her parents was revolting, unprovoked, and unforgivable, and Yuki was determined to nail that psycho-bitch and send her away for good. But for all of Yuki's determination and gifts for bringing the strongest argument to life, she was becoming famous around the DA's office — famous for *losing*. And that was killing her.

8th Confession

So this was *it*.

If Stacey Glenn got off, as much as she'd hate to do it, Yuki would go back to civil law, handle rich people's divorces and contract negotiations. That's if she wasn't *fired* before she could quit.

Yuki hunched forward in her creaky chair and shuffled a packet of index cards, each one highlighting a point she would make in summing up the People's case.

Item: Stacey Glenn had left her apartment in Potrero Hill at two in the morning and driven her distinctive candy-apple-red Subaru Forester to her parents' house forty miles away in Marin, crossing the Golden Gate Bridge.

Item: Stacey Glenn entered her parents' house between three and three fifteen a.m., using a key that was kept hidden under a particular heart-shaped stone by the front door. She went through the kitchen to the garage, brought a crowbar upstairs to the master bedroom, and bludgeoned her parents, beating both their heads in.

Item: A neighbor testified that around three that morning she saw a red Subaru Forester with off-road tires in the Glenns' driveway and recognized it as belonging to Stacey.

Item: Leaving her parents for dead, Stacey Glenn drove toward her home, going through a tollbooth on her return trip at approximately four thirty-five.

This timeline was crucial to Yuki's case because it established Stacey Glenn's movements on the night in question and *decimated* her alibi that she was home alone and asleep when her parents were attacked.

Item: Stacey Glenn was a degenerate shopper, heavily in debt. Her parents were worth nothing to her alive. They were worth a million dollars to her dead.

Item: Stacey Glenn had the means, the motive, and the opportunity—and there was also a *witness* to the crime itself.

And that witness was 90 percent of Yuki's case.

Yuki wrapped her cards with a rubber band, dropped the pack into her purse. Then she folded her hands under her chin and beamed her thoughts to her own mother, Keiko Castellano, who had died before her time and who was highly ticked off about it. Keiko had loved her only daughter fiercely, and Yuki felt her mom's comforting presence around her now.

"Mommy, stay with me in court today and help me win, okay?" Yuki said out loud. "Sending kisses."

With hours to kill, Yuki cleaned out her pencil drawer, emptied her trash can, deleted old files from her address book, and changed her too-sweet pink blouse to the stronger, more confident teal man-tailored shirt that was in dry cleaner's plastic behind her door.

At eight fifteen, Yuki's second chair, Nicky Gaines, ambled down the corridor calling her name. Yuki stuck her head out of her doorway, said, "Nicky, just make sure the PowerPoint works. That's all you have to do."

"I'm your man," said Nicky.

"Good. Zip up your fly. Let's go."

Chapter 13

YUKI STOOD UP from her seat at the prosecutors' table as the Honorable Brendan Joseph Duffy entered the courtroom through a paneled door behind the bench and took his seat between the flags and in front of the great seal of the State of California.

Duffy had a runner's build, graying hair, windowpane glasses worn low on the slope of his nose. He yanked out his iPod earbuds, popped the top on a can of Sprite, then, as those in attendance sat down, asked the bailiff to bring in the jury.

Across the aisle, Yuki's opponent, the well-regarded criminal defense attorney Philip R. Hoffman, exchanged whispers with his client, Stacey Glenn.

Hoffman was tall, stooped, six-foot-four, forty-two years old, with unruly dark hair. He wore a midnight-blue Armani suit and a pink satin tie. His nails were manicured.

Like Yuki, Hoffman was a perfectionist.

Unlike her, Hoffman's win-to-loss ratio put him in the all-star league. Normally, he commanded fees upwards of nine hundred bucks an hour, but he was currently representing Stacey Glenn pro bono. Hoffman was no altruist. The courtroom was packed with press, and their coverage of this case was worth millions to his firm.

Stacey Glenn was a stunning blue-eyed brunette with two spots of blush on her cheeks emphasizing her jailhouse pallor. She wore a frumpy suit in an unflattering olive-toned plaid, conveying schoolteacher or statistician rather than the calculating, murdering, moneygrubbing psychopath that she was.

Beside Yuki, Nicky Gaines, with his perpetual adenoidal wheeze, breathed noisily as the jurors entered the small courtroom from a side door and settled into their seats in the jury box.

Judge Duffy greeted the jurors, explained that today both sides would summarize their cases and that afterward, the jury could begin its deliberations.

Duffy took a long pull of soda right out of the can, then asked, "Ms. Castellano, are the People ready to proceed?"

"Yes, Your Honor."

Taking her notes from the table, Yuki walked to the lectern in the center of the oak-lined courtroom. She smiled at the twelve jurors and two alternates she'd come to know by their tics, grimaces, laughter, and eye-rolling over the past six weeks, said, "Morning, everyone," then, pointing to the defendant, spoke from her heart.

"Stacey Glenn is a depraved and unrepentant murderer.

"She killed her father, who adored her. She did her level

50

best to kill her mother and thought she had. She bludgeoned her parents without mercy because she wanted to collect their life-insurance payout of a million dollars.

"She did it for the *money*."

Yuki went over the timeline she'd established during the trial—the tollbooth attendant's testimony and that of the Glenns' neighbor—and she reminded them of the insurance broker Stacey had called to check on the status of her parents' policy.

Last, she asked the jury to recall the testimonies of Inspector Paul Chi, a decorated Homicide investigator with the SFPD, and Lynn Colomello, a seasoned paramedic.

"Inspector Chi and EMS Sergeant Lynn Colomello have both testified that although Rose Glenn was close to death when she was found in bed beside her murdered husband, she had *cognition* and she was *lucid*," Yuki told the jury.

"Rose Glenn obeyed the paramedics' directions. She knew who had attacked her and, most important, *she was able to convey this information to the police.*

"You know that Inspector Chi had a video camera with him when he was called to the scene of a homicide that morning. When he realized that Mrs. Glenn was still alive, he videotaped their conversation, believing it to be Mrs. Glenn's dying declaration.

"Rose Glenn knew full well who had attacked her. And on this videotape, she tells this story more powerfully than anything I can say.

"Nicky, please roll it."

Chapter 14

A VIDEOTAPE OF the dimly lit murder scene appeared on the screen to the side of the judge's bench closest to the jury.

The camera's eye focused on a bedroom dominated by a king-size bed. The linens were in disarray and dark with drying blood. A man's twisted body was on the far side of the bed, his face turned away from the camera, blood and brains spattering the headboard, deep wounds visible on his scalp and throat.

A woman's ghostly hand lifted from the bed and motioned the viewer to come closer. The sound of labored breathing intensified as the camera neared the bed.

It was shocking and horrifying to see that although her jaw was clearly smashed and one eye was gone, *Rose Glenn was alive*.

"I'm Inspector Paul Chi," said a man's voice off camera. "An ambulance is on the way, Mrs. Glenn. Can you hear me?"

Amazingly, the woman's chin moved slowly downward and then back.

"Is your name Rose Glenn?"

The woman nodded again.

"Is Ronald Reagan president of the United States?"

Rose Glenn turned her head from side to side—no.

"Rose, do you know who did this to you and your husband?"

The woman's breathing became more ragged, but she tilted her chin down and then up, nodding.

"Was your attacker a stranger?" Chi asked her.

Rose Glenn shook her head no.

"Was your attacker a family member?"

She nodded yes.

Suddenly, police radios crackled and a gurney rolled noisily into the room, blocking the camera's view. Then the scene cleared once more.

A paramedic, her blond hair pulled back in a ponytail, said in a raspy smoker's voice, "Holy Mother of God. She's *alive*."

The paramedic, who had testified before this jury, was Lynn Colomello. On screen, she hurried to Anthony Glenn and felt for his pulse. Chi asked the dying woman, "Rose, was it your son? Did your son, Rudy, do this?"

Rose Glenn shook her head in agonizing slow motion—no.

The sound of footsteps overrode the questioning as Colomello was joined by two other paramedics. They talked about emergency treatment, brought out an oxygen tank, and inserted a cannula into Rose Glenn's nostrils.

Paul Chi's voice continued, saying calmly to the paramedics, "I just need another second." Then he spoke to the victim. "Rose. Rose. Was your attacker your daughter, Stacey?"

The woman's head nodded affirmatively.

"Rose, are you saying that your daughter, Stacey, did this to you?"

The woman hissed, "Yesssssss."

It was a terrible sound, the air escaping her lungs, as if the woman was using her last breath to tell Chi who'd killed her.

And then, on Colomello's count, the paramedics lifted Rose Glenn onto the gurney — and the interview was over.

Inside the courtroom, the screen went dark and the lights came on. The jurors had seen the video before, but since this tape was Yuki's pièce de résistance, she could only hope that the blunt shock of seeing it again would reinforce its power.

Yuki cleared her throat, said, "Ladies and Gentlemen, Rose Glenn was asked many different questions that morning and was able to shake her head yes and no, and was even able to speak. When asked if her daughter had attacked her, *she said yes.*

"At no time during this trial did Rose Glenn deny what she said to Inspector Chi. She simply can't remember.

"And why can't she remember? Because her daughter bashed her head in with a crowbar, causing trauma to the extent that her doctors had never seen anyone with such severe injuries survive.

"But Rose Glenn did survive — widowed, disfigured, and partially paralyzed for life.

"*The defendant did this to her,* Ladies and Gentlemen.

"The People ask you to find Stacey Glenn *guilty* on both counts: for the murder of her father, Anthony Glenn, and for the attempted murder of her mother, Rose. We ask you to make sure that Stacey Glenn pays for these crimes to the fullest extent of the law."

As Yuki took her seat, she felt a lot of things, all of them good: the warm glow of accomplishment, Nicky's hand patting her shoulder, and her mother's presence surrounding her like a full-body hug.

"Good job, Yuki-eh," her mother said. "You make sram dunk."

Chapter 15

PHILIP HOFFMAN had never lost his composure in this jury's presence. He'd been respectful to the defense witnesses and he'd never used a five-dollar word when a nickel word would do. He felt sure that the jury liked and trusted him, and he was counting on that good feeling rubbing off on his client.

"Folks," he said, towering over the lectern, making it seem like a toy in his shadow, "Stacey Glenn is a good girl who has never harmed a person in her life. She loves her parents, and when Rose Glenn came before you at great emotional and physical cost, she told you that Stacey hasn't got a bit of violence in her. That Stacey would never, ever attack her father or Rose herself.

"You heard Rose Glenn say that she's absolutely sick at heart, that whatever she said or did when she was on the verge of death was misinterpreted and used to indict her innocent daughter."

8th Confession

Hoffman shook his head, left his notes on the lectern, and walked to the jury box, then locked his hands behind his back and swept his dark eyes over the jurors.

"The prosecution has used the crime-scene video in order to stir your emotions because that's *all* they have. And that video, as moving as it is, is not proof that Stacey Glenn is guilty of *anything.*"

Hoffman took the jury through his case, citing the two neurologists and the psychiatrist who testified that Rose Glenn was in shock when she was interviewed by Inspector Chi, that her responses were completely and totally unreliable.

He said that while the toll-taker *believed* he saw Stacey Glenn, a transaction with any driver lasted a few seconds at most and, in this case, his glimpse of said driver had taken place in the dark of night.

"There is no record of the Forester's license-plate number," Hoffman said to the jury, "and no videotape of the driver.

"Bernice Lawrence," Hoffman went on, "the neighbor who swore that she saw Stacey's car in her parents' driveway . . . well, she's a good citizen and she was trying to help. Maybe she saw a similar car or maybe she got the date of that sighting wrong—but regardless, she admits she never saw Stacey.

"Using common sense, we are unlikely to believe that my client would be stupid enough to park her car in front of her parents' house and then go inside to kill them. It's ridiculous.

"You've seen what Tony and Rose Glenn's bedroom looked like after the attack," he said. "Can you believe that a person could raise a crowbar, strike with enormous force, lift and strike again a dozen times, and not get a hair or a spot of blood on their clothing?

"Stacey was brought in for questioning within hours of the tragedy. Her hair, her hands, her whole body, was examined. Her apartment was searched, and her shoes and clothing were tested thoroughly in the crime lab.

"There was no evidence on her person. *None.*

"Stacey's car was reduced to buckets of nuts and bolts, and *no evidence* was found.

"Regarding the key left in her parents' front door, I ask you: how many of you keep a spare key under the mat or in some other obvious place where anyone could find it?

"And the call to Wayne Chadwell, the insurance broker?

"Stacey was being a good daughter. Her parents were getting old. She checked on their policy because she wanted to be sure they were *protected.*

"In sum, folks, there's no forensic evidence whatsoever linking my client to this crime. *None.*

"And because the police have the questionable testimony of a severely injured woman, they have pinned this crime on Stacey—and they never considered anyone else. Is there reasonable doubt in this case? I submit to you there's nothing *but* reasonable doubt.

"Rose Glenn lost her husband and almost died. And now the prosecution is asking you to compound this poor woman's tragedy by taking away her daughter as well.

"Stacey didn't do it, folks.

"And there's no evidence to support that she did.

"I urge you to find Stacey Glenn not guilty on all charges. And I thank you."

Chapter 16

CINDY, FRESH IN a pink wraparound dress under her coat, hair gleaming, looking as though she'd stepped from a department-store window, skirted the filthy drug addicts loitering outside the three-story redbrick building on Fifth off Townsend and thanked a toothless young man who held open the door for her.

The ground floor of "From the Heart" was one large, green room, with a cafeteria-style hot table along one wall, folding tables and chairs set up in rows, and ragged people milling—some talking to themselves, others eating eggs from paper plates.

Cindy noticed a thin black woman eyeing her from a spot near the entrance. She looked about forty years old and was wearing a bold print blouse over black stretch pants. Purple-framed eyeglasses hung from a cord around her neck, and a badge pinned to her blouse read, MS. LUVIE JUMP, DAY ROOM SUPERVISOR.

Ms. Jump continued to scan Cindy skeptically, then said, "Help you?"

Cindy told the woman her name and that she was writing a story about Bagman Jesus for the *San Francisco Chronicle*.

"I'm following up on his murder," Cindy said, taking the morning's paper out of her computer bag. She flipped it open to page three, exposed the headline above the fold.

The black woman squinted at the paper, said, "You had your coffee yet?"

"Nope," said Cindy.

"Then sit yourself down."

Luvie Jump returned a minute later with two mugs of coffee, a basket of rolls, and foil-wrapped pats of butter.

"Will you read me that story?" she asked, sitting across from Cindy, laying out plastic flatware and napkins. "I don't have my reading glasses."

Cindy smiled, said, "*Love* to. I don't get to do readings too often." She flattened the paper, said, "The headline is 'Street Messiah Murdered. Police Have No Leads.'"

"Uh-hunh. Go on."

"Okay, so then it says, 'Sometime after midnight on May sixth, a homeless man was beaten and shot to death outside the Caltrain yard on Townsend Street.

"'More than a hundred homeless people die on our streets from neglect and violence every year, and the city buries and forgets them.'"

"Can say that again," Luvie murmured.

Cindy went on, "'But this man won't be forgotten easily.

8th Confession

He was a friend to the castoffs, the shadow people of the underclass. He was their shepherd, and they loved him.

" 'We don't know his name, but he was called Bagman Jesus.' "

Cindy's throat caught and she looked up, saw Luvie Jump smiling at her, the woman's mouth quavering as if she might cry.

"He delivered my oldest child in an alley," Luvie said. "That's why he wore that baby on the cross around his neck. Jesus saves. Jesus *saves*. What can I do to help you, Cindy Thomas? Just tell me."

"I want to know everything about him."

"Where should I start?"

"Do you know Bagman's real name?"

Chapter 17

CINDY WAS IN the grip of a dead man—heart, mind, and soul. Conklin and I sat with her at MacBain's Beers O' the World Pub, a cop hangout on Bryant. The jukebox pumped out "Dancing Queen," and the long, polished bar was packed three-deep with a buoyant after-work crowd who'd streamed here directly from the Hall of Justice.

Cindy was oblivious to her surroundings.

Her voice was colored with anger as she said to us, "He delivered her *baby* and she doesn't know his *name*. No one does! If only his face wasn't totaled, we could run his picture. Maybe someone would call in with an ID."

Cindy downed her beer, slammed her empty mug on the table, said, "I've got to make people understand about him. Get their noses out of the society pages for a minute and realize that a person like Bagman Jesus *mattered*."

"We *get it,* Cindy," I said. "Take a breath. Let someone else speak!"

"Sorry." Cindy laughed. "Sydney," she said, raising a hand, calling our waitress over, "hit me again, please."

"Rich and I spent our lunch hour sifting through missing persons and running Bagman's prints."

"Your lunch hour. Wow," Cindy said facetiously.

"Hey, look at it this way," I said. "We bumped your Bagman to the top of a very thick pile of active cases."

Cindy gave me a look that said "sorry," but she didn't mean it. What a brat. I laughed at her. What else could I do?

"Did you find anything?" she asked.

Conklin told her, "No match to his prints. On the other hand, there are a couple of hundred average-size, brown-eyed white men who've gone missing in California over the last decade. I called you at two thirty so you could make your deadline. When you dump your voice mail—"

"Thanks, anyway, Rich. I was interviewing. I turned off my cell."

More beer came, and as dinner arrived, Cindy served up the highlights of her other interviews at From the Heart. It took a little while, but soon enough I realized that Cindy was pretty much playing to Conklin. So I sawed on my sirloin and watched the two of them interact.

My feelings for my partner had taken a sharp and unexpected turn about a year and a half ago when we were working a case that had brought us to L.A. We had a late dinner, drank some wine, and missed our flight back to San Francisco.

It was late, so I expensed two rooms at the airport Marriott. I was in a bathrobe when Conklin knocked on the door. About two minutes later, we were grappling together on a California King.

I'd hauled up the emergency brake before it was too late, and it felt *awful,* absolutely wrenching—as wrong as if the sun had gone down in the east.

But I'd been right to bring things to a halt. For one thing, even though Joe and I had broken up around then, I still loved him. Besides, Conklin is about ten years younger than I am and we're *partners.* I'm also his *boss.*

After that night, we agreed to ignore the moments when the electricity between us lit up the patrol car, when I'd forget what I was saying and find myself speechless, just staring into Richie's light-brown eyes. As best we could, we sidestepped the times Rich had burst into thirty-second rants about how crazy he was about me.

But this wasn't one of those times.

Right now, Inspector Hottie was grinning at Cindy, and she'd almost forgotten I was there.

I could argue that Cindy and Rich would make a terrific couple. They are both single. They look good together. They seem to have a lot to talk about.

"Rich," Cindy was saying, "I'm having another beer. Think you could make sure I get home okay?"

"I'll drive you," I said, putting a sisterly hand on Cindy's arm. "My car's out front and I can swing by your apartment on my way home."

Chapter 18

YUKI NEARLY BUMPED into Phil Hoffman as he stepped out of the elevator.

"What do you think this is about?" Hoffman murmured.

"Weird, huh?" Yuki replied.

It was ten a.m., two days after she and Hoffman had made their closing arguments, and they'd just gotten calls from the judge's clerk saying that their presence was required in Courtroom 6a.

With Hoffman looming a full fourteen inches above her, Yuki walked beside him down the long buff-painted corridor toward the courtroom, with Nicky Gaines trailing behind.

"Could be nothing," Yuki said. "I had a jury ask for a calculator once. Thought they were adding up the award for my client. Turned out a juror was doing his income tax during the lunch break."

Hoffman laughed, held open the first of two sets of doors to the courtroom. Gaines held open the second set, then the three lawyers walked to the front, took seats behind their respective counsel tables.

Judge Duffy was at the bench, the court reporter and clerk in their places, the sheriff's deputy standing in front of the jury box, patting down his mustache.

Duffy shoved his glasses to the top of his head, closed his laptop, and asked both counsel to approach, which they did.

"The foreperson sent out a note from the jury," Duffy said. A smile pulled at his mouth as he unfolded a quartered sheet of paper, held it up so Yuki and Hoffman could see the twelve hangman's gallows that had been drawn on the paper with a black marker. A note had been penned underneath the gallows: "Your Honor, I think we have a problem."

"Nooo way," Yuki said. "They're hung after…what? Ten hours of deliberation?"

"Your *Honor*," said Hoffman. "Please. Don't let them quit so soon. This is absolutely *bizarre!*"

Yuki couldn't read Duffy's expression, but she could read *Hoffman's* and knew he felt the same anxiety, anger, and nausea as she did. It had taken months to prepare this case for trial. Dozens of people had been deposed. There'd been uncountable man-hours of prep and six weeks of what Yuki thought to be pretty flawless presentations in the courtroom.

If there was a mistrial, the People might decide not to spend the resources required to retry. Hoffman's firm would probably pull the plug as well.

And that meant Stacey Glenn would go free.

"Take a seat, you two. No need to transport the defendant."

Duffy called out to the sheriff's deputy, "Mr. Bonaventure, please bring in the jury."

Chapter 19

AS THE JURORS put their bags down beside their seats, Yuki's mind whirled like cherry lights on a police cruiser. She scrutinized the jurors as they filed in, looked for telling signs on their faces and in their body language.

Who had believed Stacey Glenn was innocent? How many of them had voted to acquit—and why?

The foreperson, Linda Chen, was Chinese-American, forty years old, with an Ivy League education and a successful real estate business. She had a no-nonsense manner countered by a wide and easy smile, and both Yuki and Hoffman had felt comfortable with Chen when they'd cast the jury. Even more so when she'd been voted foreperson.

Now Yuki wondered how Chen had let the jury quit so soon.

Duffy smiled at the jury, said, "I've given your note serious thought. I understand that six weeks of trial is an ordeal and many of you are quite ready to go home.

"That said, this trial has been expensive—not just in terms of money, although it's cost the State of California plenty, but for the better part of a year, both sides have labored to put together this case for you to judge.

"Where things stand now," said Duffy, "*you* are the experts on the *People versus Stacey Glenn*. If you can't arrive at a unanimous decision, this case will have to be tried again, and there's no reason to believe that any other group of people would be more qualified or impartial, or have more wisdom to decide this verdict, than you."

Duffy explained to the jury that he was going to ask them to continue their deliberations, not to give up deeply held ideas based on the evidence but to reexamine their views with an open mind in order to try to reach consensus.

The judge was giving the jury the "Allen charge," the so-called dynamite charge designed to bust up logjams in deadlocked juries. It was considered coercive by legal purists.

Yuki knew that this was the best option available, but the Allen charge could backfire. A resentful jury could push back and deliver whatever verdict would end its service the fastest.

It was obvious to Yuki that the easiest, least-nightmare-provoking decision would be a unanimous vote to acquit.

Judge Duffy was saying, "I want you to have maximum seclusion and comfort, so I've arranged for you to be sequestered in the Fairmont Hotel for as much time as you need."

Yuki saw the shock register on every one of the jurors'

faces as they realized that the judge was locking them up in a hotel *without any warning,* denying them TV, newspapers, home-cooked meals, and other comforts of daily life.

They were not pleased.

Duffy thanked the jury on behalf of the court and, taking his can of Sprite with him, left the bench.

Chapter 20

YUKI'S PHONE RANG the moment she returned to her office.

"It's me," said Len Parisi, the deputy district attorney who was also her superior, her champion, and her toughest critic. "Got a minute?"

Yuki opened her makeup kit, applied fresh lipstick, snapped her purse shut, and stepped out into the corridor.

"Want me to come with?" Nicky Gaines said, raking his shaggy blond mop with his fingers.

"Yeah. Try to make him laugh."

"Really?"

"Couldn't hurt."

Parisi was on the phone when Yuki rapped on his open door. He swung his swivel chair around and stuck his forefinger in the air, the universal sign for "I'll be a minute."

Parisi was in his late forties, with wiry red hair, a pear-shaped girth, and a heart condition that had nearly killed him a year and a half ago. He was known around town as "Red Dog," and Yuki thought the name pleased him. Called up images of a drooling bulldog with a spiked collar.

Parisi hung up the phone, signaled for Yuki and Nicky to come in, then barked, "Did I hear this right? The jury hung?"

"Yep," Yuki said from the doorway. "Duffy dropped the Allen charge and then he sequestered them."

"No kidding. What do you think? There were one or two holdouts?"

"I don't know, Len," Yuki said. "I counted six jurors that wouldn't meet my eyes."

"Jesus H. Christ," Parisi said. "I'm glad Duffy put the squeeze on, but don't get your hopes up." He shook his head, asked rhetorically, "What's the hang-up? Stacey Glenn did it."

"I'm guessing it's Rose Glenn's testimony," Yuki said. "When she said, 'My baby would never hurt us.' It's got to be that—"

Parisi had stopped listening. "So, okay, we wait it out. Meanwhile, Gaines, get a haircut. Castellano, help Kathy Valoy after lunch. She's swamped. That's it. Thank you."

Parisi picked up his ringing phone, spun around in his chair, faced his window.

"I would have gone for it," Nicky was saying as he and Yuki walked back down the hallway. "But he didn't even look at me. I couldn't get a quip in edgewise. Or a retort. Or even a pun."

Yuki laughed.

"And believe me, I've got jokes ready to go. Have you heard the one about the priest, the rabbi, and the hippo who walk into a bar—"

Yuki laughed again, a musical chortle that was just short of manic. "You made *me* laugh," Yuki said. "That's something. You did good, number two. I'll see you later."

Yuki left Gaines in the bull pen, took the stairs down to the lobby, and drafted behind a large cop who strong-armed the heavy steel-and-glass doors leading out to Bryant Street.

Yuki quickly scanned the reporters loitering on the steps outside the Hall. No one had seen her — yet.

Which was good.

Sometimes when the press fired questions at her, she wanted to answer and often couldn't prevent her thoughts from stampeding out of her mouth unchecked. So when Yuki saw Candy Stimpson, a feisty reporter from the *Examiner,* she walked quickly down the steps, making a straight line for the corner.

The reporter called after her, "Yuki! Is the Glenn trial going into the crapper? How are you feeling right now? I just want a *quote.* One stinking *quote.*"

"Outta my face, Candy," Yuki snapped, turning her head toward the reporter, maintaining her forward motion as she stepped off the sidewalk. "I've got nothing to say."

Candy Stimpson screamed, *"Yuki, no!"*

But Yuki didn't get it.

Chapter 21

THE LIGHT SHINING in Yuki's eyes was blinding.

"*Mom!*" she yelled. "*Mommy!*"

"It's okay," said a man's reassuring voice. "*You're* okay."

The light went off, and she saw gray eyes rimmed with blue, then the rest of his face. She didn't know him, had never seen him before in her life.

"Who *are* you?"

"Dr. Chesney," he said. "John. And your name is...?"

"Ms. Castellano. Yuki."

"Good." He smiled. "That checks with your ID. I have a few questions—"

"What the hell? What's going *on?*"

"You're in the emergency room," Dr. Chesney told her. He appeared to be in his early thirties. Looked like he worked out. "You walked into an oncoming car," he said.

"I did *not.*"

"It was stopping for the light, lucky for you," Chesney continued. "Your CAT scan was negative. Just a minor concussion. You've got a couple of scrapes, a few stitches, an impressive bruise on your left hip, but no broken bones. How many fingers am I holding up?"

"Two."

"And now?"

"*Three.*"

"Okay. Do this. Close your eyes. Touch your nose with your left forefinger. Now, same thing with the right. Excellent. And what's the last thing you remember?"

"I have an impressive bruise on my hip."

Chesney laughed. "I meant, what do you remember from before the accident?"

"A reporter was hounding me..."

"You remember her name?"

"Candy Bigmouth Stimpson."

"Okay. Very good. She's waiting outside. I want to keep you here overnight, just for observation—"

But Yuki was staring around, starting to recognize the emergency room, her guts turning to Jell-O. She gripped the sides of the bed. "What hospital is this?"

"San Francisco Municipal."

Mommy died here.

"I'll want to check you over again in the morning—"

"Hell with *that*," Yuki said. "I'm fine."

"Or you can leave," said Chesney. He produced a form on a clipboard, said, "This is a release that says you're checking out against medical advice. Sign here."

"Got a pen?"

Chesney clicked his Bic, and Yuki signed where he indicated. He said, "I recommend acetaminophen. It's not too late to change your mind about staying overnight, Yuki."

"*No.* No, no, no."

"Your decision," Chesney said. "Don't wash your hair for at least three days—"

"Are you *crazy?* Don't wash? I have to *work*—"

"Listen. Look at me, Yuki, and pay attention. You'll want your doctor to take those stitches out in ten days. If you can wait thirty or forty seconds, a nurse will bring your clothes. I suggest you go home and get some sleep."

"Sorry?"

"*Get some sleep.* And I'm not joking. Watch where you're walking."

Chapter 22

YUKI THOUGHT, *I have to get out of here. Have to!*

She finished dressing, stepped into her shoes, threw open the curtains around the stall, and fled. After taking a wrong turn into obstetrics and a detour through the cafeteria, she found the door leading to the waiting room.

Candy Stimpson stood up when she saw Yuki.

"Oh *God,* Yuki, I'm so sorry."

Candy had big curly hair and enormous breasts. She embraced Yuki, who withstood the hug briefly, then struggled free and headed toward the exit, saying, "What time is it? How long have I been here?"

Candy kept pace with Yuki, talking all the way.

"It's after five. I've got your briefcase and your handbag and all your instructions and paperwork. In the interest of full disclosure, I opened your wallet. Had to get your insurance card and...oh! I also have the name and number of the driver who hit you. She wants to make sure you're okay. Probably worried because she hit a lawyer with her Beemer, for God's sake...ha! Oh, and give me that prescription, Yuki. We'll stop at a pharmacy. Do you have food in your apartment? Does your head hurt?"

"My head?"

Candy looked at her, nodded dumbly.

Yuki lifted her hand to the left side of her scalp, felt stubble, a prickly line of stitches.

"Oh nooooo. A mirror. *I need a mirror.*"

Candy dug into her purse, located a two-by-two plastic clamshell case, and handed it to Yuki. Yuki opened the mirror and angled it, staring at herself wide-eyed and disbelieving, finally getting the complete picture.

Her head had been shaved in a three-inch-wide swath starting at her left temple, then swooping in a long, graceful curve all the way behind her left ear. Black stitches, like a prickly caterpillar, marched along the center of that neatly sheared road.

"Look at me! I'm a *freak!*" Yuki shouted to the reporter.

"On you, freaky looks *cool.* Lean on me, honey. I'm driving you home."

Chapter 23

IT WAS ANOTHER freaking *brilliant* night at Aria. The Wurlitzer was pounding out mob hits and opera classics, tourists were giddy on killer martinis, and the regulars were high on gin and tonics, on seeing and being seen.

"Pet Girl" sat alone at the crowded bar, nursing her secret like it was a just-hatched baby bird.

She was a petite brown-eyed blonde, looked ten years younger than her thirty-three years, a woman who could slip in and out of a room like she was wearing a cloak of invisibility, like she was a freaking superhero.

That was the silver lining.

Pet Girl left a ten on the bar. Taking her Irish coffee, she drifted back to the VIP room, where McKenzie Oliver, the recently deceased rock star and her former boyfriend, lay in state, his bronze coffin squared up on the pool table.

Pet Girl's love affair with McKenzie had lasted for six

months or twenty-seven years, depending on how you counted it, but anyway it ended badly a few days ago.

That sucked. And she still didn't totally understand *why*. She'd loved him, the real person he was, the kid with a concave chest and flat feet, that way he had of looking cool and scared at the same time, just like in their sandbox days, when he was Mikey and she was his friend.

Clearly none of that had counted with him—evidence the underage, weeping junkie waif with tattoos on her face and rings in her nose, McKenzie's "real" girlfriend, whom he'd been seeing the whole time she'd been seeing him, and Pet Girl had been the last to know.

When she'd caught them in the act, McKenzie had given her that *look* that said, *Come* on. *Look who I* am. *What did you expect?*

He hadn't even said "I'm sorry."

Now Pet Girl peered into the satin-lined casket and had to admit that McKenzie looked good. He looked clean, anyway—in both meanings of the word. She felt her nose prickle, her eyes fill up, a shot of grief slamming into her heart—what she'd least expected, when she'd least expected it.

She swiped at her tears with the palm of her hand, slipped his front-door key into the breast pocket of his leather suit jacket, whispered to the dead man, "*Bite me,* asshole." Then she signed the guest book before dropping into a sofa so she could watch the party from the sidelines.

And what a party McKenzie was having.

The guys from his band were snorting lines off the pool table. Bono huddled in a corner with his manager. Willie Nelson dropped by to pay his respects, and all the others blah-blahed about the tragedy, the people she'd known her whole life, people who thought they knew her but who didn't really know her at all.

Pet Girl closed her eyes and listened to J'razz, the lead vocalist from McKenzie's band, sing "Dark Star," McKenzie's tribute to himself. After the applause, J'razz lifted his glass to the corpse, saying, "Too bad you died so fucking young, man."

The lights went out. Candles glowed. Everyone joined J'razz in singing "A Hole in the Night," McKenzie's friends and fans all thinking it was the drugs that killed him.

But Pet Girl knew that the drugs had nothing to do with it.

McKenzie Oliver had been murdered.

She knew, because she had done it.

Part Two

THE UPPER CRUST

Chapter 24

PET GIRL SAT on the floor of the children's former nursery, her back against the wall. She was wearing welder's gloves and steel-tipped boots, had her precious Rama safe inside her bag. And she listened to the Baileys' muted shouts through the plaster.

"Pig!"

"Slut!"

"Shut up, shut up, shut up!"

The fools didn't even know she was sitting ten feet away in the dark, that she'd been waiting for hours for them to come home and screw themselves to sleep.

She'd used the time well, ran the Grand Plan through her mind again. She was prepared. She knew their habits, the floor plan, the best way in, the quickest way out.

And she knew the code.

It was a good plan, but Pet Girl also had a Plan B—what to do if she got caught. *And she had the nerve to do even that.*

On the other side of the wall, Ethan Bailey accused his wife of screwing around, and Pet Girl didn't doubt that she had. Isa had been a pretty competent flirt when they were in class together at Katherine Delmar Burke School.

And since then, Isa had truly mastered the art of casual seduction. Like Gwyneth Paltrow on a really good day.

But that wasn't why Pet Girl despised Isa.

It was deeper than that, had to do with when her life had shattered to pieces—when Pet Girl was ten and her dad had died, and Isa had hugged her hard at the funeral and said, "I'm sooooo sorry. But don't ever forget that I love you. We're best friends *forever*."

"Forever" had lasted a couple of weeks.

Once her dad's fortune and protection shifted entirely to his *real* family, it was as if Pet Girl and her mother had never existed. No more private school or dance classes or birthday parties on Snob Hill for her. Pet Girl had plummeted through the delicate web of those who had it to the flat and dismal plains of "Who cares?"—where the bastard daughter of a married man belonged.

Isa, on the other hand, had graduated at eighteen and married Ethan Bailey in a hand-beaded Carolina Herrera gown at twenty-two, a wedding attended by the entire West Coast Social Register. And everything else followed: her two clever children, her charities, her place at the gleaming peak of high society.

Pet Girl's mother had said, "Move, sweetheart. Start over." But Pet Girl had her own roots in this city, deeper and more historic than even Isa's midnight-blue bloodlines.

8th Confession

And so, this was Pet Girl's life after the fall, working for the Baileys and their revolting ilk, walking their neurotic dogs, taking their disgusting furs into cold storage, addressing invitations to their snobby friends, people who called her "Pet Girl" and who talked about her when she was close enough to hear.

For so long, she thought that she was handling it.

But if she'd learned anything from McKenzie Oliver, it was that "handling it" was overrated.

Pet Girl stared around the room, filled now with racks of outrageous, never-worn clothes and mountains of unopened boxes of pricey purchases bought on a whim.

It was sickening. The decadence of the very rich. The twenty-four-karat-gold crap.

Inside the bedroom, the shouting stopped. Pet Girl pressed her ear to the wall, listened to the Baileys grunt and groan, Isa calling out, "Oh yes, that's good, oh!" the two of them making what they called *love,* Isa's voice giving Pet Girl even more reason to bring her down.

And then there was silence.

Pet Girl gripped the handle of her canvas bag.

It was time.

Chapter 25

PET GIRL OPENED the door to the Baileys' bedroom, dropped to a crouch as the pugs, Wako and Waldo, ran over to her, all snuffling and wriggling. She shushed and rubbed them, watched them trot back to their baskets under the window, circle, and lie down again.

Pet Girl stood rock still, listening to the Baileys' rhythmic breathing coming from their vast moonlit bed. At the windows, silk taffeta curtains billowed, the rustling covering her own excited breathing and the whooshing of traffic on the street below.

She could see that Isa was nude, lying on her stomach under the thousand-thread-count sheets and 100-percent goose down comforter, her long, dark hair fanned out over her shoulders. On her left, Ethan lay on his back, his snores scenting the air with alcohol.

Pet Girl walked to Isa's side, homed in on her exposed

shoulder. Her heart was thudding. She felt as high as if she'd jumped from a plane and was waiting to pull the rip cord.

She put down her canvas bag, opened it, and reached inside with her gloved hand. Just then, Isa stirred, half rose up in her bed, and, seeing Pet Girl's stooped silhouette, called out, "Who's there?" her voice slurry with drink and sleep.

Pet Girl croaked, "Isa, it's just *me.*"

"What are you...doing here?"

Pet Girl's feet had frozen to the floor. Had she been crazy? What if Isa turned on the lights? What if the dogs went nuts? What if Ethan woke up?

Plan B was satisfactory, but it was far from ideal.

"I picked up your prescription. I made a special *trip,*" Pet Girl whispered, vamping madly. Ethan stirred, rolled onto his side facing away from her. He pulled the comforter up under his arm. He was *out.*

"Put it on my nightstand and get the hell out, okay?"

"That's what I'm *doing,*" Pet Girl said, sounding pissed off now, believably so. "Did you hear me? I made a special *trip.* And you're *welcome.*"

Isa's shoulder was only inches from Pet Girl's hand. She struck softly, precisely.

"What was that?" Isa asked. "Did you pinch me?"

"Yeah, bitch. Because I *hate* you. I wish you'd *die.*"

Isa laughed. "Don't hold back, darling."

"No," said Pet Girl, "not me."

But a new idea was forming. *Call it Plan C.*

Willing her pulse to slow, Pet Girl walked to Ethan's side of the bed, picked up a paperback off the floor, returned it to the night table, eyed his hairy arm lying across the top of the comforter.

"What are you doing now?" Isa asked.

"Tidying up," Pet Girl said.

And she struck again.

Oh yes, it's so good. Oh.

"Go to sleep," Pet Girl said, snapping her bag closed. "I'll be back in the morning for the dogs."

"Don't wake us up, chickadee."

"Don't worry. Sweet dreams," she said, her voice rising giddily. With the handles of her canvas bag slung over her shoulder, Pet Girl ran quickly down two flights of stairs in the dark and punched Isa's code into the keypad at the front door, disarming and then arming the alarm again.

Then she stepped outside as free as a chickadee. "Sweet dreams, darlings," sang the voice in her head. "Sweet dreams."

Chapter 26

IT WAS AROUND LUNCHTIME on Monday when Jacobi loomed over our desks, said to me and Conklin, "I need you both to get over to Broadway and Pierce before the bodies are moved. Boxer, relieve the swing shift and take over the case."

"Take over the case?" I said dumbly.

I shot a look at Conklin. We'd just been talking about the Baileys, who'd been found dead a few hours ago in their bed. We'd been glad we hadn't caught a case that was guaranteed to be surrounded by media high jinks all the time, live updates on the hour.

"The mayor is Ethan Bailey's cousin," said Jacobi.

"I know that."

"He and the chief want you on this, Boxer. Asked for you by name."

As flattering as that was meant to be, I nearly gagged. Rich and I were drowning in unsolved cases, and not only would a high-profile crime be micromanaged by the brass but our other twelve cases would not go away. They'd just get cold.

"No bitching," Jacobi said to me. "Yours is to protect and serve."

I stared at him, mouth closed so I wouldn't say bad things.

But I saw that Conklin was having a whole different reaction. He cleared off a space on his desk, and Jacobi put his butt down, still talking.

"There's a live-in housekeeping staff at the Bailey house, and they have their own wing. The head of housekeeping, Iraida Hernandez, found the bodies," Jacobi said. "You'll want to talk to her first."

I had my notebook out. "What else?" I was in the frying pan, felt the flames lapping at the edges.

"The Baileys had dinner with a friend last night. Interior designer, name of Noble Blue, might be the last person to see them alive. After Hernandez called nine one one, she called Blue, and Blue phoned the mayor. That's all we've got."

Well, there would be more. Lots more.

The Bailey family history was common knowledge.

Isa Booth Bailey was a fourth-generation San Franciscan, descended from one of the railroad magnates who'd forged train lines over the prairies in the mid-1800s. Her family was in the billionaire league.

Ethan Bailey's line also went back to 1800s San Francisco, but his family had been working-class. His great-grandfather was a miner, and from there his family worked their way up, notch by notch, through everyday commerce. Before Ethan Bailey died sometime in the dark hours, he'd owned "Bailey's," a chain of restaurants featuring all-you-can-eat buffets for $9.99.

Together and separately, they'd been the focus of San Francisco socialites and wannabes. There were rumors of Hollywood lovers, kinky combinations, and all the parties money could buy: red party, blue party, and party hearty.

I tuned back in to what Jacobi was saying. "This Noble Blue is some kind of fancy fruit. Said he can fill you in on the Baileys' crowd from soup to nuts. And he's not kidding about the nuts. Boxer, take anyone you need to work the case— Lemke, Samuels, McNeil. I want updates and I'll be sticking my nose in."

I gave him the evil eye but said, "Fine. You know what I'm praying for?" I took the file out of Jacobi's hand, stood to put on my jacket.

Jacobi's face flattened. "What's that, Boxer?"

"That the Baileys left suicide notes."

Chapter 27

CONKLIN TOOK THE WHEEL of our unmarked Chevy, and we pulled out heading north on Bryant. We bucked through stop-and-go traffic until I said, "This is nuts," and flipped on the siren. Fifteen minutes later, we were parked across from the Baileys' home.

The fire department was there, as well as an assortment of marked and unmarked police cars and the CSI mobile that was blocking the front walk.

There aren't many Hollywood types in San Francisco, but if we had a star map, the Baileys' house would be on it. A three-story buff stucco giant with white crossbeams and trim, it was planted on the corner of Broadway and Pierce, running a half block to both the south and the east.

It looked more like a museum than a house to me, but it had a glamorous history going back to Prohibition, and it was the best that fifteen million bucks could buy: thirty thousand square feet of the city's most prime real estate.

I greeted the first officer at the door, Pat Noonan, a kid with stuck-out red ears and a growing reputation for immaculate police work. Samuels and Lemke came up the path, and I put them back on the street to canvass the neighborhood.

"Forced entry?" I asked Noonan.

"No, ma'am. Anyone entering the house had to have an alarm code and a key. Those five people over there? That's the live-in staff. They were all here last night, didn't hear or see anything."

I muttered, "Now there's a shock." Then Noonan introduced us to the head housekeeper, Iraida Hernandez.

Hernandez was a wiry woman, immaculately dressed, late fifties. Her eyes were red from weeping, and her English was better than mine. I took her aside so we could speak privately.

"This was no suicide," Hernandez announced defiantly. "I was Isa's nursemaid. I'm raising her kids. I know this whole family from conception on, and I tell you that Isa and Ethan were happy."

"Where are their children now?"

"Thank God, they spent the night with their grandparents. I want to be sick. What if they had found their parents instead of me? Or what if they'd been home—no, no. I can't even think."

I asked Hernandez where she'd been all night ("In bed, watching a *Plastic Surgery: Before and After* marathon"), what she saw when she opened the Baileys' door ("They were dead.

Still warm!"), and if she knew anyone who might have wanted to hurt the Baileys ("Lots of people were jealous of them, but to kill them? I think there's been some kind of horrible accident").

Hernandez looked up at me as if she were hoping I could make the bad dream go away, but I was already thinking over the puzzle, wondering if I'd actually taken on some kind of English-style drawing-room whodunit.

I told Hernandez that she and the staff would be getting rides to the station so that we could take exclusionary prints and DNA. And then I called Jacobi.

"This wasn't a break-in," I told him. "Whatever was going on in this house, the staff probably know about it. All five had unrestricted access, so —"

"So chances are good that if the Baileys were murdered, one of them did it."

"There you go. Reading my mind."

I told Jacobi that I thought he and Chi should do the interviews themselves, and Jacobi agreed. Then Conklin and I ducked under the barrier tape and logged in with a rookie in the foyer who directed us to the Baileys' bedroom.

The interior of the house was a wonderland of tinted plaster walls, elaborate moldings and copings, fine old European paintings and antiques in every room, each chamber opening into an even grander one, a breathtaking series of surprises.

When we got to the third floor, I heard voices and the static of radios coming from halfway down the carpeted hallway.

A buff young cop from the night tour, Sergeant Bob Nardone, walked into the hall, called out to me as we came toward him.

I said, "Sorry about having to take over, Bob. I have orders."

For some reason, I expected a fight.

"You're joking, right, Boxer? Take my case, please!"

Chapter 28

CHARLIE CLAPPER, head of our crime lab, was standing beside the Baileys' bed. Clapper is in his midfifties, and having spent half his life in law enforcement, he's as good as they come. Maybe better. Charlie is no showboater. He's nitpickingly thorough. Then he says his piece and gets out of the way.

Clapper had been at the scene for about two hours, and there were no markers or flags on the carpet, meaning no blood, no trace. As techs dusted the furniture for prints, I took in the astonishing tableau in front of me.

The Baileys lay in their bed, as still and as unblemished as if they were made of wax.

Both bodies were nude, sheets and a comforter were draped over their lower trunks. A black lace demibra hung over the massive carved-mahogany headboard. Other clothing, both outer- and underwear, was scattered around the floor as though it had been tossed there in haste.

"Everything is as we found it except for an opened bottle of Moët and two champagne flutes, which are headed back to the lab," Clapper told Conklin and me. "Mr. Bailey took Cafergot for migraines, Prevacid for acid reflux. His wife took clonazepam. That's for anxiety."

"That's some kind of Valium, right?" Conklin asked.

"Similar. The directions on the bottle were for one tablet to be used for sleep at bedtime. That's minimal."

"How much was in the medicine bottle?" Conklin asked.

"It was nearly full."

"Could clonazepam have a lethal interaction with champagne?"

"Put her to sleep is all."

"So what are you thinking?" I asked Clapper.

"Well, I look at the positions of the bodies and hope that'll tell me something. If they were holding hands, I'd be thinking suicide pact. Or maybe something a little more sinister."

"Like the killer staged the scene after the victims were dead?"

Clapper nodded, said, "Exactly. Some kind of forethought or afterthought. But here are two apparently healthy people in their thirties lying in natural sleeping positions. There's semen on the sheets but no blood, no other substances. And I don't see any signs of struggle, no marks or wounds."

"Please, Charlie, give us *something*," I said.

"Well, here's what it's *not*: carbon monoxide. The fire department did a thorough sweep, and it was negative. Also, the Baileys' dogs slept here," Clapper said, pointing to the dog beds near the window, "and both are alive. According to the housekeeper, the dog walker came for them at eight, and when she brought them back, she told Hernandez that the dogs were fine."

"Lovely," I said. "Perfect, really."

"I'll get back to you on the prints and leave the rest to the ME when she gets here. But you're right, Lindsay. This crime scene is too clean. If it *is* a crime scene."

"And that's all?"

Charlie winked. "That's all. Clapper has spoken."

Chapter 29

THE BAILEYS GOT the best of everything, even in death. We got search warrants without a grilling. First time ever. Then Deputy DA Leonard Parisi came by and asked for a tour of the so-called crime scene.

His presence told me that if this was homicide and there was a prosecutable suspect, Red Dog was going to try the case himself. I showed him the victims, and he stood silently, respectfully.

Then he said, "This is ugly. No matter what happened here, it's grotesque."

No sooner had Parisi left when Claire walked in with two assistants. I briefed her as she took photos of the Baileys: two shots from each angle before she touched the bodies.

"Any thoughts you can share?" I asked as she pulled down the bedsheets, took more pictures.

"Hang on, baby girl. I don't know *what* the hell I'm thinking yet."

She harrumphed a few times, asked for help in turning the bodies, said, "There's no rigor. Lividity is blanching. They're still warm to the touch. So I would certainly put time of death at twelve hours or under."

"Could it be six?"

"Yes."

"Anything else?"

"Yeah. They're rich, thin, beautiful, and dead."

Claire then gave me the usual disclaimer: she wouldn't say anything official until she'd done the posts.

"But here's what's unusual," Claire told my partner and me. "Two dead folks, the rigor is pretty much the same, the lividity is pretty much the same. Something got these people at the *same time*, Lindsay.

"Look at them. No visible trauma, no bullet wounds, no bruising, no defensive wounds. I'm starting to think of poisoning, you know?"

"Poisoning, huh? Like maybe two homicides? Or a homicide-suicide? I'm just thinking out loud."

Claire shot me a grin. "I'll do the autopsies today. I'll send out the blood. I'll let you know what the labs come back with. I'll tell you what I know as soon as I know it."

Conklin and I worked the top floor of the Baileys' museum of a house while Clapper's team did the kitchen and baths. We looked for signs of disturbance and we looked for notes and journals, found none. We confiscated three laptops: Isa's, Ethan's, and the one belonging to Christopher Bailey, age nine, for good measure.

8th Confession

We methodically tossed the closets and looked under the beds, then searched the servants' quarters so the staff could return to their rooms when they got back from the Hall.

I checked in with Claire as the deceased were being zipped into body bags, and she looked at my frown, said, "*I'm not worried, Linds, so relax yourself. The tox screens will give us a clue.*"

Chapter 30

"HERE WE GO," said Conklin, nodding in the direction of the fortyish, sandy-haired man in shorts and a hot-pink T-shirt waving to us from a tiki hut, one of several similar cabanas grouped around an oval-shaped pool.

If there was ever a place where Conklin and I stood out as cops, this was it. The Bambuddha Lounge had been the epicenter for hipster-richies since Sean Penn had held a party here after wrapping his Nixon film. As we crossed the patio, eyes shifted away, joints were snuffed out. I half expected someone to shout, "Cheese it, the fuzz."

"I'm Noble Blue," said the man in pink.

We introduced ourselves. I ordered mineral water to Noble Blue's mai tai, and when we were all comfortable, I said, "I understand you had dinner with the Baileys last night."

"Can you imagine?" Blue said. "They were having their last meal. In a million years, I would never have guessed. We were at the opera before dinner. *Don Giovanni,*" he told us. "It was terrific."

The word "terrific" got caught in his throat, and tears spilled down his tanned cheeks. He grabbed a tissue and wiped them away. "Sorry," Blue said. "It's just that Isa and Ethan saw so many of their friends there. It's almost as if they'd had a big night out because they knew..."

"Could they have known?" Conklin asked. "How did they seem to you?"

Blue told us that they were "a hundred-percent normal." Isa had flirted at dinner with a man at a nearby table, and, as usual, that made Ethan wild.

"How wild?" I asked.

Blue smiled, said, "I don't mean *violent,* Sergeant. It was part of their foreplay."

Conklin asked, "Can you think of anyone who might have wanted them dead?"

"No. I mean, not in my wildest. But people felt snubbed just as a matter of fact. Everyone wanted to be around the Baileys, and it just wasn't possible."

Blue brought up committees that Isa chaired and people who were slighted by that. He spoke of other big-name couples and the not-so-friendly competition among them to see who could be mentioned most often in the *Chronicle*'s lifestyle pages.

And he went into a kind of rhapsody as he described Isa's thirtieth-birthday party in Paris, what she had worn, the fact that Barbra Streisand had performed and that their three hundred guests had been treated to a week of exorbitant luxury.

Conklin had been taking notes, but the three-hundred-name guest list stopped him.

"There's a list of the guests somewhere?"

"Surely there is. I think it was published. You could Google it?" Blue said helpfully. He blew his nose, sipped his drink, and added thoughtfully, "Sure, people hated them. Ethan and Isa attracted envy. Their money. Their fame. And they were both so hot, they perspired pearls."

I nodded, but after Noble Blue's hour-long virtual tour of the Baileys' lifestyle, I was exhausted by so much information that had yielded so little.

At the same time, Noble Blue had managed to hook me. I found that I cared about these two people who'd seemed lucky and blessed until their lives were canceled—as if someone had thrown a switch and simply shut them down.

I thanked Blue, unfolded my cramped legs, and stepped down from the tiki hut in the center of the Tenderloin.

"I know less now than when Jacobi lobbed this hot potato to us," I said to Conklin as we walked out to Eddy Street.

"You," Conklin said, unlocking the car.

"Me, what?"

He gave me his lady-killer grin, the one that could make me forget my own name. "You," my partner said again. "Jacobi lobbed this hot potato to *you*."

Chapter 31

THE COPS on the Bailey investigation were loosely arranged around the grungy twenty-by-thirty-foot squad room we often think of as home.

Jacobi sat behind my desk, saying into the phone, "They just got here. Okay. As soon as you can."

He hung up, told us, "Clapper says there were no suspicious prints in the bedroom or bath. There was nothing interesting in the glasses or the pills or the bottle of champagne.

"Claire's on her way. Paul, why don't you start?"

Paul Chi is lithe, upbeat, resourceful, and a first-class interrogator. He and Jacobi had interviewed the Baileys' live-in staff, and Chi gave his report from his seat.

"First up, the gardener. Pedro Vasquez, forty-year-old Hispanic. Seemed twitchy. He volunteered that he had some porn on his laptop," Chi said. "But it turned out to be legal-age porn. I spent an hour with him, don't see a motive, not yet, anyway. His prints were *not* found in the Baileys' bedroom. Vasquez told me he'd never been above the ground floor, and at this point, we've got no reason to think that's a lie.

"Two: Iraida Hernandez," Chi said, flipping the page in his notebook. "Hernandez is a nice lady."

"Your professional opinion, Chi?" Lemke asked mildly.

"Yes," said Chi, "it is. Hernandez is a naturalized citizen, Mexican, fifty-eight, employed for more than thirty years by Isa Booth's family and by the Baileys. As expected, her prints are all over the Baileys' bedroom.

"She's got no record, but as for motive? It's a maybe."

"Really?" I said.

Chi nodded. "She says she's probably in the Baileys' will, so you never know, but my Grift-O-Meter didn't go off. Iraida Hernandez does things by the book. She's loyal. She didn't have a bad thing to say about anyone, so as I said, 'Nice lady.'"

"What about the cook?" Cappy McNeil called out. Cappy's a big guy, two hundred fifty, and if the doughnuts and the stairs don't get him, he could get promoted out of here to a good lieutenant's job in a small town down the line. That's what he's shooting for. Calls it "going coastal."

"As I was about to say," Chi said to his partner, "number three: the cook is Miller, Marilyn, white, forty-seven years old. Moved here from somewhere in flyover country." Chi looked at his notes. "Ohio. Only been working for the Baileys for a year. Has a clean record. No prints upstairs. All I got off her was 'What's going to happen to me now?' I see no motive. What's she got to gain? But like the rest of the staff, access to the Baileys was a given. And if we're thinking poison..."

Chi shrugged as if to say, *She's the cook.*

8th Confession

Jacobi said, "I told Miller not to leave the city, and I got two teams from the Special Investigation Division. They'll be on her at all times."

Chi was finishing up his report on the remaining two of the Baileys' live-in staff, a second housekeeper and the mechanic, both as clean as cat whiskers, when Claire stomped into the squad room in her sneakers and scrubs.

She looked around and said, "Are you all thinking, *Now that Claire's here, the party can begin?* Think again."

Chapter 32

CHI WHEELED A CHAIR over for Claire. She sat down, propped her feet up on a desk, said, "Ladies and Gentlemen, the Baileys' bodies were so pristine, I expected them to start breathing. No pills in their stomachs, no abrasions, contusions, or lacerations. Negative for carbon monoxide. And since I never let skin stand between me and my diagnosis, I did a layerwise dissection on both necks, and the backs of their necks as well.

"In sum, I looked at everything but their dreams. The autopsies were completely negative."

Everyone groaned. Even me.

"I spoke with Ethan Bailey's physician," Claire continued. "I spoke with Isa's gynecologist. Both doctors had complete and recent medical histories of their patients, and the Baileys passed their physicals with five stars each, ten stars total. Those kids knew how to take care of their bodies.

8th Confession

"So as I hung up the phone after talking to you ten minutes ago," she said to Jacobi, "the rushed toxicology report walked in the door.

"I was ready to opine that if there was poison involved, one of the Baileys whacked the other and then took poison him- or herself, so we'd have homicide-suicide or double suicide. But I got surprised—and not in a good way."

Claire had us by the eyeballs.

No one spoke. Maybe no one breathed.

Claire waved a computer printout, said, "Toxicology was negative. No poison, no opiates, no narcotics, no nothing. Cause of death? No idea. Manner of death? No idea. Something stinks, and I don't know what," she told us, "but the likelihood of these two individuals, with completely negative autopsies and completely negative toxicologies, expiring at the same time is statistically *astronomical*."

"Oh, man," I muttered. "So much for 'The tox screens will give us a clue.'"

"Okay, okay, I was wrong about that, Lindsay. Since there's no such thing as 'sudden adult death syndrome,' we're thinking homicide. Until we've got something to go on, I'm giving Ethan and Isa Bailey Chinese death certificates."

Chi spoke up, said, "Claire, my darling, that's a new one for me. What's a Chinese death certificate?"

"Pen Ding," she cracked. "Case open. Any other questions?"

"Yep," said Jacobi. "What now?"

Claire took her feet off the desk, stood up, and said, "I'm going home. Going to kiss my baby. Then I'm going to eat an entire turkey potpie followed by a bowl of chocolate pudding with whipped cream, and no one better try to stop me."

She gazed around the room at our faces, slack from the long day and gray from the overhead fluorescent lights. I was pretty sure we looked like the living dead.

Jacobi in particular looked awful. He would be the one telling the family and the press and the chief and the mayor that at the end of the day, we were clueless.

"I know you're just getting started, and so am I," said Claire, her smile beaming a small ray of hope into our collective gloom. "I sent the samples back to the lab. Let the night crew take a crack at this," she said. "I'm asking them to run the tests again, this time instructing them to look for the weird, the strange, and the *bizarre*."

Chapter 33

CONKLIN AND I spent seven full hours interviewing Isa and Ethan Bailey's friends, family, and the short list of their non-live-in personal employees: Isa's secretary; the dog walker, who was also a gal Friday; and the children's tutor.

Nothing popped. We filled our notebooks and moved on.

While the rest of my team went back to the neighborhood canvass, Conklin and I went to see Yancey and Rita Booth, Isa's indescribably wealthy parents, who tearfully invited us into their magnificent Nob Hill home.

We spent hours with the Booths, mostly listening and taking notes. The Booths were in their sixties, devastated by Isa's death, and needed to talk their way through the shock by telling us about the Booth and Bailey family histories.

According to Yancey Booth, there was a hundred-year-old dispute between the Booths and the Baileys, ongoing to this day, that had started with a plot of land with ambiguous boundary lines.

We learned that Ethan Bailey had three brothers, none of them successful, and that little fact opened a door to a new branch of the investigation.

We looked at the Booth family photos going back to the gold-rush days, and we met the grandkids, or rather *they* met *us,* demanding to be let in to see the police.

At five in the afternoon we turned down an offer to stay for dinner. We left our cards and assurances that Isa Booth Bailey was our number one priority—and then we got the hell out of there.

As we walked down the front steps, I grumbled to Conklin, "We're going to be working this case until we retire."

We got into the car and sat there, talking over what we knew about the lives of Isa and Ethan, wondering if this case would ever come together.

I said to Conklin, "Her parents are never going to get over this."

"They sure loved her," he said.

"When Mrs. Booth broke down—"

"Heartbreaking. I mean, I think she could really die of this."

"And those little boys."

"Just old enough to understand. When the smaller one, Peter, said, 'Please tell me why anyone would do this to Mommy and Daddy...'" Conklin sighed. "See? Isa and Ethan couldn't have done it. I don't see one killing the other. Not with kids like that."

"I know."

I told Conklin about my sister's kids, Brigid and Meredith,

who are about the same age as the Bailey boys. "I'm going to call my sister tonight. I just want to hear the little girls' happy voices."

"Good idea," Conklin said.

"We were supposed to visit them. Me and Joe. He had to go on a business trip."

"That's too bad. But you can see Cat when he gets back."

"That's what he said."

"You like kids, Lindsay," Conklin said after a moment. "You should have some."

I turned away, looked out the window as all those forbidden thoughts tumbled over one another, how close Rich and I had become, the taboo words and deeds, the smell of his hair, what it had felt like to kiss him, the part of me that regretted saying no because now I would never know how we would have fit together.

"Lindsay? You okay?"

I turned to him, said, "I'm just thinking," and when I looked into his eyes, there was that hit, that arc of electricity going from me to him to me.

A phone rang in the distance.

On the third ring, I grabbed my cell off my belt, feeling mad, sad, and glad—in that order. It was Jacobi calling, but I wouldn't have cared if it had been a wrong number.

I'd been saved by the bell.

Because in another moment, I might have suggested doing with Conklin what I was thinking—and all that would accomplish would be to make me feel *worse*.

Chapter 34

CLAIRE STOOD IN the center of the squad room again, but this time she looked weird, like she'd taken a punch.

"For those of you who haven't heard my lecture, there are two types of cases—one type is circumstance-dependent and the other is autopsy-dependent."

She was pacing now, talking as much to herself as she was to the ten of us, who were waiting to hear about the second tox run.

"That homeless guy, you know the one, Bagman Jesus. He had trauma all over him, six gunshot wounds to the head and neck, plus a postmortem beat-down. His body was found in a neighborhood frequented by drug dealers—but I don't even *need* to know the circumstances.

"Six gunshot wounds. That's a homicide.

"Now we've got two dead people found in their beds. Got a completely negative autopsy, completely negative environment..."

She stopped speaking. Swallowed.

"The tox run for the weird, the strange, and the *bizarre*," I said, trying to give her a little push.

"Negative. Completely negative, so thanks, girlfriend, I almost forgot what I was saying. But now I remember: the Bailey case is circumstance-dependent.

"And a circumstance-dependent case means we need police work. You all know what I'm getting at. What were their finances like? Anyone having an affair here? Anyone leading a double life? You gotta help me out, give me a direction, because I'm twisting in the wind."

So that was it. Claire was *stumped*. I wasn't sure I'd ever seen her stumped before. Ever.

"This is the press release I've got to give in the morning," Claire said. She took a piece of paper out of the pocket of her scrubs and began to read from it.

"The Bailey case is under active investigation by the medical examiner's office. Since these deaths are suspicious, we are treating them as homicides. I'm not going to comment because I don't want to undermine the overall investigation."

Claire stopped reading and looked up.

"And then the press is going to beat the hell out of me."

"You're not saying you're finished, are you?" Jacobi said.

I felt worried for Claire. She looked pained and scared.

"I'm gonna get a consult. I've got calls in to two very knowledgeable board-certified forensic pathologists, asking them to come in and take a look," said Claire. "You have to tell the families, Jacobi. Tell them that they can't have their children's bodies yet, because we're not done."

Chapter 35

YUKI WAS STARING into his blue-gray eyes again, this time across a small table in the hospital cafeteria, Dr. John Chesney working on his vegetarian chili, saying, "Finally having lunch, fourteen hours into my day."

Yuki thought he was *adorable,* felt giddy just looking at him, knowing full well that adorability didn't mean he was good or honest or *anything.* She even flashed back on a couple of handsome *rats* she'd dated in her life, not to mention more than a few gorgeous *killers* she'd faced in court—but never mind!

Not only was John Chesney adorable but he was damned *nice,* too.

She could almost feel her mother's breath on the back of her neck, her mom whispering, "Yuki-eh, this doctah John, he good man for hus-band."

Mom, we know nothing *about him.*

Chesney sipped his Coke, said, "I'm not sure I've *met* San Francisco yet. I've been here for four months and my schedule is get off work, jog home, fall asleep in the shower."

Yuki laughed. Imagined him naked, ash-blond hair plastered to his head, water sluicing down his compact, muscular body...

"When I wake up, I'm here again. It's like *Groundhog Day* in a war zone, but I'm not complaining. This is the job I've always wanted. What about you? You're a lawyer, right?"

"Yep. I am."

Yuki told John that she was currently waiting for a verdict on a pretty high-profile case, maybe he'd heard about it.

"Former beauty queen kills her father with a crowbar, tries to do the same to her mother—"

"That's *your* case? We've all talked about the mother surviving five solid blows to her head. Jeez, a caved-in cranial vault, broken orbital socket, and smashed jaw. Man, she wanted to *live*."

"Yeah. It was a real kick in the pants when she recanted what we call her 'dying declaration'..." Yuki started thinking about Rose Glenn, ran her hand over her new buzz cut, looked up to see Chesney smiling, turning those eyes on her approvingly.

"That's a great look on you, Yuki."

"Ya think?"

"You know I had to do it, don't you?"

"Well, good intentions are no defense, Doctor. You started this with your clippers, did you not? Used them like a lawn mower. Gave me the worst haircut I've ever had in my life, isn't that so, Doctor?"

Chesney laughed, said, "Guilty of inciting a bad haircut. But I gave you very neat stitches."

Yuki laughed with him, then said, "John, I called because I want to apologize. I'm sorry I was such a crazy bitch when I was here."

"Ha! You were the best mad patient I've ever had."

"Come on!" She laughed again.

"Really. You didn't threaten me, didn't hit me or stick me with a needle. I've got a guy in the ER right now with three broken ribs and a concussion, and he won't give up his cell phone. 'I'm *working*,' he says. Took three of us to wrench his phone out of his hand."

And just then, Chesney's beeper went off. He looked at it, said, "Damn. I've got to get back. Um, Yuki, would you want to do this again sometime?"

"Sure," said Yuki. "I'm only a taxi ride away."

"Maybe we could go somewhere *else*. Maybe you could show me the city."

Yuki gave him a coy smile, said, "So I guess I'm forgiven."

John put his hand over hers. "I'll let you know."

She laughed and so did he, and their eyes locked until he took his hand away—and then he was gone.

Yuki was already waiting for his call.

Chapter 36

CINDY TOOK A right turn out of her apartment building, cell phone pressed to her ear, listening to Lindsay say, "I wish I could do something, but we're *drowning* in the Bailey case. *Drowning.*"

"My editor is holding page one of the Metro section for my story. I've got a *deadline.* You're saying you've got nothing at all?"

"You want the truth? Conklin and I were kicked off Bagman Jesus on day one. We tried to work it on our own time—"

"Thanks anyway, Linds. No, really," Cindy said, snapping her phone closed. Enough said. *No one was working the case.*

Cindy walked up Townsend Street to the corridor between her apartment and the spot where Bagman Jesus had been murdered. She stopped at the humble shrine outside the train yard, blood still staining the sidewalk, newly wilted flowers and handwritten notes woven into the chain-link fence.

She stood for a while reading the messages from friends telling Bagman Jesus that he'd be missed and remembered. These notes were heartbreaking. A good man had been killed, and the police were too busy to find his killer. So who was fighting in Bagman's corner?

She was.

Cindy moved on, keeping pace with pedestrians exiting the train station. She turned onto Fifth Street and made her way toward the brick building in the middle of the block that housed the soup kitchen called From the Heart.

On one side of the soup kitchen was a hole-in-the-wall liquor store. On the other side was a fast-food Chinese restaurant that looked really low, like it served tree squirrel sautéed with brown sauce and peanuts.

In between the restaurant and the soup kitchen was a black door. Cindy had a date behind that door. She hoisted her computer bag higher up on her shoulder, turned the knob, and gave the door a shove with her hip. It opened at the foot of a dark and sour-smelling stairway.

Cindy began the steep climb, the stairs wrapping around a small landing, rising again to a floor with three doors, the signage identifying them as a nail salon, a massage parlor, and, toward the front of the building, PINCUS AND PINCUS, ATTORNEYS-AT-LAW.

Cindy pressed the intercom button on the panel beside the door, gave her name, and was buzzed in. She took a seat in the reception area, an alcove filled wall-to-wall with a cracked leather sofa and a coffee table. She leafed through an old copy of Us Weekly, looking up as someone called her name.

8th Confession

The man introduced himself as Neil Pincus. He was dressed in gray slacks, a white button-down shirt with the sleeves rolled up, no tie. He had a receding hairline and a pleasant, unremarkable face, and he was wearing a gold wedding band. He put out his right hand and so did she.

"Nice to meet you, Mr. Pincus."

"Neil. Come on in the back. I can give you only a few minutes, but they're all yours."

Chapter 37

CINDY SAT ACROSS from the attorney's desk, her back to the dirty window. She glanced at a grouping of framed photos on the credenza to her right: the Pincus brothers with their good-looking wives and teenage daughters. Neil Pincus stabbed a button on his telephone console, said to his brother, "Al, please take my calls. I'll be just a few minutes."

Then he said to Cindy, "How can I help you?"

"You've got a heck of a reputation in this neighborhood."

"Thanks. We do what we can," Pincus said. "People get arrested and either get a public defender or they ask us."

"Nice of you to do this work for free."

"It's pretty rewarding, actually, and we're not alone. We work with a group of businesspeople around here who kick in money for legal costs and special needs. We have a needle-exchange program. We run a literacy program—"

The phone rang. Neil Pincus peered at the caller ID,

turned his eyes back to Cindy, and talked over the ring tone. "I'm sorry. But I think you should tell me why you're here before the phone drives us both crazy."

"I'm doing a five-part piece about Bagman Jesus, the homeless man recently found dead."

"I read your story."

"Okay. Good. So this is it," Cindy said. "I can't get the police interested in his death. They don't think his murder is solvable."

Pincus sighed, said, "Well, that's typical."

"I need Bagman's real name in order to get a fingerhold on his past and work forward from there. I'm hoping he may have been a client of yours. If not, maybe you could lead me to someone who knew him."

"Ah. If I'd known what you wanted, I could have saved you a trip. I've seen him on the street, sure, but Bagman Jesus never came here, and if he had, I probably wouldn't tell you."

"Lawyer-client privilege?"

"Not exactly. Look, Cindy, I don't know you, so I shouldn't be telling you what to do. But I will anyway.

"The homeless aren't stray puppies. They're homeless for a reason. Most of them are drug addicts. Or they're *psychotic*. Some are violent. I'm sure you're well-meaning, but this fellow was *murdered*."

"I understand."

"Do you? You're a pretty girl in pretty clothes, walking around the Tenderloin alone asking who killed Bagman Jesus. Just suppose for a minute that you find his killer—and he turns on *you?*"

Chapter 38

WHEN CINDY LEFT Neil Pincus, she was irritated and just as determined as before. The lawyer had called her a *girl*. Like she was one of his kids. He'd underestimated her tenacity, and he didn't get that she was a working journalist who covered *crime*.

She was careful. She was experienced. She was a pro.

And what she hated most? He'd gotten to her.

She shook off a wave of anxiety, opened the door to From the Heart, looked around at the hundred ragged people going through the food line, others hunched over their plates, protecting their bacon and eggs. Three men in dirty clothes rapped in the corner.

For the first time, she wondered if someone in this place had killed Bagman Jesus.

She looked for but didn't see the day supervisor, Luvie

Jump, so Cindy made a bullhorn of her cupped hands and shouted for attention.

"I'm Cindy Thomas from the *Chronicle*," she said. "I'm writing a story about Bagman Jesus. I'm going to be sitting right outside," she said, pointing through the window to two plastic chairs on the sidewalk. "If anyone can help me, I'd be grateful."

Voices rose and echoed around the large room.

Cindy went out the door and took a seat in the more stable of the two chairs. She opened her laptop and a line formed, and from the first interview, Cindy learned something: "I'd be grateful" was code for "I'll pay for information."

An hour after making her announcement, Cindy had collected thirty stories of personal contact with Bagman Jesus, scraps of barely intelligible and frankly meaningless conversations, nothing solid, useful, or even interesting.

The price for this crazy pastiche of information had added up to seventy-five bucks, including all the change at the bottom of her handbag, plus a lipstick, a penlight, the barrette in her hair, a tin of Altoids, and three gel-ink pens.

It would make a hilarious expense report, but her story hadn't advanced even an inch.

Cindy looked up as the last person, a black woman in a red stocking cap and purple-framed eyeglasses, took the chair opposite hers.

"I'm out of cash, but I've got a BART card," Cindy said.

"Cindy? You taking up permanent residence here? Because that's not allowed."

"Luvie! I'm still working this darned story. Still getting nothing, not even Bagman's real name."

"Tell me who you talked to."

"Cindy scrolled to the top of her computer screen. "Noise Machine. Miss Patty. Salzamander. Razor, Twink T, Little Bit—"

"Let me stop you there, honey. You see, your *problem* is also your *answer*. Street people use their aliases. You know. 'Also known as.' Some of them got records. Or don't want their families to find them. They *want* to be lost. That could be why Bagman Jesus doesn't have a real name."

Cindy sighed, thinking how she'd been hustled all morning by the nameless, homeless, and hopeless, feeling remorse for snapping at Lindsay, who was right to till more fertile ground.

Mentally kissing her deadline good-bye, Cindy thanked Luvie, packed up her computer, and walked toward Mission, thinking that Bagman Jesus had disconnected from his past by his own design. His death was the end of his story.

Or was it?

An idea bloomed.

Cindy phoned her editor, said, "Therese, can you give me some time in about five minutes? I want to run something by you. Something with *legs*."

Chapter 39

AFTERNOON SUN FILTERED through the skylight and haloed Sara Needleman's head as she gave Pet Girl holy *hell*.

"What were you thinking when you left the Baileys' place cards on the table?"

"I wasn't in charge of the place cards, Sara."

"You *were*. I specifically asked you to check the place cards against the guest list. Are Isa and Ethan on the guest list?"

"No, of course not."

"I could kill you, I really could. Those two empty seats at table four. Everyone is thinking about the Baileys as it is."

"I'm sorry, Sara," Pet Girl said, but she was decidedly *not* sorry. In fact, elation was rising in her like champagne bubbles. She had to stifle a laugh.

Place cards! Like place cards were important!

Pet Girl and two other gal Fridays sat behind the reception table in the magnificent Loggia of the Asian Art Museum, welcoming the guests to an engagement dinner for Sara Needleman's niece, Frieda.

The guests were the cream of San Francisco society: senators and doctors of medicine and science, publishers and movie stars. They came up the grand staircase in their tuxedos and custom-made gowns, found their seat assignments at the reception table, and were directed to Samsung Hall.

From there, they could enter the galleries to view the priceless works of art from Japan and China and Korea before sitting down to a table dressed with raw silk and calla lilies. Then they'd be served a seven-course dinner prepared by the eminent chef Yoji Futomato.

But that would be later. Right now Sara Needleman wound up her tirade with a final flourish. "You can leave now," she snapped. "Only a few people have yet to arrive."

"Thanks, Sara." Pet Girl smiled. "Still want me to walk the dogs in the morning?"

"Yes, yes, please do. I'll be sleeping in."

"Don't worry," Pet Girl said. "I won't wake you."

Pet Girl said good-bye to the other gals. She took her annotated copy of the guest list and stashed it in her handbag, already mulling over the two hundred people she'd greeted this evening—who had acknowledged her, who had not, how many points each had scored.

And she thought ahead to her evening alone.

She'd make a little pasta. Drink a little wine. Spend a couple of pleasant hours going over the guest list.

Sort out her notes.

Make some *plans*.

Chapter 40

CLAIRE HAD PLANTED her hands on her hips and said, "We need police work" — and we'd done it. Conklin and I had strip-searched the Baileys' house for the fourth time that week, looking for God only knew *what*.

We'd been through all thirty thousand square feet: the ballroom; the two poolrooms, one with a pool *table* and one with a *pool*; the bedroom suites; the kitchens; the pantries; the sitting rooms; the playrooms; the dining rooms and living rooms. We'd opened closets, boxes, and safes; dumped drawers; and flipped through every book in the whole flippin' library.

"I forgot what we're looking for," I groused to Conklin.

"That's because whatever killed them isn't here," said Rich. "Not only am I out of *good* ideas but I don't have any bad ones either."

"Yes, and haven't we done a fine job of trashing the place?" I said, staring around the main salon.

Every doorknob and flat surface and objet d'art was smudged with black powder. Every mirror, every painting, had been taken down from the walls.

Even the benign and wise Charlie Clapper was disgusted: "The Baileys had a lot of friends and a lot of parties. We've got enough prints and trace to short out the crime lab. For a *year.*"

Conklin said, "How about it, Sarge?"

"Okay. We're done."

We turned out the lights as we worked our way to the front hall, bumped into each other in the dark as Conklin locked the front door behind us. Then he walked me to my car.

He held the door open, and as I stepped up to my Explorer's running board, my foot slipped, throwing me off balance. Rich caught me, his hands gripping my shoulders, and there was a fraction of a moment when I could see the danger.

I closed my eyes.

And as if we'd planned it, his mouth was on mine and my arms were around his neck, and I felt like I was falling off the face of the earth.

I held on tight, the heat burning me up, my hair blowing around our faces as cars streamed past us. I heard a driver calling out his window, "Get a room!"

And with that, gravity dropped me back to earth with a jolt.

What the hell are we doing?

Before Rich could say, "That man has the right idea," I

panted, "Damn, Richie. I don't know who's crazier, you or me."

His hands were at the small of my back, pulling me tight against his body.

I gently disengaged from his arms. His face was all twisted up from our kisses, and he looked . . . stung.

I said, "I'm sorry, Rich. I should've . . ."

"Should've what?"

"I should've watched my step. Are you okay?"

"Oh yeah. Just have another thing to pretend never happened."

My lips were still tingling, and I felt ashamed. I couldn't look at his hurt face any longer, so I turned away, placed my shaky foot firmly on the running board, and hauled my stupid ass into the driver's seat.

"See you tomorrow," I said. "Okay?"

"Sure. Yes, Lindsay, yes."

I closed the door and put the car in gear, and as I backed out, Rich motioned for me to roll down my window. I did.

"*You.* Since you asked, you're crazier," he said, putting both hands on the window frame. "Between you and me, it's *you.*"

I leaned out the window, put my arm around Rich's neck, and drew him to me so that our cheeks touched. His face was warm and damp, and when he put his hand in my hair, I almost melted from his sweetness. I said, "Richie, forgive me."

I pulled back, tried to smile. I waved and then headed out to the empty apartment I shared with Joe.

I wanted to cry.

For all the reasons being with Rich was wrong before, it was still wrong. I was *still* about ten years older, we were *still* partners—and I *still* loved Joe.

So why, I asked myself, driving away from Rich—*speeding* away, as a matter of fact—*does doing the right thing feel so bad?*

Chapter 41

YUKI AND PHIL HOFFMAN sat in easy chairs in Judge Duffy's chambers. The court stenographer was sitting behind her machine near the judge's desk, and Yuki was thinking, *What now? What the hell is it now?*

Judge Duffy looked frazzled, as though he'd misplaced his hallmark nonchalance. He tapped an audiocassette on its side, called out edgily, "Corinne? Got that player ready?"

The clerk came into the wood-paneled office and placed the cassette player in front of the judge, who thanked her and then pressed the tape into the box.

Duffy said to Yuki and Hoffman, "This is a tape of a phone call made from a monitored pay phone at the women's jail to juror number two. It's crackly but audible."

Yuki looked at Hoffman, who shrugged as the judge pressed the *play* button.

A young woman said, "Can you hear me okay?" A second

woman, recognizable by her nasal twang as juror number two, the retired postal worker Carly Phelan, said, "Lallie, I can't talk long. I'm supposed to be in the little girls' room."

The judge pressed the *stop* button, said, "Lallie is the juror's daughter."

Hoffman said, "The juror has a *daughter* in detention at the women's *jail?*"

"So it seems," said Duffy.

The judge pressed the *start* button, and the tape played again. There was some back-and-forth conversation between the two women: how Lallie's defense was going, how her mother liked the hotel accommodations, what was happening with Lallie's son now that both mother and grandmother weren't home.

Duffy said, "It's coming now. Listen to this."

Yuki strained to make out the words under the static.

"I saw your defendant in the shower this morning," said Lallie. "That Stacey Glenn?"

"Crap," Hoffman said.

Duffy hit *rewind*, played it again.

"I saw your defendant in the shower this morning. That Stacey Glenn? She's talking to the matron, saying if she *had* done that murder, she wouldn't have done it with no crowbar when she's got a perfectly good handgun at home."

Yuki felt light-headed and a little sick.

First, Carly Phelan had lied by omission during voir dire. If she'd said she had a daughter in jail, she would have been excused because one could logically infer that she'd be prejudiced against the prosecution.

The DA's office was trying to put her daughter away!

Second, and worse, Lallie Phelan was carrying news about the defendant to her mother. If Carly Phelan gossiped to anyone on the panel, the whole jury would be tainted.

"You're declaring a mistrial?" Hoffman asked.

"No. I'm not."

"Then I move for a mistrial, Your Honor. I have to preserve my client's rights," Hoffman countered, singing a different tune from the week before.

Duffy waved his hand dismissively. "I'm going to dump juror number two and substitute an alternate."

"I have to object, Your Honor," Hoffman said. "This conversation took place last night. Phelan could have poisoned the whole jury by now. Her daughter told her that my client has a *handgun*."

"Your Honor, I'm with *you*," said Yuki. "The sooner you get Phelan off the jury, the better. The alternates are ready to go."

"So noted. All right," said Duffy. "Let's get on with it."

Chapter 42

HOFFMAN AND YUKI walked out of the judge's chamber and down the buff-painted hallway toward the courtroom, Yuki stepping double time to keep up with the lanky opposing counsel.

Hoffman raked his hair back with his fingers, said, "The jury is going to spit blood when they hear this."

Yuki looked up at Hoffman, wondering if he thought she was green or stupid or both.

The jury would be pissed, all right. A new juror meant that they had to put aside all their earlier deliberations and start fresh, comb through the evidence all over again, beginning at day one as if it were all new.

Yuki's fantastic closing argument would be lost in the mists of time, and all that the jurors would be thinking about was how to vote so they could get out of that hotel.

Yuki knew that Hoffman was laughing inside.

8th Confession

He'd had a secret weapon all along in Carly Phelan and hadn't even known it. If Phelan had tainted the jury, it would have been in favor of the *defense.*

"Give me a break, Phil."

"Yuki, I don't know what you mean."

"Like hell."

What they both knew was that if the jury voted to convict, Hoffman would appeal. Just the fact that Carly Phelan had lied during voir dire was enough to get the conviction reversed.

On the other hand, if the jury hung again, and it very well could, the judge would *have* to declare a mistrial.

Judge Duffy didn't want a mistrial. He wanted this case over and done with.

He needn't worry, Yuki thought. It would take a year or two to mount a second trial, and by then the DA would weigh the cost and likely say, "Drop it. We're done with Glenn."

Of course, the jury could always vote to *acquit.* Either way, young Stacey would be just as free.

Yuki thought, *My damned losing streak is still going strong.* Win, lose, or draw, odds were that Stacey Glenn, that heinous frickin' father-killer, was about to walk.

Chapter 43

CINDY STOOD in front of the chain-link fence outside the Caltrain yard the next morning, put the hot new Metro section down on the sidewalk, weighted it with a couple of candles.

The headline over her story was big and bold: $25,000 REWARD.

Underneath the headline, the lead paragraph read, "The *San Francisco Chronicle* is offering a $25,000 reward for information leading to the arrest and conviction of whoever killed the man known as 'Bagman Jesus.'"

There was a tug on Cindy's arm. She pulled back, spun around, was a whisper away from a woman of about thirty with stringy hair, a blotchy complexion, a short black coat, and clothes reeking faintly of urine.

"I knew Bagman. You don't have to look at me like that. I may be strung out, but I know what I'm talking about."

"That's great," Cindy said. "I'm Cindy Thomas."

8th Confession

"Flora Gold."

"Hi, Flora. You have some information for me?"

The woman looked both ways at the stream of foot traffic, commuters coming from the white-bread suburbs to their offices in big software companies, Ms. Gold seeming by contrast like a troll who'd crawled up out of a manhole.

She turned her jittery gaze back to Cindy.

"I just wanted to say that he was a good person. He took care of me."

"How do you mean, 'took care of me'?"

"In *every* way. And he gave me this."

The woman opened her coat, dragged down the neckline of her sweater, showed Cindy a tattoo above her breast. It was done in black ink, the lettering having an Asian cast. Looked to Cindy like it had been etched by an amateur, but the message was clear.

SAVED BY JESUS & I LOVED IT!

"He's the only one who ever gave a crap about me," said Flora. "He looked out for me after I left home last year."

Cindy tried not to show her shock: Flora had been living at home until last year?

"Yeah. I'm seventeen," said Flora. "Don't look at me that way. I'm doing what I want with my life."

"You're using meth, aren't you?"

"Yeah. It's like heaven. Sex on 'ice' gives you orgasms that take your head off and last for a week. You can't imagine. No, you should *try* it."

"It's going to kill you!"

"Not your problem," Flora said, snapping her coat closed. "I just wanted to speak up for Bagman."

Flora turned away from Cindy and started a fast, loping walk up Townsend.

Cindy ran after her, called her name until Flora stopped, turned around, and said, "*What?*"

"How can I find you again?"

"You want my pager?" the teenager sneered. "Maybe I should give you my e-mail address?"

Cindy watched Flora Gold stride away until she dissolved into the distance. Flora Gold. She got it now. It was the name of a product used to keep flowers fresh longer.

And what about that tattoo?

SAVED BY JESUS & I LOVED IT!

Cindy tried to make sense of it. How had Bagman saved Flora? She was a meth head. An addict. She was going to die.

Flora had said that Bagman Jesus had given her the tattoo, yet the wording was strange, sexual. It almost seemed like a brand claiming ownership.

What kind of saint branded a devotee?

Chapter 44

A SECURITY GUARD knocked on the conference room door. Cindy looked up, as did everyone else in the editorial meeting.

"Miss Thomas, there's a vagrant standing outside. A lady. Says she has to talk to you and won't leave. Causing a real scene down there."

"Well, this was bound to happen," said Cindy's editor, Therese Stanford. "Post a twenty-five-thousand-dollar reward..."

"Can you just take her name or something?"

The guard said, "Says her name is Flora and that you want to talk to her."

Cindy told the group that she'd be back in five minutes and took the elevator down to the lobby, then walked through the revolving door and out to the street.

"I've been thinking," Flora Gold said without preamble. "About the reward?"

"Yeah. What does it mean, 'leading to the arrest and conviction'?"

"If you tell me something that the police can use to arrest Bagman's killer, and if the killer goes to court and is found guilty, then you get the reward."

Flora pulled at her tangled hair, thinking.

Cindy asked, "Do you know who killed him, Flora?"

The young woman shook her head no. "But I do know something. Maybe it's worth a hundred dollars."

"Tell me," Cindy said. "I'll be fair, I promise."

"Bagman Jesus loved me. And I know his name."

Flora handed Cindy a metal tag with a name stamped in raised letters. Cindy stared. Thinking about Flora Gold's pseudonym and yesterday's street-person hustle, she asked, "Is this true?"

"As the sky is blue."

Cindy pulled her checkbook out of her handbag.

"I don't have a bank account."

"Oh. Okay. No problem."

Cindy walked with Flora to the ATM on the corner, withdrew a hundred dollars, and gave fifty to Flora.

"You get the other fifty if this lead pans out."

Cindy watched Flora count the bills, then roll them up and tuck them in the top of her boot.

Cindy said, "Give me a couple of days and then find me, okay? Like you did today."

Gold nodded, gave Cindy a tight smile, mouth open just enough for Cindy to see that her front teeth were gone. Then the reporter headed back to the Chronicle Building.

Editorial meeting forgotten, Cindy went directly to her

office and wheeled her chair up close to her desk. She called up Google and typed, "Rodney Booker."

Less than a second later, information rolled up on the screen. Cindy sat back in her chair, watching her story crack wide open. It was a miracle. A miracle she'd *earned*.

Bagman Jesus had been decoded.

He had a name. He had a past.

And he had a family living in Santa Rosa.

Chapter 45

CINDY SAT IN the comfortable sunroom of a million-dollar Craftsman-style house in Santa Rosa, feeling anything *but* comfortable. Had she been rash? Yes.

Intrusive? Absolutely.

Thoughtless? She ought to get an *award* for blinding insensitivity.

What had she been thinking? Of course, that was the problem. She'd been thinking about her story, not about real people, so she'd launched herself into the Bookers' lives like a live hand grenade.

And the moment Lee-Ann Booker opened her front door, her sweet, momsy face shining with anticipation, Cindy realized it was too late to unpull the pin.

They were all in the sunroom now.

Lee-Ann Booker, a fair Clairol blonde in her midsixties, clutched a charm necklace of crosses and semiprecious stones and Mexican good-luck charms. She sat beside Cindy on the rattan sofa, sobbing into tissues, hiccuping and sobbing again.

Her husband, Billy Booker, brought Cindy a mug of coffee.

"You sure you don't want something *stronger?*" he asked. It sounded like a threat.

Booker was black, also in his sixties, with a military bearing and the lean body of a dedicated runner.

"No thanks, I'm good," Cindy said.

But she wasn't.

She couldn't remember any time in her life when she'd caused anyone so much pain. And she was also very afraid.

Booker took the chair opposite the sofa, leaned forward, rested his elbows on his knees, and scowled at Cindy.

"What makes you think that this 'Bagman Jesus' is our son?"

"A woman saying she was his close friend gave me this," Cindy said. She dug in her purse, pulled out the tin ID tag stamped RODNEY BOOKER on one side, PEACE CORPS on the other. She handed it to Booker, saw a spasm of fear cross his face.

"Is this supposed to *prove* something? Mother and I want to see his body."

"No one claimed him, Mr. Booker. He's at the ME's office. Uh, they don't show bodies there, but I can make a call—"

Booker sprang out of his chair and kicked a rattan footstool across the room, spun back around to face Cindy.

"He's in a freezer like a dead fish, that's what you're saying? Who tried to find us? No one. If Rodney was *white*, we would have been notified."

"To be fair, Mr. Booker, this man's face was beaten beyond recognition. He had no ID. I've been working hard to learn his identity."

"Good for you, Miss Thomas. Good for you. His face was busted up and he had no ID, so I'm asking again, how do you know that dead man was our son?"

Cindy said, "If I could have a good, clear photo of Rodney, I think I could clear this up fast. I'll call you tomorrow."

Lee-Ann Booker eased a photo out from the clinging plastic leaves of an album and passed it to Cindy, saying, "This was taken about five years ago."

In the picture, Rodney Booker was sitting on the same rattan love seat Cindy sat on now. He was handsome, light-skinned, broad-shouldered, had close-cropped hair and a beautiful smile.

Cindy strained to find a resemblance to Bagman Jesus in Rodney's build and skin color, but when she'd seen Bagman's remains, he'd barely looked *human*.

"You've been to Rodney's house?" Billy Booker asked.

"Rodney has a house?"

"Well, *damn it*, girl. My son could be *home* right now watching a ball game while you're out here scaring us to *death*."

Lee-Ann Booker wailed, and Cindy's mind scrambled again. House? Bagman Jesus was homeless, wasn't he? How could he have a house? What if Rodney Booker was alive and well—and she was totally wrong?

Billy Booker snatched a pen and notepad from the coffee table, scratched his son's cell phone number and address on the top sheet, ripped it off and handed it to Cindy.

"I get his voice mail when I call. Maybe you'll do better. So what's your plan, Miss Thomas? Tell me *that*. Then I'll know what *I'm* going to do."

Cindy left the Bookers' house, sure that her well-intentioned pop-in visit had not only blown up but shown all the signs of becoming a *scandal*.

Chapter 46

AS SHE DROVE BACK from Santa Rosa to San Francisco, Cindy obsessed. She'd promised the Bookers she'd let them know *tomorrow* whether or not Bagman Jesus was their son.

How was she going to do that? How? And yet she would have to do it or die trying.

She stirred the contents of her purse with her right hand, found her cell phone, and speed-dialed Lindsay's office number. A man's voice answered, "Conklin."

"*Rich*, it's Cindy. Is Lindsay there?"

"She's out, but I'll tell her—"

"Wait, Rich. I've got a solid lead on Bagman Jesus. I think his name is Rodney Booker."

"You doing police work now, Cindy?"

"*Someone* has to."

"Okay, okay. Take it easy."

8th Confession

"Take it *easy?* I just walked in on this unsuspecting old couple, told them their son was dead—"

"You did *what?*"

"I had his *name*, Rich, or thought I did, so I went to interview Bagman's parents, logical if you think about it—"

"Oh man. How'd that go over?"

"Like a *bomb*, like a freaking *bomb*. Billy Booker, the father? He's a Vietnam vet, former sergeant major in the marines. He's saying the police are *racist*, that's why they didn't work the case."

"Bagman Jesus was black?"

"Booker has Al Sharpton's home number and he's threatening to use it. What I'm saying is, I've got to get ahead of this story before I *become* the story. Before *we* become the story."

"We, huh?"

"Yeah. The SFPD and me. And I'm the one who feels the moral obligation. Rich, listen. Rodney Booker has a *house*."

"You're losing me, Cindy. Wasn't Bagman *homeless?*"

"Look him up. Please."

"Entering 'Rodney Booker.' Here ya go. Huh. Cole Street. That's off Haight. Nice neighborhood."

It wasn't.

It was the badlands, the turf of small-time drug dealers.

And that made sense.

If Bagman Jesus wasn't lying when he told Flora Gold that his real name was Rodney Booker, and if Flora wasn't lying to *Cindy,* then the house on Cole could turn out to be where Rodney Booker, aka Bagman Jesus, had hung his bag.

Cindy said to Conklin, "Can you check it out, Rich? Because if you won't, I've got to."

"Stand down, Cindy. My shift is over in twenty minutes. I'll run over and take a look."

"I'll meet you there," said Cindy. "Wait for me."

"No, Cindy. I'm the cop. *You* wait for *me.*"

Chapter 47

THE HOUSE ON COLE was painted roadkill gray, one in a block of distressed Victorian homes, this particular residence having boarded-up bay windows, trash-littered front steps, and an air of melancholy that had not lifted since the end of the '60s.

"It's condemned," Conklin said to Cindy, tilting his chin toward the notice nailed to the door.

"The lot alone is worth some dough. If this house belonged to Bagman, what made him homeless?"

"That's rhetorical, right?"

"Yeah," Cindy said. "I'm thinking out loud."

Cindy stood behind Conklin as he knocked on the door, touched the butt of his gun, then knocked again, this time louder and with meaning.

Cindy's hands were shaking as she cupped them and

peered through a sidelight. Then, before Conklin could stop her, she pushed in the door.

A startled cry came from inside, and piles of rags rose up from the floor, ran toward the back of the house. A door slammed.

"This is a crash pad," Conklin said. "Those were squatters, crackheads. It's not safe, Cindy. We're not going in."

Cindy rushed past and headed for the staircase, ignoring Conklin, who was yelling her name.

She'd made a promise.

The air was damp and cold, smelling of mildew and smoke and rotting garbage. Cindy ran up the stairs, calling, "Rodney Booker? Are you here?"

No one stirred, not even a mouse.

The top floor was brighter and more open than the floors below. The windows were bare, and sunlight lit up the one large bedroom.

A brass bed was centered on one wall, the mattress covered with dark-blue sheets. Books were scattered everywhere. A crack pipe was on the top of a scarred dresser.

"Cindy, I don't have a search warrant. *Do you understand?*" Conklin said, coming up behind her. "Nothing we find here can be used as evidence." He gripped her shoulders, gave her a little shake. "Hey, do you hear me?"

"I think Bagman Jesus lived here until he died."

"Really. Based on what?"

Cindy pointed to the mural behind the bed. It was crudely drawn in black and white on plaster, images of writhing people, their hands reaching upward, fire and smoke swirling around them.

"Read that," Cindy said.

Here was the proof Cindy had been looking for, that Rodney Booker and Bagman Jesus were one and the same.

Written within the hellish scene were two words in the same primitive lettering Cindy recognized from Flora Gold's tattoo.

The letters spelled out JESUS SAVES.

Chapter 48

CONKLIN AND I were working the phones at half past six p.m. when Jacobi stopped by our desks, took a twenty out of his wallet, put it on my desk with a stack of take-out menus, and said, "I'll check in with you later."

"Thanks, Boss."

It was discouraging work.

We still didn't know if the Baileys' deaths were an accident, a homicide-suicide, or a double homicide—only that Claire's consultants had come up with nothing and the public was having a collective heart attack.

So Conklin and I did all we could do. We worked our way down the Baileys' endless list of friends and associates and asked the questions: When did you last see the Baileys? How were their moods? How did they get along? Do you know of anyone who would have wanted to harm Isa or Ethan Bailey?

8th Confession

Do you know of anyone who would have wanted them *dead?*

I was dialing a number when I heard my name, looked up to see Cindy breeze through the wooden gate in front of our assistant, Brenda Fregosi, Brenda calling out, *"No,"* stabbing the intercom button, her voice blatting over the speaker on my desk.

"Cindy's here."

Waving a newspaper, Cindy floated around the day crew, who were putting on their coats as the night crew punched in. She plopped down in the side chair next to my desk, angling it so she could look at Conklin, too.

Hate to admit it, but she brought light into the gloom.

"Want to see what tomorrow's paper will look like?" she asked me.

"No."

"I'm a rock star, Richie. Look," she said, slapping the paper down on my desk. Conklin tried to stifle a laugh and failed.

I said to Cindy, "You've heard the expression 'misery loves company'?"

"You're miserable and I'm company. What's your point?"

"Misery loves *miserable* company."

Conklin snorted and Cindy har-de-har-harred and I couldn't keep stone-faced for another second.

Cindy gloated, "Don't you just hate it when I'm right?"

She lovingly smoothed out the newspaper so I could see the picture on the front page of the Metro section, the photo of Rodney Booker, aka Bagman Jesus, under the headline $25,000 REWARD. DO YOU KNOW WHO KILLED THIS MAN?

So there it was: Rodney Booker *was* Bagman Jesus.

Rodney Booker had been identified by his father from the morgue photos, which showed three raised lines on Rodney's shoulder, a crude slash-and-rub-with-ashes tattoo he'd gotten while in Africa.

Rodney Booker's death was a homicide. And *my* name was associated with his case file. All I needed to do was find out who killed him, and while I didn't have the time to do that, Cindy Thomas was both high on success and hot on the trail.

"I've been thinking," Cindy said. "I can just keep working the case, turn over anything I find out to you. *What,* Lindsay?"

"Cindy, you can't work a homicide, okay? Rich, tell her."

"I don't need your permission at *all*," Cindy said. Then, eyes brightening, "Here's an idea. Let's go to Susie's and map out a plan we can all live with—"

I rolled my eyes, but Conklin was shaking his head and grinning at Cindy. He liked her!

I was ready to call Jacobi, let *him* straighten her out, when Claire blew through the gate, stomped toward us with a bad look in her eyes.

"*Dr. Washburn* is on her way back," Brenda's electronic voice cawed from my intercom.

Claire was busy. She didn't like to pay house calls to Homicide. Cindy, oblivious, called out, "Claire! We're off to Susie's. Come with us."

Claire fixed her eyes on me.

"I can't go to Susie's," she said, "and neither can you. Another one just came in. Killed just like the Baileys."

Chapter 49

THE DRAPED BODY on the autopsy table was female, thirty-three, her skin as white as my mom's bone china. Her hair was a shimmering shoulder-length cut in four shades of blond. Her finger- and toenails had been lacquered recently, oxblood red, no chips.

She looked like the sleeping princess in the fairy tale waiting for the prince to chop through the briars and kiss her awake.

I read her toe tag. "Sara Needleman."

"Positively ID'd by her personal assistant," said Claire.

I knew Sara Needleman by her photographs in *Vogue* and *W*. She was a big-name clothing designer who made custom gowns for those who had thirty grand to throw down for a dress. I'd read in the *Gazette* that Needleman often did gangs of bridesmaids' dresses, each gown related in color but distinctly different in style, and that during the debutante season, Needleman's shop was in overdrive, designing for both the moms and the debs.

Surely Sara Needleman knew the Baileys.

Claire picked up her clipboard, said, "Here's what I've got. Ms. Needleman called her personal assistant, Toni Reynolds, at eight this morning complaining of abdominal cramps. Ms. Reynolds says she told Sara to call her doctor and that she'd check in on her when she got to work.

"Sara did call her doctor, Robert Dweck, internist, and was told she could come in at noon."

"She didn't make the appointment," Conklin said.

"No flies on you," Claire said to Conklin. "Sara Needleman called nine one one at ten-oh-eight. EMS got there at ten fifteen, found Sara dead in her bedroom."

"She *died* of stomach cramps? Something she ate?" I asked.

Claire continued, "To be determined, girlfriend. To be determined. Stomach contents and blood are at the lab.

"Meanwhile, I spoke with the medics who brought Sara in. There was no vomit or excrement in the house."

"Why do you think her death is like the Baileys'?"

"At first I didn't. There was a lull when she came in, so I got to her quick, thinking I knew what to look for."

Three of Claire's assistants tried to look busy, but they were hanging close enough to hear her report. I could already see the words "Breaking News" under a glamour shot of Sara Needleman interrupting our regularly scheduled programming. I could feel the public linking Needleman's death to the Baileys', the barometric pressure falling.

Big storm coming in.

8th Confession

Claire ticked off the possible causes of Sara Needleman's death.

"Leaving poison aside for now, stomach cramps are often caused by a perforated ulcer or an ectopic pregnancy gone bust."

"But not this time," Conklin guessed.

"Correct, Mr. Man. So the cramps could've been unrelated to her death. I checked for aneurysms, stroke, heart attack—found nothing. I examined all her organs. You could gift wrap them, tie 'em with a bow. Show 'em to med students to let them know what normal organs look like."

"Huh."

"No marks on her body, no bruises of any kind. Nothing wrong with Sara Needleman except that she's dead."

Conklin said, "She was on my list of names. I hadn't gotten to her yet."

"Too late now," I muttered.

Claire said, "So now I'm thinking we've got the Baileys and Needleman. Same social circle. Could be same cause of death. So when I sent out Sara's blood, I ordered the works. I've got sections holding at minus seventy for testing by someone who's going to be looking for something other than the usual herbs and spices," Claire said glumly. "What am I going to say now, compadres?"

Conklin said it. "More police work."

"Bingo, Ricardo. Someone's got to figure this out, because I've hit the wall."

Claire turned to Sara Needleman's body, put her hand on the woman's sheeted torso, and said, "I hear hoofbeats coming down the road, Sara darlin', I'm thinking 'horse.' *You* are a definite *zebra*."

Part Three

PARTY ALL THE TIME

Chapter 50

THE MORNING AFTER Sara Needleman died, Chief Anthony Tracchio called to say, "The mayor's on my ass. Drop everything except this case, and don't screw up."

I said, "Yes, sir, Tony. No screwing up," but I wanted to scream, *"What are we looking for?"*

Lieutenant Michael Hampton, a twenty-year veteran of the Special Investigation Division (SID), had also been assigned to our dead-millionaires case, and he looked half as happy as I was. We met in Hampton's office, broke down the tasks, and divvied up the list.

Hampton deployed a team to Dr. Dweck's office to collect Sara Needleman's records and interview the doctor and his staff. Another SID team shot over to Needleman's showroom and office to interview Sara's personal assistant, Toni Reynolds, and the rest of Needleman's staff.

Conklin and I drove out to Needleman's house in Cow

Hollow with my four guys caravanning behind. Conklin parked on the street. Chi and McNeil, Lemke and Samuels, started the neighborhood canvass while Conklin and I found the main entrance to Needleman's house.

Sara Needleman's place wasn't as *Architectural Digest* as the Bailey manse, but by any standard, it was stunning. The caretaker, a twentysomething hipster sporting black denim and a goatee, name of Lucas Wilde, met us at the door. He took us through the eight-thousand-square-foot house, a home Sotheby's would be listing as soon as Disaster Masters cleaned up CSU's mess.

After the tour of the seven-bedroom house, including the bi-level Japanese garden in back, we invited Lucas Wilde to come to the squad room and tell us what he knew about Sara Needleman.

He willingly complied.

"I know everyone who comes and goes," he said.

Conklin left us in Interview Room Number Two, ran Wilde's name, got nothing on him, came back with a legal pad and coffees all around.

We spent another hour with Wilde, and he dumped all his thoughts about Sara Needleman and the company she kept.

"Poofs and phonies, mostly. And then there were her clients."

The young man laboriously listed all of Sara's visitors, both friends and workers, including the housekeeper, the dog walker, the Japanese gardener, the tile man, the koi keeper, the yoga teacher, and the caterer.

"What kind of relationship did you have with Sara?" I asked.

8th Confession

"We got along fine. But I was no Lady Chatterley's lover, if that's where you're going. I was the gofer and the handyman, which is what she wanted, and I was happy to have the job and the cool place to live."

Wilde told us that he saw Sara briefly on the morning of her death. He brought her newspaper in from the gate, and she seemed okay to him.

"She just cracked the door, took the paper. She wouldn't have told me if she was sick."

"Got any ideas?" I asked Wilde. "If Sara Needleman was killed, who would've killed her?"

"I wouldn't know where to start," Wilde said. "Sara was a snob. If you were a mover or a shaker, she was a sweetheart.

"Otherwise, man, she could be *cold*. I don't know her friends from her enemies, and frankly I don't think she knew either."

Chapter 51

SARA NEEDLEMAN was still chilling in the morgue that evening when the teams working her case were summoned to Chief Anthony Tracchio's office with its high view of Bryant Street and a photographic panorama of the Golden Gate Bridge mounted across from his mahogany desk.

Tracchio was a bureaucrat by trade, had come up through the ranks by political appointment. He had no street experience, was squishy around the middle, and had a silly hairsprayed comb-over, but I was starting to appreciate that he was politically shrewd, a quality that I lack entirely.

Tracchio was agitated in a way I'd rarely seen him. He said, "People, tell your families you won't be home until we've got this case wrapped up. And buck up. Whoever solves this thing is going to be a hero. Or hero*ine*," he said in my direction.

Teams reported, and Tracchio, Hampton, and I questioned them before they were tasked to new assignments.

Conklin and I collected the names of every person inter-viewed regarding Sara Needleman, then went back to our desks to compare them with a similar list on the Baileys.

"Compare and contrast" was eye-glazing work, but it had to be done. I pulled my chair over to Conklin's desk and read off names.

Whenever we had a match, Conklin slapped the Staples Easy Button and it squawked, "That was easy."

By nine that night, our empty pizza box was in the round file. We'd eliminated the Baileys' live-in household staff and a few hundred others, but still the lists yielded dozens of over-lapping names.

The Baileys and Sara Needleman went to the same gym, were all members of the opera society, frequented the same restaurants and clubs. They even shared the same dry cleaner.

"Sara Needleman was thirty-three and so was Isa Bailey. Bet they went to the same school," said Conklin.

I nodded. It was something.

Something that expanded the search.

I drained my soda can, tossed it in the trash, and said, "I read about a lab experiment. First up were the rats. Two lights, one flashes green, one flashes red. Guess the light that's about to flash, and if you go to the correct light, you get food. Eight out of ten times, the green one flashes."

"Go on."

"The green light flashes so many times, the rats go to that chute every time. Why not? They're rewarded eighty percent of the time.

"Now the behaviorists did the same experiment with humans."

"Never been high on rat chow myself."

I laughed. "The humans got M&M's."

"I *know* this is going somewhere," said my partner.

"The people tried to *predict* when each light would go on. They were looking for a *pattern*—so many reds before a green, like that. And they were rewarded only sixty-seven percent of the time."

"Proving that rats are smarter than people."

I shook my head no.

Conklin tried again. "Proving that we should interview every name on both lists whether they're red people or green?"

I laughed, said, "Proving that sometimes people think too much."

"You're tired, Linds."

"Let's compare the lists again. And this time, we don't overthink. We just pull the names of the rats who had keys to the victims' houses."

Rich hit the Staples button, and it yapped, "That was easy."

Chapter 52

PET GIRL WAS handing over Sara Needleman's dogs to the caretaker, Lucas Wilde-boy, she liked to call him, when the squad car pulled up to the curb and two familiar cops got out. The woman cop was tall, blond, looked like Sheryl Crow had landed a gig on *Celebrity Cops*.

The guy cop was a couple of inches taller than the blonde, buffed, maybe thirty.

Sheryl Crow showed her badge, reintroduced herself as Sergeant Boxer and her partner as Inspector Conklin, and asked if Pet Girl would mind coming with them to the Hall of Justice to answer some questions.

Pet Girl said, "Okay."

She was cool. All she had to do was *play* along, and they'd *move* along — just like they'd done the last time, when they'd questioned her about Isa and Ethan Bailey.

She slid into the backseat of the squad car, thought about

the night she'd done it, pretty sure she hadn't forgotten anything.

She flashed on Wilde-boy, positive that he hadn't seen her go into Sara's house because he'd walked naked past his window, the light going on in his bathroom, and she'd heard the shower running before she'd gone in the main entrance.

She remembered doing it to Sara when "the dame with the golden needle" was so boozed up, she couldn't even open an eye. Pet Girl felt a thrill, like she wanted to laugh or maybe *pee*.

And she listened to the two cops gabbing in the front seat, talking to Dispatch, joking and stuff, seemed to Pet Girl that they weren't acting like they had a *killer* sitting behind them.

More like they'd already forgotten she was even there.

She stood silently between the two cops as they went up in the elevator, turned down the offer of a soft drink when they showed her to the interview room.

"Are you sure?" the sergeant asked her. "Maybe a bottle of water?" Like the cop *cared* instead of wanting to get a DNA sample, a trick so old it was amazing anyone ever fell for it.

"I want to help," Pet Girl said sweetly. "Whatever you want to know."

Inspector Conklin was cute, had light-brown hair that flopped over his eyes. He pushed it away as he read to himself whatever notes he had written about her. And then he asked her where she'd been over the last forty-eight hours.

Pet Girl knew they were locking in her story in case they ever interrogated her again, and hey, no problem.

"I walked the Baileys' dogs four times, morning and evening both days. I wonder what's going to happen to the dogs..."

Then she'd detailed her tight calendar of dog-walking and running errands, including walking Sara Needleman's AKC champs this morning after Lucas Wilde called her to say that Sara Needleman was dead.

"See anything or anyone unusual in this neighborhood in the last week or so?" Sergeant Boxer asked her.

"Nope."

"What do you think of Lucas Wilde?"

"He's okay. Not my type."

"What was your relationship like with Sara Needleman?" asked Inspector Conklin.

"I *loved* Sara," she told him. Found herself giving him a flirty smile. Couldn't hurt. "Sara was smart and funny and generous, too. She gave me samples from her collection. That's just the way she was."

"How often did you walk her dogs?"

"Maybe once a week. She liked to walk them herself. Anyway, if she got into a time crunch, she'd call me and I'd pitch in."

"And the Baileys?"

"Same. Walk the dogs. Run errands. I work for a lot of people in their crowd. *Dozens.* I've got references."

"Sounds pretty good," Inspector Conklin said. "You make your own hours." Then, "Did Sara have any enemies?"

"Christ, yeah. She had three ex-husbands and about thirty ex-boyfriends, but I'm not saying they'd want to kill her."

"Anyone on that list of exes who may have also held a grudge against the Baileys?"

"If you only knew how *little* those people told me about anything."

"Do you have keys to the Needleman house and the Bailey

house?" Sergeant Boxer asked her. Pet Girl reached into a side pocket of her backpack, pulled out a key ring the size of a boat anchor.

"I've got lots of keys. That's kind of the point. I keep out of my clients' way. I'm the silent type, and they like that about me. I come in, walk the pets, bring them back. Pick up my check. Most of the time, nobody even knows I've been there."

Chapter 53

AFTER THE dog walker left, I said to Conklin, "You know, *my* dog sitter has had my keys and my alarm code for years and I've never thought a thing of it. Martha *loves* Karen. I trust her."

"So what are you saying now, Sarge-of-My-Heart? You're throwing out the 'rats with keys' theory?"

"I don't know, bud. The dog walker's got access, but what's her *motive*? What's she got to gain by killing her employers?"

My intercom buzzed, and Brenda's voice came over, sounding breathy and a little coy. "Lindsay, you have a visitor."

I looked across the squad room. Didn't see anyone.

I pressed the intercom button, asked Brenda, "Who is it?"

"He's on his way back."

I heard him before I saw him, the whir of rubber rolling over linoleum flooring, and then St. Jude was there, doing a wheelie, parking his chair up to my desk, a huge grin on his bearded face.

"Boxer, you look great, kid. Better and better."

I got up and hugged the legendary Simon McCorkle, known around the state as "St. Jude, the patron saint of lost causes." McCorkle had been shot in the back while on duty, was paralyzed from the waist down but refused to retire. Since that dark day twenty years ago, "St. Jude" had been in charge of cold cases, worked out of an office suite at the crime lab.

"Thanks, McCorkle. I see a little gray in your beard. Looks fine on you."

"Give me your hand, Boxer. No, the left one. Not married? So I still have a chance."

I laughed, introduced McCorkle to Conklin, and they gripped paws like long-lost brothers of the shamrock, and pretty soon we were telling St. Jude about the case of the deceased millionaires, an investigation that was driving us crazy.

McCorkle said, "That's why I'm here, girl-o. When I saw Sara Needleman on the tube this morning, I added it to the Baileys—and guess what, Boxer?

"It rang a bell."

Chapter 54

McCORKLE REACHED BEHIND his chair with one of his massive, heavily tattooed arms and pulled a backpack onto his lap.

"I brought you a present," he said, winking at me.

"I can't even guess, but I'm hoping for chocolate."

He took a murder book out of his backpack, a three-ring binder thick with notes and documents from a homicide case. The book was lettered across the cover with a broad-tip marker: PANGORN, 1982.

Two more murder books followed the first, one marked GODFREY, 1982, and the other, KENNEDY, 1982.

"What is all this?" I asked as McCorkle shifted the three binders to my overflowing desk.

"Patience, my pretty. This is the final one. Christopher Ross. He was the last to go, died in December nineteen eighty-two."

"McCorkle, my man, fill me in."

"I'm going to tell you everything, and maybe you, me, and Conklin here are all going to get some closure."

I leaned back in my chair. There were people in the world who lived for an audience, and Simon McCorkle was one of them.

It partly came from being in that lab all the way out there on Hunters Point. It also came from obsessing about cold cases and colder bodies.

But there was another thing. Whether he solved the crime today or next month, St. Jude was always sinking free throws, scoring points that wouldn't have been made without him. His job made for excellent storytelling.

"Here's what these victims all had in common." McCorkle leaned forward in his chair, put a beefy arm across the folders so that I was staring at a hairy, half-naked hula girl on his personal tattoo beach.

"The victims were all high-society types. They all died showing no signs of foul play. But the last victim, this Christopher Ross—the killer left the murder weapon at the crime scene. *And a very distinctive weapon it was.*"

I was just out of school when this terrible killing spree ended, so I hadn't fastened on the particulars of this case—but it was coming back to me now, why those cases were unsolved.

McCorkle grinned as he watched the dawn breaking inside my poor, tired brain. I did remember.

"It was a distinctive murder weapon, all right," I said to my Erin go bro. "Those victims were killed by *snakes.*"

Chapter 55

RICH CONKLIN had dinner that evening with Cindy at a Thai restaurant across the street from her apartment.

It was not a date, they'd both been very clear about that, but she was twinkling at him as she passed him the files she'd printed out, all the stories on the "high-society murders of nineteen eighty-two" that had run in the *Chronicle* before the personal computer was as common as the telephone.

"I'm *trusting* you," she said. "If you tell anyone I gave you this stuff from our 'morgue,' I'm going to be in the soup."

"Wouldn't want any soup on you," Conklin said.

"So fair's fair," said Cindy. "I share, you share."

Cindy had a rhinestone clip in her hair. Very few girls older than eight could pull off rhinestone barrettes at the same time they were wearing pink, but Cindy somehow looked 100-percent delicious.

And Conklin was absolutely mesmerized watching her

strip the meat from a chicken wing with her lips, so delicately and at the same time with such pleasure.

"*Rich,*" she said, "fair's *fair.* It's clear that you see a connection between the Baileys and Sara Needleman and the nineteen eighty-two society killings. But are you thinking that the killer from all those years ago has gone back into the murder business?"

"See, the question is, can I trust *you,* Cindy? Because, actually, you're not so trustworthy."

"Awwww. You just have to say the magic words."

"Please, Cindy."

"Richieee. What you want to say is 'off the record.' I'd go to jail before I'd go back on 'off the record.' "

Rich laughed, sat back, let the waiter take away the remains of his sea bass, said, "Thanks for telling me. I don't want you to go to jail. But you realize I'd be in more than soup if I leaked this story to your paper."

"You don't have to worry. Number one, I promise." She made the Girl Scout oath hand sign, three fingers up, thumb over her pinky. "Two, you're going off the record. And three, it's not my story," she said. "I'm working the Bagman Booker case, remember?"

"Okay, *off the record,* Cindy. You read the files. Back in eighty-two rich people were killed, turns out by snakebites, and yeah, maybe the killer is coming out of retirement. Maybe he's bored. Wouldn't be the first time. The BTK killer, for instance."

"Oh man, *that* guy," said Cindy, shaking her head, rhinestones flashing. " 'Bind them, torture them, kill them.' That guy still gives me the creeps. Worked for a home-security company, I seem to remember. Mr. Regular Dad, Kiwanis Club, Rotary Club, whatever."

"Yep. He was a homebody for about twenty-five years after his last killing. Then one day he realizes life had more punch when he was taunting cops, getting headlines. So he starts sending letters out to newspapers and TV stations. His ego trips him up and he gets nailed."

"So you're thinking the society killer of nineteen eighty-two is the same guy who killed the Baileys and Sara Needleman?"

Conklin signaled the waiter for the check. "Possibly."

"Wouldn't that be something?" Cindy said.

She was looking at him like he'd done something wrong, so he said, "Oh, sorry, did you want anything else? Ice cream or something?"

"I was just thinking. I'm not finished talking about this. I finally unpacked my cappuccino machine, Rich."

Conklin watched her twirl a curl around her finger. He smiled and said, "Are you inviting me over for coffee?"

Chapter 56

McCORKLE AND I were in the squad room having congealed Chinese take-out as we went over the murder books.

McCorkle flapped open the one marked PANGORN, said, "April Pangorn was a beautiful young widow, only twenty-eight and very wealthy. According to Inspector Sparks's notes, she had many chums of both sexes."

"Says here Ms. Pangorn was found dead in her bed, no marks or bruises," I said. "Just like the Baileys and Sara Needleman."

"Right you are, which is why it wasn't considered a homicide until Frank Godfrey dropped dead."

McCorkle gnawed on a cold sparerib, tossed the bone into the trash as I opened the Godfrey book, started flipping the pages to follow along as St. Jude narrated.

"Godfrey, Frank. White male, forty-five, retired prize-fighter, owned a piece of Raleigh's.

8th Confession

"It's closed now, but then it was a very old-school club, red velvet on the walls, humidors on the bar, gambling in the back room. Frankie kept busy in his *de*luxe apartment in the sky. Very busy. He liked women—in multiples—and he liked to spend money. Look here, Lindsay. The photo of the scene."

The victim was lying facedown on the bedroom floor, looked to me like he might have been crawling to the bathroom just visible at the edge of the frame.

McCorkle was saying, "Homicide thought maybe Frank was murdered, but the ME couldn't find the cause. Negative autopsy, negative toxicology. Positive mystery.

"Next up. Patrick Kennedy was a banker," said McCorkle, reaching across the table, grabbing the third book. "He was gay, a top secret fact that came out when he died, because *everything* was shaking out.

"There were three ultrarich people dead in a couple of months under suspicious circumstances. Things got a little desperate here in the Southern Division. A Lieutenant Leahy took over for Inspector Sparks, spent about a month interviewing every gay man in San Francisco." McCorkle laughed. "Half of them 'knew' Paddy. Sorry," he said. "But think about it. And then, a month later, Christopher Ross died."

"And what was his story?" I asked. I broke open a fortune cookie, read the little squib of paper to McCorkle. "'A good friend will give you the answer.'"

I gave McCorkle a soft punch to one of his humongous arms. "Get on with it, buddy. How did the cops find out about the snakes? *Spill it, Jude.*"

Chapter 57

McCORKLE LAUGHED at me.

"Boxer, I'm talking as fast as I can."

"Talk *faster.*"

I pounded the Godfrey murder book in jest, but I was starting to get really scared. Four society people had mysteriously died in '82. We already had three similar, if not identical, deaths within the same week.

I hadn't fully believed that our unmarked deaths were homicides—but I did now. And I could see that if we were looking at the same killer, he was slippery, smart, and very organized.

"Christopher Ross," I said. "The final victim."

"Christopher Ross," said McCorkle, opening the fourth murder book to one of the morgue photos. "He was a forty-two-year-old white man. Rich as God. Born into old money.

He was a family man who fooled around on the side. Some said he even had another family right here in town.

"Look at his kisser there, Boxer. Even dead, Chris Ross was a looker. His wife was one of those women who just put up with his breaking his vows. People said Chris was her life-long sweetheart, and she loved him. And then, suddenly, he was found stone dead in his own bed—and this was why."

McCorkle turned to the back of the Ross murder book.

"Here's your murder weapon," he said.

It was what I'd been waiting for—and it was nothing like what I expected. The snake was pinned to a board alongside a yardstick showing that the reptile was twenty-one inches long.

I just couldn't drag my eyes away from that snake.

It was delicate, banded in bluish-gray and white, looked more like jewelry than a killer.

"This snake is a krait," McCorkle was saying. "Incredibly lethal. Comes from India, so someone imported it. Illegally. No signs of a break-in at any of the victims' houses."

"So how did the snake get there?"

McCorkle shrugged expansively.

"And this one snake killed the other victims?" I asked.

"Maybe not this particular snake, Lindsay, but a snake just like it. The first three bodies were exhumed and examined microscopically. The ME, a Dr. Wetmore, found the bite marks on all four victims.

"And according to Dr. Wetmore, the marks were damned hard to see with the naked eye. They were like pinpricks, easily missed if you weren't looking for them. And according to his report, there was no swelling or discoloration around the bite marks."

"What about suspects?" I asked.

"Mrs. Christopher Ross inherited fifty million bucks. She was interrogated repeatedly, kept under surveillance. Her phones were tapped, but no one believed she did it. She had her own money. She had everything."

"Is she still alive?"

"Died in a car accident two or three years after her husband's death. And there never was another serious suspect."

"Simon, did the victims know one another?"

"Some did, some didn't, but one thing they all had in common was that they were all very rich. And something else, maybe you can use it.

"The lead investigator, Lieutenant Leahy, made an unfortunate aside to his deputy at a press conference and the mic was open. A reporter ran with it."

"Don't make me beg, McCorkle."

"Leahy said, and I quote, 'The victims were twisted—sexually and morally corrupt.'"

McCorkle was telling me that the sky fell on Leahy after his comment ran in the *Chronicle,* that he relocated to Omaha not long after that. But I was far from Omaha. I was thinking about a dainty little Indian snake that left almost imperceptible bite marks.

Claire didn't know anything about this.

I had to call her.

Chapter 58

RICH'S EYES ADJUSTED to the dim light in Cindy's apartment. He'd been here a year and a half ago when a murdering psycho was at large in the building—a situation that couldn't possibly be more different from this.

He and Cindy were alone. They'd been drinking. And Cindy was fussing with her multipart cappuccino machine as if she were really going to make *coffee*.

How had this happened?

Had wishing made it true?

As Cindy piled coffee-machine parts onto the countertop, Rich's mind deleted her pink sweater and her tight pants, ran his hands all over her, refusing to peer any farther into the future than, say, an hour from now.

He couldn't think about later.

He hadn't planned for *this*.

"What's your bird's name?" he asked, walking over to the

large brass cage on a table near the window. The bird was white and peach, with scaly claws and a black beak. Reminded him of a junkyard dawg.

"That's Peaches," said Cindy, coming up behind Rich, standing so close he could feel her breasts pressing against his back. "He was lonely in the pet store..."

Rich turned to Cindy, and her arms went around his neck. He drew her close and kissed her.

It was a perfect first kiss, no clashing of noses or teeth, Rich smelling flowers, tasting watermelon lip gloss and white wine, Cindy's strong little body pressing hard against him, making him feel like he was going to burst out of his clothes like the freaking Hulk, when Peaches shrieked, "Kill the bitch! Kill the bitch!"

"He was abused," Cindy said softly, with a melting look on her face as much as saying, "Take me to bed."

"That's too bad," Rich said.

He reached into her hair and unfastened the rhinestone clip, and a torrent of blond curls jumped into his hand.

"Ohhhh," Cindy said.

Still standing in front of the bird, Rich gently removed Cindy's diamond studs, placing first one and then the other on the table, seeing her skin flush from the V of her sweater up to her eyes as her breathing cranked to about sixty miles per hour.

She hooked her hand around his belt.

He kissed her again and she moaned, then opened her hazy blue eyes and said, "You're a little fast for me, Rich, but please. Don't stop."

He grinned at her, said, "How about a coffee break?"

"Later," she said, taking his hand, pulling him through the living room and back to her bedroom.

Once there, she turned on the bedside lamp with its pink bulb and gauzy shade, stood in front of him, and lifted her arms like a little girl. He pulled off her sweater. He ran his fingers across the tops of her breasts, which were swelling out of her pink lace demibra, her nipples hardening behind the lace.

She unhooked her bra, breasts spilling out, sat down on the bed, and wriggled out of her pants. He ripped his shirttails from his waistband, and Cindy leaned forward to help with the last of his shirt buttons, undo his belt buckle, and hug him around the waist, resting her cheek against his zipper.

His clothing flew into the corner of the room, and then they were lying side by side in her bed, glued together, all panting and skin-on-skin, Rich slipping his hands into the flimsy fabric of her panties, making them disappear.

There was a fumbling moment, Cindy finding a square of foil in her nightstand, opening the packet with her teeth—and then he was inside her, making love to the beautiful woman with the curly blond hair who breathed, "Oh, oh, oh," into his ear, and he held her tight until the shock waves overtook him and he cried out into her pillow.

Rich was awoken sometime later by the sound of the telephone on the nightstand, Cindy silky and warm in his arms, whispering, "Let's not tell Lindsay."

"Why not?"

"She'll spoil it."

Rich nodded his agreement—he would have agreed to

anything—and then he heard Yuki's voice coming over Cindy's answering machine.

"Cindy. Cindy, pick *up*. Where *are* you? I have to talk to you. *Damn*. Call me, okay? Love you."

Cindy held Rich's face with one hand, reached down with the other hand and gave him a little tug, breathed, "Richie? Can you stay?"

Chapter 59

CLAIRE AND I were huddled around her office computer at seven fifteen in the morning, caffeine free, reading an e-mail to Claire from Michelle Koo, a senior herpetologist at Berkeley.

Claire read aloud, " 'Dear Claire, two of the most familiar families of venomous snakes are the Elapidae and the Viperidae,' " she said, neatly rounding the corners of the Latin, " 'or, rather, elapid snakes and viperid snakes. Kraits are in the Elapidae family. The venom of elapids are neurotoxins, are typically faster-acting than viperids, and leave better-looking corpses.' "

"Better-looking corpses, indeed," I said, breathing over her shoulder. "You could even say museum quality."

" 'The kraits' bites are often painless,' " Claire read on, " 'and this gives the victim a false sense of security.' "

"So that's why the Baileys didn't call for help."

"I'm thinking the same thing, Linds. Or maybe they never

knew they were in trouble. The Baileys had high blood-alcohol. Needleman, too. In medicalspeak, they were all zonked.

"Here," Claire went on, "Michelle writes, 'The symptoms can include stomach cramps and dizziness, dilated pupils and slurred speech, inability to swallow, heart arrhythmia, respiratory failure, and falling into a coma. Death can come in six to eight hours.'"

I had stopped reading the text and had fastened on the photo of the krait, the same beguilingly lovely elapid I'd seen lined up along a yardstick in the Christopher Ross murder book.

"Michelle says, 'Death is directly due to the neurotoxicity of the venom as it acts on fundamental chemical pathways that keep our muscles working.' And that's the main thing, girlfriend. The muscles can't work. So the victim can't breathe. And the neurotoxin is metabolized so fast, even if you knew what to look for—which we didn't—*nothing* shows up on the tox screen."

I said to my best friend, "So if there's no neurotoxin left in the victims' bodies by the time they die, how can you prove what killed them?"

Claire opened a desk drawer, rooted around, cried, "Gotcha!" and pulled out a magnifying glass the size of a saucer.

"I'm going to do *precisely* what old Doc Wetmore did. Go over my patients' bodies with a glass and a bright light," she said. "Look for itty-bitty puncture wounds that might've been caused by *fangs*."

Chapter 60

WE WERE ALL crowded into Jacobi's votive holder of an office, Cindy in the worn desk chair in front of Jacobi's desk, Conklin and I squeezed in between stacks of paper on his credenza.

"I've known you how long now?" Jacobi was saying to Cindy.

"Six years or so."

"And I've never asked you for a favor before, have I?"

"Warren, I told Rich and I told Lindsay that I'm not even *working* the high-society murder story."

Jacobi leveled his hard gray eyes at my friend, and frankly I admired her ability to hold her own. He'd intimidated depraved killers with that same stony look.

"It's not just that it's not your story," said Jacobi. "It's that you know something we want to keep in the vault for now."

"All of those files I pulled for Rich are in the public record,"

Cindy said, showing Jacobi her palms. "Anyone could find out what I know, including someone else at the *Chronicle*."

"It's *buried* in the public record," said Jacobi. "And we need it to *stay* buried for now. That's why we're going to make you an offer you can't refuse."

Cindy laughed. "I love it when you guys offer me an exclusive when I've already done the work."

"Cindy, let's not start talking personal gain, okay? We've got four unsolveds from the eighties and three probable homicides from the last week. We'll give you the first clear shot, and that's a promise."

My cell phone rang, and I glanced down at my hip. I didn't recognize the number, so I let the phone ring again before I snatched the receiver off the hook and growled, "Boxer," as I edged out of Jacobi's office.

Joe was laughing.

"Ohh man, I'm sorry," I said.

"Forget it, Blondie, it's good to hear your voice, no matter how snarly you are."

"I've got good reason to snarl."

I caught Joe up fast, telling him about Sara Needleman's death and that Jacobi was restraining Cindy in virtual handcuffs so that our snake killer didn't slither down a hole.

"Any leads on the doer?"

"Too many and *none*," I said. "We're going to start throwing darts at the phone book pretty soon. And by the way, when are you coming home?"

As I paced a circle around Cappy McNeil's desk, Joe said he was hoping that he'd be back in a week or so and that we should make plans to do something fun, dress up, celebrate his return.

I kissed the little holes in my cell phone, heard kisses in my ear, and then I went back to Jacobi's office. I sat down next to Conklin cheek-to-cheek on the cheap credenza, the warmth of his hip and arm making me think about him and about Joe, and making me ask myself yet again why each man had a grip on me that clouded my feelings for the other.

Conklin leaned forward, almost parking his nose in Cindy's hair, saying to her, "Like you said, it might be the same killer coming out of retirement. Or he might be a *copycat*."

"Either way, he's a repeater," Jacobi growled. "We can't tip him off. We need every advantage because we're *nowhere*, Cindy, and I'll give you any odds: if he can, this guy is going to kill *again*."

Chapter 61

YUKI WAS SCARED out of her mind.

She couldn't remember *any* day when she'd felt as special as she did with John "Doc" Chesney. And it seemed that the feeling was fantastically mutual.

Oh God. Twice now, he'd played his eyes over her face until her cheeks burned and she had to say something, *anything,* because she just couldn't take so much attention.

Doc had met her early that morning out at the beach. He was wearing a navy-blue parka over his jeans, a color that turned his eyes bluer, his sandy hair blonder, the dazzling entirety of his being enough to make Brad Pitt jealous.

Yuki had cautioned herself not to get too gaga on their first real date, not to let her moony eyes show, reminded herself that she'd been a *bitch* when she'd first met Doc and he'd *liked* that about her.

And so she'd gotten a grip on herself and they'd spent the

day exploring Crissy Field, a very pretty park that ran along the shoreline from Marina Green to Fort Point, a Civil War fort that was lodged underneath the Golden Gate Bridge.

She'd jogged a bit faster along the path than Doc did, laughed at him for not keeping up until he sprinted past her, kicking up a little sandstorm and calling over his shoulder, "Hey, girlie, just try and catch me."

She'd collapsed on a weathered bench, laughing and panting, and he'd come back to her, also blowing hard, dropping down beside her, the smell of him filling her up, making her knees shake.

"You're a show-off, you know?" he'd huffed, staring at her until she'd said, "Oh, look," and pointed to the bobbing heads in the bay.

"Coconuts?"

"You're kidding me, right? Those are *sea* lions."

"You like all this nature stuff?" he'd said, untying his Reeboks, shaking out the sand. "All this big sky, these creepy life-forms—"

"Crabs and jellyfish—"

"As I was saying, you nature-lover—"

"Oooooooh, Doc, that really hurts." Yuki laughed. "By the way, New Yorkers don't have a lock on skyscrapers. I like cities as much as you do."

"Yeah? Prove it." He'd grinned, showing her that his whole act was just that—an act.

But she'd proved it anyway, named her top-ten architects, seven of whom turned out to be his favorites, too, and told him about San Francisco landmarks, putting her Golden Gate Bridge up against his Throgs Neck any day of the week, her

Folsom Street against his Fifth Avenue, and then she'd asked him what ocean he could see from midtown Manhattan.

Doc gave her props for "the ocean thing," and they walked together to the Warming Hut, where they sat now at a small table, hot cocoa in hand, their cheeks flushed, grinning at each other as if their feelings were gold coins they'd found in the back pockets of their jeans, never having seen them before.

"You know, you're gorgeous," he said.

"Come on."

"Yeah, you are."

He reached over and rubbed her bristly head, and she touched the back of his hand and rested her cheek in his palm, waiting for the bubble to burst, which it did when his cell phone went off to "Somebody to Love."

Doc sighed, removed his warm palm from her cheek, opened his phone, and announced, "Chesney," into the speaker.

"I'm not on call," he said. "Isn't that *his* problem? Okay, okay. I can make it in an hour."

Doc put his phone away and grabbed both of Yuki's hands in his. "I'm sorry, Yuki. It's going to be this way until I move up in the pecking order."

"I understand," she said.

They walked back to their cars together, arms around each other's waists, covering new territory, Yuki liking the feeling so much and equally relieved that the day had closed at the best moment. She was attracted to Doc, and she was scared.

He draped an arm over her shoulder, brought her to him, and kissed her, sweetly, softly, so she kissed him again, even more so.

8th Confession

When they broke apart, Yuki blurted, "I haven't had sex in almost two years."

A look passed over Doc's face that she couldn't read. It was like an eclipse of the sun. He hugged her, got into his car, and said out the window, "I'll call you."

"Okay," she said, too softly for him to hear over the sound of the engine as he drove away.

What had she said to him?

Why had she said that?

Chapter 62

CINDY SAT IN a booth of a diner called Moe's, just down the block from Bagman's condemned Victorian house that had decayed into a crash pad for druggies.

Her grilled cheese and coffee were cooling, and Cindy was making notes for a sidebar: how many homeless died before the age of forty, how many were under the influence of alcohol or drugs when they died—65 percent.

She was taking the data off the SFPD Web site, so it was automatic writing, not creative, but it was distracting her from the delicious aches and twinges caused by spending another entire night wrapped around Richard Conklin, this time at his place. And those memories only made her want to call him, make another date to wrap herself around him again.

She was in that luminous and dangerous state of mind when she felt a tug on her hair, turned to see a woman peering over the back of the booth at her and saying her name.

8th Confession

Cindy thought the woman looked familiar but at the same time didn't recognize her.

"Sorry. Do I know you?"

"I've seen you at From the Heart."

"Okay, sure," Cindy said, pretty certain that she didn't recognize this young woman from the soup kitchen—but she couldn't place her anywhere else.

"Want to join me?" Cindy said, forcing herself to make the offer, because you just never knew. This woman with the messy blond hair could be the one who knew who killed Bagman Jesus.

"You look busy."

"It's okay," Cindy said, shutting the lid of her laptop as the woman took the seat across from her.

Cindy could see the beginning of the woman's decline into an extreme meth makeover: the graying skin, the huge pupils, the high agitation.

"I'm Sammy."

"Hi, Sammy."

"I read your last story. About Bagman being a guy named Rodney Booker. That he went to Stanford."

"Yes, he did."

"I went to Stanford, too."

"You dropped out, I'm guessing."

"School can't compete," Sammy said.

"With what?"

"With *life*."

Cindy blinked into the young woman's face. She was remembering the cautions, not to speak too fast, move too quickly, appear in any way a threat. That as long as the meth addict was talking, it was safe enough. Silence meant she might be getting paranoid — and dangerous.

Cindy tried not to look down at the fork and knife on the table. She said softly, "Do you know who killed Bagman, Sammy? Do you know we're offering a twenty-five-thousand-dollar reward?"

"What's *your* life worth, Cindy?" Sammy said, her eyes darting all around the diner, then back to Cindy. "Would you sell your life for money you'll never get to spend? That's what I want to tell you. You're wasting your time. No one's going to say who the people are who killed Bagman Jesus. *No one would dare.*"

Chapter 63

I WAS IN THE squad car with Conklin, heading toward a dive of a bar in the Mission, where our new and only suspect was said to work from three p.m. until midnight.

Henry Wallis's name had come to us by way of an anonymous tip, but what made this tip different than the hundreds of others that had fried our phone lines was that Henry Wallis was on our short list.

He was a bartender, had worked the Baileys' parties, and had dated Sara Needleman — until she dumped him. And the tipster said he'd seen Wallis driving down Needleman's street, passing in front of her house several times in his one-of-a-kind junker the night before Needleman died.

Wallis's sheet listed his arrests for violent crimes.

He'd been convicted of domestic violence and assault and battery, and he'd been charged with attempted murder when he and a couple of other drunken bullies had worked over a customer in an alley behind the bar and nearly killed him.

The witnesses to the beating had differing stories. The evidence was thin. Wallis was found not guilty. Case dismissed.

Stats said that Wallis was white, five ten, 165 pounds, and, most important, forty-six years of age. That meant he was old enough to have read about the high-society murders in the '80s.

Hell, he was old enough to have *committed* them.

Conklin and I wondered if Wallis had keys to both the Bailey and Needleman houses. It seemed probable, even likely.

The photo we had of Wallis was four years old, but he was good-looking, even in the scathing high-contrast flash of the Polaroid camera.

He had muscular arms, jailhouse tats on his knuckles.

But what had sent me and Conklin out to the car was the tattoo on Wallis's left shoulder: that of a snake twining through the vacant eyes of a skull.

Conklin was quiet as he drove, and I understood why.

We were both imagining the variety of ways the scene could play out in the Torchlight Bar: what we'd do if Wallis drew a weapon, if he ran, how we'd manage whatever came down without causing collateral damage.

Conklin parked on Fifteenth between Valencia and Guerrero in front of the Torchlight Bar and Grill, a white clapboard building surrounded by bookstores and cafés.

I unbuttoned my jacket, touched the butt of my gun. Conklin did the same. And we entered the dark atmosphere of the bar. There was a TV overhead, tuned to a recap of yesterday's ball game — the A's were getting pounded.

8th Confession

The bartender was six-foot-two, weighed one eighty, and was bald. It was gloomy in that bar—dim light cast by neon signs—but even so, I could see from thirty feet away that the bartender wiping beer mugs with a dirty towel wasn't Henry Wallis.

I stood just inside the doorway as Conklin went to the bartender, flashed his badge, talked quietly under the television's blare. The bartender's eyes went to me, then back to Conklin.

Then he pointed to a man at the head of the bar who was sipping a beer and looking up at the TV screen, unaware that we'd come through the door.

Conklin signaled to me, and we approached Henry Wallis. Maybe he had eyes in the back of his head, or maybe the guy next to him saw us and gave Wallis a nudge, but he whipped his head around, saw my hand going for my piece, and made for the rear exit.

Conklin yelled, "*Freeze!* Wallis, stay where you are."

But the man took a turn around the kitchen and kept running until he reached the back door, which banged shut behind him.

When we opened the door seconds later, Wallis was inside his rusty black Camaro and was shooting down Albion Street like a cannonball.

Chapter 64

I CALLED DISPATCH, requested backup as Conklin floored our car up the deserted street.

The no-nonsense voice of the dispatcher Jackie Kam came over the radio and declared a code 33—silence on our wave band—and alerted all cars in the area that we were in pursuit of a black Camaro heading up Sixteenth toward Market.

This was bad.

School was out, the worst time for a high-speed chase, dangerous for me and Conklin, potentially lethal for other drivers and pedestrians.

I flipped on our sirens and grille lights. Wallis had at least thirty seconds on us, and as he pulled away going seventy, it was clear that he wasn't slowing down for anything or anybody.

"I can't read his plate," I said to Dispatch. But we were almost close enough when the harsh screech of metal on metal, accompanied by panicky horns, preceded the sight of a taco van tipping over.

Wallis's car backed up, then hauled ass, whipping around the fallen van, fishtailing across both lanes, and caroming off a parked station wagon. Then Wallis jammed down the pedal, leaving rubber on the asphalt and the disabled van in the middle of Market.

I called in the collision, urgently requested EMS. As we blew past the van, the driver staggered out into the street with blood on his forehead, trying to flag us down.

We couldn't stop. I swore at the son of a bitch Wallis as Conklin floored our car toward the intersection of Market and Castro.

I had the plate number now, and I called it in: "Foxtrot Charlie Niner Three One Echo heading toward Portola."

Portola is a twisting grade, and we were flying around those turns at fifty, the Camaro getting even farther out in front of us. All along Portola, vehicles ran up on the curb and bikes hugged the sides of buildings.

We assumed more patrol cars were on their way, but for now we were still alone following Wallis.

"Dispatch! Any casualties?"

"Walking wounded only, Sergeant. What's your location?"

I told Kam we were on Twin Peaks Boulevard, the top of a small mountain in the center of the city. I'd busted teenagers making out under our main radio tower on that spot, but now I was hanging on to the dashboard as Conklin screamed, "Bastard!" and sped up the insanely treacherous road lined with two-foot-high guardrails, dented where cocky drivers had gone ballistic.

We were closing in on Wallis as he began his high-speed descent toward Clayton, a snaky and steep slide that sent my guts into my throat. I clenched the microphone so hard I put fingernail marks in the plastic.

I called in our location again: we were heading into the Upper Haight, a residential area of Tudor and Victorian houses occupied by young families who lived on the genteel tree-lined streets.

A child, a woman, and a dog appeared in our windshield. I screamed, *"Noooo!"* Conklin leaned on the horn and the brakes, took us up on the sidewalk, our wheels flying over the curb, our siren wailing like a wounded banshee as we slammed back onto the street.

Conklin grunted. "Everything's under control."

Who was he kidding?

I looked behind us and saw no bodies in the street, but still my heart was airborne. Were we going to survive this joyride? Would we kill people today?

"Where is this asshole taking us?" I asked the air.

"To *hell*. He's taking us to *hell*," Conklin said.

Did he know?

I think he did. Somehow Conklin instinctively knew where Henry Wallis was heading.

It took me another minute to get it.

Chapter 65

I GRIPPED THE DASHBOARD, stared out as the streets blew by and we played dodge 'em with innocent bystanders, wondering if Henry Wallis was our man. Had he killed three people last week?

Had he killed a total of seven?

How many more would he kill before we stopped him?

"Hang on, Linds," Conklin said, wrenching the steering wheel hard. We squealed onto Haight Street, where the likelihood of mowing down punks, retired flower children, old people getting in or out of their cars, was close to 100 percent.

"Haight dead-ends at Stanyan!" I shouted.

We followed the fool in the Camaro, speeding a hundred feet in front of us, sparks coming off his right rear bumper, which now dragged in the street.

Wallis still outran us because he simply didn't care what he hit—and he refused to be boxed in. He made the right turn down Stanyan, drove nearly a block before pulling an illegal left across two lanes of traffic to go into Golden Gate Park.

The imposing Conservatory of Flowers, a giant greenhouse originally from another century, rose up on our right. I envisioned a colossal spinout in my mind, a James Bond–worthy scene of that greenhouse exploding into a trillion shards.

But Wallis skidded and avoided a crash.

I yelled, *"Rich, look out!"*

We followed the Camaro into a cacophony of horns and squealing tires, the bumper-car chase carrying us forward because we had no choice.

In the heart-stopping minutes we'd been on the Camaro's tail, I hadn't seen another cop car, marked or otherwise. I could hear sirens in the distance, but we were alone, powering our Crown Vic at warp speed, Wallis's junker a half block ahead of us as he took the park drive toward Ocean Beach.

We drafted behind him as the terrain sloped sharply downward. Runners with dogs jumped out of the way. My God, I wanted to cover my eyes, but I couldn't.

The boat pond was on our right, filled with seniors and kids driving remote-control ships, and then our two cars screamed past soccer fields with high-school teams standing openmouthed as we passed.

We were climbing again, the road heading straight up to Sutro Heights, almost to land's end, when Wallis veered out of the park and onto Point Lobos Avenue, four fast-moving lanes.

As I yelled our location into the mic, Wallis took a hard left over the median strip and pointed his car like a rocket up toward the Cliff House, a landmark restaurant perched on the western edge of the continent over a rocky cliff that plunged straight down to the Pacific.

I could see it now: Wallis was going for a dramatic *Thelma & Louise* exit, but his would be a solo flight. As the Camaro crashed through guardrails and left the road, I saw the frankly unbelievable: the driver's-side door opened and Wallis jumped out.

But he'd mistimed his jump.

As the Camaro made its wobbly one-way passage off the cliff toward the gray water below, Wallis plummeted alongside his car, both vehicle and man dropping in slow-motion, as if in a dream.

Rich braked our car in front of the broken wall, and we peered over the promontory in time to see the Camaro explode in flames.

"There," I said. "He's there!"

Wallis's body was fifty feet below us, a tangle of bloodied flesh. It was an impossible climb down, a straight 180 degrees over wet and jagged rocks. Conklin took my hand and I gripped his, stood hypnotized as the fire crackled and burned.

I heard Jackie Kam's voice behind me, calling over the car radio, "*Sergeant Boxer, what is your location? Lindsay? Lindsay, please answer me.*"

Rich let go of my hand and leaned over the cliff, facing into the wind as he called down to Henry Wallis's fresh corpse.

"*Did you enjoy yourself, asshole? Get what you wanted?*"

I used my cell phone to call Dispatch, but the cars were already screaming to a halt all around Point Lobos.

Jacobi jumped out of one of them before it came to a stop. He ran toward us, calling, "*You okay? You okay?*"

I was so shaken I couldn't talk.

"Take it easy, Boxer," Jacobi said, putting his hands on my shoulders. My good friend. "Try to breathe."

Tears leaked out of the corners of my eyes, but I wasn't sad. It was something else—surprise and relief that I was alive.

I breathed in the smoke-filled air and said, "I don't get it, Warren. Wallis jumped out of his car! Was he trying to escape? Or was that how he wanted to die?"

"Whatever," Conklin said beside me.

I nodded. *Whatever.* Henry Wallis, the man with the snake-and-skull tattoo on his shoulder, was dead.

Chapter 66

JACOBI TOOK ME and Conklin out to dinner at Restaurant LuLu, *the* place for homey Provençal cooking, rich casseroles and pizzas grilled in a hickory-wood oven. The sunken dining room was packed, conversation was humming all around us, and our waiter really knew the wine list, long considered one of the best in town.

I knew why Jacobi was celebrating.

The chief and the mayor had given him a big ol' "attaboy." TV newscasters were brimming with the drama: the chopper shots and the news that life was safe again for the rich and famous.

But I couldn't stand this, and I had to say it. "Warren, is everyone crazy? You feel comfortable saying that Henry Wallis is the guy who killed our millionaires?"

Jacobi answered with a question: "Can't you let something

good into your life, Boxer?" And then another: "Can't you just be happy for an hour?"

"I guess not," I said, scowling at him. "What's wrong with me? Or am I just too smart for this charade?"

Conklin nudged me under the table with his knee, and I didn't know what the hell was wrong with him either.

A man had died.

We'd almost followed him off a cliff.

We were lucky we weren't looking up at Claire from her table or seeing a story on TV of dead children, their tearful parents threatening to sue the city for another fatal high-speed chase, the sad-faced anchorperson saying, "The funeral services for the little Beckwith children will be at Our Sisters of the Sacred Heart on Sunday."

The waiter poured the wine, and Jacobi tasted it, pronounced it excellent, and, over the clamor of fat-walleted diners chatting happily all around us, raised his glass to me and Conklin.

"Thanks," he said, "from the chief, the mayor, and especially from me. I love you guys."

Jacobi smiled, something I've seen him do maybe twice in the last ten years, and he and Conklin tucked into their pan-roasted mussels and rotisserie duck.

I had no appetite.

The muscles in my face had gone rigid, but my mind was whirling around on its brain stem.

Was Henry Wallis really the high-society killer?

Or was he just some loser of an ex-con with something to hide—so he'd freaked out and ended his life?

Did anyone care but me?

Chapter 67

AGAINST EVERYONE'S GOOD JUDGMENT, I found an ADA in her office at nine that night, the indefatigable Kathy Valoy. She called a judge and got us a search warrant for Henry Wallis's apartment, and now, at midnight, Conklin and I were there.

Wallis had lived in a three-story walk-up on Dolores Street, a few blocks from the Torchlight Bar.

We rang the buzzer until we woke up the building's owner, a squat man by the name of Maury Silver. He was balding, with loose dentures, bad breath, and a stained work shirt hanging long over his boxers.

Silver looked at our warrant through the cracked door, read every page back and front, and then let us enter the building.

"What happened to Henry?" he asked. "Oh *no*. You telling me he's the one who drove off the cliff? Henry's a *killer?*"

Wallis's apartment was on the ground floor, rear.

We flicked on the ceiling lights, closed the door on Mr. Silver, and simply tossed the place. Didn't take long.

Like a lot of ex-cons, Henry Wallis kept his furniture minimal and his few possessions neat.

Conklin took the bedroom and bath while I searched the small living room and kitchen. We called out to each other from time to time: when Conklin found the plastic-wrapped bricks of pot in the kitty-litter box and when I found a book on tattoos, corners folded down on the pages featuring snakes.

But that was it.

No *old* newspaper clippings, no *new* newspaper clippings, no shrines to himself, no trophies from rich people. And most of all no snakes.

No snake figurines, no snake artifacts, no books on snakes.

"No reptiles other than these," I said, showing Conklin the tattoo book.

He said, "Take a look at this."

I followed him into the bedroom and checked out his find: a drawerful of XL women's underwear.

"Unless he had a big girlfriend, and I don't see any pic-tures, cosmetics, anything that would indicate that," Conk-lin said, "Henry Wallis was a cross-dresser."

"A cross-dressing drug dealer. Kudos to Sara Needleman for dumping him. Let's lock this joint up," I said.

"I live only a few blocks from here," said Rich as we closed and padlocked the door. "Come have a drink. Talk all this out."

I said, "Thanks anyway. This has been the longest day of my life, Rich. I need to go home. Get naked. Go to bed."

8th Confession

Conklin laughed. "Is that an order, Sergeant?"

I laughed along with him as I walked to my car, feeling just a little silly, thinking maybe Dr. Freud was having the *real* laugh.

"Okay," I said, one hand on my door, being very careful when I stepped up on the running board. "One drink only."

Chapter 68

THE DIFFERENCE BETWEEN Conklin's place and Henry Wallis's dump was extreme. Conklin lived on a similar block, both streets lined with unremarkable two- and three-story houses from the '50s made of cheap and ordinary materials, but once we were inside, Conklin's place felt lived-in and warm.

His living room was welcoming: good lighting, deep couches grouped around a fireplace, and the requisite bachelor must-have—a fifty-two-inch plasma-screen TV.

Rich stooped down near the entertainment unit, flipped through a stack of CDs, said, "Van Morrison okay with you?"

I said, "Sure," and looked at the photos on the wall, black-and-white blowups of sailboats on the bay, their spinnakers full of summer wind, light spangling the waves, three different shots, all of them breathtaking.

"You take these, Rich?"

8th Confession

"Uh-huh."

"They're wonderful."

Van Morrison was singing "Brown Eyed Girl," a tune that made me want to sing along. I smiled when Rich handed me a glass of wine, and I watched him sit down on the far end of the couch, put his feet up on a burnished hatch cover he'd turned into a coffee table.

I sipped from the frosty glass of chardonnay, kicked off my shoes, and sat on the *other* side of the same oversize couch. The tension left my body as the wine slid down my throat, cold and dry and good.

"See, what I'm wondering is, how could this be over?"

Conklin nodded, encouraging me to go on.

"A man is *dead*. There's going to be fallout that Tracchio and Jacobi just don't want to see. Wallis is going to have a family somewhere. There are going to be questions, and we both know, Rich, that Wallis didn't do it. Here's what I think happened: we just contributed to the death of a *red herring*."

Conklin laughed, said, "You paint a wonderful word picture."

I told him, "And you've got a great laugh, Rich. I love to hear you laugh."

He held my eyes until I blinked first.

The only clock in the room was on the DVR, and I was too far from it to read the flashing digits, but I knew that it was late. Had to be somewhere around two in the morning, and I was feeling keyed up, starting to get some ideas about seeing the rest of Rich's apartment. And maybe the rest of Rich.

My mind and body were overheating, and I don't think Rich meant to cool me down when he went to the kitchen to retrieve the chilled bottle. While he was gone, I undid a shirt button.

And then another.

In the process, I adjusted my position on the couch, felt something hard and sharp down between the cushions. I wrapped my fingers around the object, pulled it out, and saw a hair clip, a rhinestone barrette between my fingers.

The shock of that two-inch sparkler chilled me to the core. Cindy's barrette could have found its way to this couch only if Rich and Cindy had been grappling on it.

I placed the barrette on the coffee table, looked up as Rich returned with the bottle. He saw the barrette, saw the look in my eyes. Opened his mouth to say something—but nothing came out.

I averted my eyes, made sure he wouldn't see my pain.

I muttered that it was late and thanks for the wine. That I'd see him in the morning.

I left with my shoes half tied and my heart half broken. I found my car on the street where I'd left it, and I talked to myself as I drove home.

"What are you, jealous?" I shouted. "Because being jealous is stupid! Attention, brain cells: Rich plus Lindsay? That is really, really stupid!"

ing, hairy man-boobs. "Stay
get to know you better."

"Yeah, right after I figure
Pet Girl said. She turned o
this occasion and made l
throng. She stopped to retrie
brought, then quickly walke

Chapter 69

BY THE TIME Pet Girl arrived at Molly Caldwell-Davis's Twin Peaks house with its astounding city view, the party had been going on for hours. Pet Girl pressed the doorbell, banged the knocker until "Tyco" opened the door and the postdisco camp of the Scissor Sisters boomed out into the night.

Tyco was wearing his party clothes: a feather boa around his slender shoulders, nipple rings, and a black satin thong. He handed Pet Girl a flute of champagne, kissed her on the lips, said, "Hi, sexy," in a jokey way, so that Pet Girl laughed instead of saying thank you.

Pet Girl pushed past Tyco and entered the main room with its dizzying decor: tables and sofas in stepped-Alice-in-Wonderland heights, black-painted walls, leopard-print carpeting, bodies entwined on the floor pillows, the whole place feeling more like a bordello than the home of a girl who worked in a tea shop and had an eight-digit trust fund.

Pet Girl found the
low-slung sofa, crouche
through a silver straw.
beats behind the music,
ware billionaire Brian C

"Look. Who's. Here,"
nakedly sleazy, she want

"Molly," Pet Girl said,
tle of Moët & Chandon,

"Just put it anywhere
Girl as Tyco brought ove
with delight as she pawe
boy had taken of guests f

As suddenly as Molly
from Pet Girl, it boomera

"Don't you *smell* tha
burning. Why are you jus

Pet Girl blunted her e:

She went to the kitc
mushroom quiche from tl
on toast—worth three h
dog's bowl. Then she ston

She called Molly's na
stare beneath her blank, E

Pet Girl said, "I fed Mi
walk him?"

"Tyco will do it."

"All right then. Au rev

"But you just got here.
his black silk pajamas had

Chapter 70

IT WAS ALMOST MIDNIGHT when Pet Girl got out of the
cab and walked four blocks under the stars, the warm, moist
air blowing off the ocean as she approached the run-down
apartments at the farthest end of the Presidio.

She opened her front door, hung her backpack on a peg in
the hallway, and went to the kitchen. There, she used a key
to unlock the small pocket door, sliding it into its slot in the
wall. Then she entered the long, narrow room that had once
been a pantry and was now her private world.

Pet Girl hit the switch, throwing light on the half dozen
aquariums stacked on restaurant racks lining the back wall.
She sensed her beauties uncoiling their sleek bodies even
before she saw them slithering silently across the bark-and-
leaf litter—alert, hungry, eager to feed.

Pet Girl opened a cabinet and removed her tools: the tongs
with the pistol grip, her steel-toed boots, and the welder's

gloves, which were made of deerskin, lined with Kevlar, and thick but flexible, with elbow-length cuffs.

When she was dressed, she stepped over to Vasuki's cage, admired the snake's strong, muscular body, the intelligence in her eyes, feeling an almost telepathic communication with her favorite krait.

She shifted the heavy lid capping Vasuki's cage and captured the snake with her tongs, saying, "You can feed when we get back home, baby."

She dropped Vasuki carefully into a pillowcase, put the whole into a pet carrier, and snapped the locks closed.

Then she removed one of the baby garter snakes from a breeder tank and dropped it into Vasuki's cage so that her favorite pet's reward would be waiting for her when they returned.

Taking a last look around to make sure that all was well, Pet Girl exited her snake farm and locked the door.

She reached into her blouse and pulled out the antique locket she wore on a solid-gold chain. It had been a gift from her father, and his picture was inside.

Pet Girl raised the locket to her lips, kissed it, said, "Love you, Daddy," then turned out the lights.

Chapter 71

THE SCENE IN Molly's place had melted down since Pet Girl had been there two hours ago. Dozens of candles guttered in their holders, food trays were empty, and the party guests who'd passed out on the floor were snoring and twitching but were definitely *out*.

There was a sound coming from the kitchen, metal scraping the floor. Pet Girl froze, ducked behind a sofa, prepared to pretend that she'd been here all along. But when a body slammed her in the dark, she almost screamed.

"Mischa! Shhh." She stroked the springer's silky head, willing her heart rate to slow.

"Did Tyco take you for a walk?" she whispered, unclipping the dog's leash from his collar. Mischa wagged his tail, squatted, and piddled on the carpet, then ducked his head, expecting a reprimand—but he didn't get one.

Pet Girl told the dog to stay, then quickly ascended the

staircase that wound dramatically up to the second floor. Molly's bedroom was at the end of the hall, no light showing under the closed door.

The brass knob turned in Pet Girl's hand.

What if someone wakes up?

What then?

She entered the room and closed the door behind her, stood silently in the shadows, her pulse throbbing in her ears, her senses sharpened by the danger—the incomparable thrill of it.

The bed was directly in front of her, placed between two windows, crowded edge-to-edge with a tangle of naked bodies. A mottled sheet, some kind of animal print, was twisted almost like a rope, loosely tying the bodies together.

Pet Girl tried to determine which body parts belonged to which person, and when she felt ready, she tugged on her gloves and lifted Vasuki out of the carrier.

The snake, alert to the new environment, tensed in Pet Girl's hands, and Pet Girl felt Vasuki's pure lethal power. Like all kraits, Vasuki was nocturnal, aggressive at night. And she hadn't eaten in three days.

Vasuki's head swayed as Pet Girl held her over the bed. She hissed—and her steel cable of a body suddenly twisted in her owner's hands. It took only that one part of a second for the snake to slip from Pet Girl's grasp, drop to the sheets, and slide between the folds of the bedding.

She was instantly camouflaged. Completely invisible.

Pet Girl gasped as if she were in actual pain.

Vasuki was gone. Her plan had spiraled out of control.

For one crazy moment, Pet Girl imagined turning on the

lights to look for Vasuki and making up a story if someone woke up—but Molly wouldn't buy anything she said.

It just wouldn't play.

Disgusted with herself, horrified at what would happen to Vasuki if she was found, Pet Girl took a last futile look over the moonlight-washed bed. Nothing moved.

She packed up the pet carrier and left Molly's bedroom, closing the door again so that Mischa, at least, would be spared.

Outside the house, beginning the long walk down Twin Peaks Boulevard, Pet Girl assured herself that everything would be okay. As awful as it was to lose Vasuki, there was no ID on that snake.

No one could ever tie Vasuki to *her.*

Chapter 72

MOLLY CALDWELL-DAVIS LOOKED at me as though she were trying to break through a profound case of amnesia when Conklin and I interviewed her in her breakfast room. Her eyes were red, and she croaked out microsentences between long blank moments as she strained to remember the night before.

Conklin said, "Molly, take it slow. Just start at the beginning and tell us about the party last night, okay?"

"I want. My lawyer."

Footsteps thumped overhead.

EMS had come and gone, but Molly's bedroom swarmed with CSIs. Also, Claire and two of her assistants waited upstairs in the hallway for CSU to leave so that they could do their jobs.

Claire's voice floated down over the banister. "Lindsay, can you come up? You've got to see this."

"Do you *need* a lawyer, Molly?" Conklin was asking. "Because you're not a suspect. We just want to understand what happened here, you see? Because something did happen."

Molly was staring over Conklin's shoulder into the middle distance as I got up from the table and headed for the stairs. Charlie Clapper greeted me in the hallway, nattily dressed, good-natured, his irony freshly pressed this afternoon.

"It's a rerun, Lindsay. Lotsa fingerprints, no weapons, no blood, no suicide note, no signs of a struggle. We've bagged six bottles of prescription meds and some street junk, but I don't think we're looking at drug overdose. I think this was either Sodom or Gomorrah, and God weighed in."

"Honestly, I didn't know you were so conversant with the Old Testament," I said while peering around Clapper to better gawk at the vignette on the bed behind him.

"I'm Old Testament on my mother's side," he said.

I would have laughed, but my glimpse of the crime scene had suddenly made everything too real. I mumbled, "Keep in touch," and walked past Clapper into Molly's bedroom suite, where two naked men lay dead.

The boy was lying on the floor, head to one side, looked to be in his teens. His platinum-blond hair was spiked, and his green eyes were still open. Looked as though he'd been crawling toward the door when he succumbed.

The older man was on the bed in a half fetal position, his apron of belly fat obscuring his genitals. His eyes, too, were open. He hadn't died in his sleep.

This was what death by krait looked like. Central nervous system shut down, resulting in neuromuscular paralysis. The victims hadn't been able to breathe.

"When did they die?"

"They're still warm, Lindsay. Love to narrow it down for you, but I gotta say they died six to twelve hours ago. Did Molly volunteer anything useful?"

"Nope. Just the four bad words: 'I want my lawyer.'"

Claire sighed. "Before she stopped talking, Molly told me that the dead kid was her houseboy, name of Jordan Priestly. She called him 'Tyco.'"

"Tyco, like the toy company? Oh. I get it. Boy toy."

"But I didn't need her to identify this here father figure. He's Brian Caine."

"Uh-oh."

"Yeah. *That* Brian Caine. Tony Tracchio better put on his cast-iron jockstrap," Claire said, "because Caine Industries is going to be all over him."

Claire instructed her assistants to snap up the corners of the fitted bottom sheet, wrap it around Caine's body to preserve any trace before putting it all in the body bag.

Claire said to me, "You and Conklin can meet me at the morgue when you're done here. I'm going to take my time with these gentlemen, give them a better external exam than their mamas gave them when they were *born*."

Chapter 73

I WENT BACK down to the breakfast room, saw that Christine Rogers had joined Molly and Conklin.

Rogers was a celeb in her own right, a rich person's all-purpose attorney. She was trim and pretty, a gray-eyed blonde looking deceptively young for a senior partner in a big-time law firm that had her name on the door. Just guessing, but Ms. Rogers probably charged a thou an hour.

I had to ask myself why Molly Caldwell-Davis needed a cannon when even a slingshot was overkill.

We hadn't been looking at Molly as the doer.

Were we wrong?

Questions darted through my mind like a school of minnows. Did Molly know the Baileys? Sara Needleman? Where was Molly when they were killed? Did she have any connection with the victims of the snake killings of the early '80s?

8th Confession

Was this half-stoned rich girl stealthy enough, smart enough, motivated enough, to be a serial killer?

If so, what had possessed her to kill people in her own bed?

Christine Rogers's face was weary, but her hair shone, her blouse was starched, and her pin-striped Armani suit cost what I made in a month. She may have had the crazy schedule of a senior partner, but the attorney was all business.

"Ms. Caldwell-Davis wants to cooperate completely," she said. "When she went to bed around one thirty a.m., Brian Caine and Jordan Priestly were alive. When she woke up sometime after ten, they were dead."

I looked Rogers in the eye and said, "Maybe if she collects her *thoughts,* one or two of them will give us a *clue.*"

"Whatever happened, my client slept through it and was miraculously spared," Rogers said. "I want the police, the brass, the press, everyone, including God, to know that Molly had nothing to do with the deaths of her good friends. She's sick that they're dead. And she has nothing to hide."

"Wonderful," Conklin said. "So, Molly, this is square one. We need a list of everyone who was here last night, including the caterer, the delivery people, and whoever walks your dog."

Molly looked at Conklin with her big red-rimmed eyes. There was dried spittle in the corners of her mouth.

"Tyco walked my dog. I cooked for the party, and Brian tended the bar. I didn't know half the people who showed up, and that's the truth. People brought people who brought other people."

"Let's start with the ones you know," said Conklin.

Chapter 74

IT WAS LATE AFTERNOON when Conklin and I entered the autopsy suite and saw Tyco's body lying on a slab. His eyes were closed, but his collection of nipple rings and studs winked from a stainless-steel bowl under the lights.

"I'd almost given up," Claire said. "But look here."

She raised the boy's left arm, handed me the magnifying glass so I could see what she was calling "two defined pinpoint punctures."

Beside me, Bunny Ellis, Claire's number one assistant, pulled down the zipper on the second body bag, the one holding the remains of Brian Caine.

I turned—and for a terrifying moment I thought Brian Caine was *alive.*

The sheet Caine was wrapped in moved—but as I watched in horror, I saw that it wasn't Caine that was moving. It was something slim and banded, barely discernible against the mottled pattern of the sheet.

I screamed, "*Snake!* That's the *snake!*"

The animal seemed liquid as it poured out of the body bag and slid down one of the legs of the gurney onto the floor, head flattened in strike mode, winding across the gray ceramic tile toward *Claire.*

"*Don't move!*" Conklin yelled out.

His gun was in his hand, and he fired at the swiftly moving target, once, twice, again and again, the weapon bucking, bullets pinging off the tiles, gunfire echoing in the suite.

He was oh for six.

My hands were over my ears, my eyes wide open. I stared as the snake kept coming, now only a yard away from the tips of Claire's bootees.

I read the terror on her face. Moving would attract the snake, but Claire had no choice. She bolted for the stepladder that she used to shoot overhead pictures.

I broke for the hallway.

The firebox was on the wall. I smashed the glass with my gun butt, cleared the shards, reached for the fire ax, and ran back to the room.

Conklin was aiming again. Claire was standing on the ladder's top rung, and her assistants were screaming, as good as climbing the walls.

I lifted the ax, brought the blade down on the snake, divided it neatly in two at midpoint.

Both halves of the snake continued to writhe.

"It's dead, right?" I called out, my voice shrill, sweat pouring down the inside of my shirt. "It can't do anything, can it?"

My mind was suddenly swamped with images of sharks lying on boat decks—presumed dead—that "came back to life" to clamp their jaws around fishermen's legs.

This snake was still wriggling, mouth open, lethal fangs exposed.

We all stared, transfixed by the killer that wouldn't die. Then Conklin came out of his trance, disappeared into Claire's office, and returned with a metal trash can, which he upended over both parts of the snake.

He sat on the trash can.

The look on his face told me that he felt like he was sitting on a *bomb.*

"No, this is *good,*" he said to me, red-faced, perspiring, eyes bugging out just a little. "Good a time as any to get over my fear of *snakes.*"

Animal control arrived at the morgue forty minutes later. They relieved Conklin and lifted the trash can.

Both parts of the krait were still wriggling.

The front end gnashed at the air.

Chapter 75

YUKI WAS CLEANING out her fridge, listening to Faith Hill, thinking about piebald ponies and long-legged strangers, when her cell phone rang.

Her stomach clenched instantly — *Is it Doc?*

She dropped the sponge in the sink, wiped her hands on the back of her jeans, and went for the phone that was warbling on her mom's coffee table.

The caller ID read SF DOJ. Yuki stabbed the *receive* button with her thumb, said, "Castellano."

An hour later she was sitting in a leather armchair in Judge Brendan J. Duffy's chambers, waiting for Phil Hoffman to arrive.

Duffy looked perturbed, but he wouldn't even hint to Yuki about why he'd called until Hoffman was present. So Yuki used the time to study the judge's bookcase and consider the multiple possibilities. But only one possibility seemed *probable,* and that was that the damned, cursed jury who'd been charged with deliberating Stacey Glenn's case hadn't arrived at a verdict.

The jury had hung—again.

So it followed that Duffy would declare a mistrial and that the sassy beauty queen who'd bludgeoned her helpless, loving parents would do the catwalk strut out of the jailhouse.

Duffy didn't make small talk. He had gone into work mode, opening files, making notes, tossing papers into his out basket as the rays of afternoon sun lengthened across his Persian rug, and Yuki's heart continued to beat an SOS inside her ribcage.

Finally she heard Hoffman's voice in the outer office.

He ducked as he walked in the doorway, ran a hand through his rumpled black hair, said, "Sorry, Your Honor. Yuki. My wife and I were in Sausalito. The ferry couldn't be hurried."

"Sit down, Phil," Duffy said.

Hoffman sat in the second armchair, asked, "Did you hear from the jury?"

Yuki had already concluded that at this point Hoffman would be as happy with a mistrial as he would be with an acquittal. He'd spent too much time on this case. If there was a mistrial, his client would be released—and he could go back to getting *paid*.

"I've got bad news," Duffy said. "There was a fight at the jail."

"What happened?" Hoffman asked.

"Your client acquired a girlfriend over the last couple of weeks, and as I understand it, her girlfriend already had a girlfriend. There was a fight in the showers, and Stacey Glenn lost," Duffy said. "Ms. Glenn's girlfriend grabbed her around the neck, the other girl grabbed Stacey around the waist, and they both pulled."

Duffy shook his head as they all imagined the scene, but Yuki still couldn't visualize what had been so terrible.

"I'm sorry, I don't get it, Your Honor."

"My fault. I'm not explaining this well. Stacey Glenn's head was separated from her spinal cord." He put a hand around his own neck, said, "The neck itself—the muscles and so forth—was still in place, but the spine was severed. Medically speaking, Ms. Glenn suffered an internal decapitation."

"I've never heard of an internal decapitation," Hoffman said.

"First for me, too, but that's what I got from the Department of Corrections, based upon their autopsy findings, and I quote," Duffy said, reading from a notepad, " 'Those stupid bleeps turned Stacey Glenn into a bobblehead.' "

Yuki stood up, stumbled out of Judge Duffy's office, kept going even as Phil Hoffman called her name. She went for the stairs, kept a firm grip on the handrail as she wobbled down the steps, thinking about how the case had ended.

By the time she reached the lobby, she knew that she had to get ahold of Parisi. They had to really think through what they would put out to the public, and *he* had to handle it, because it wouldn't be right to let the public see her almost irrepressible elation.

Stacey Glenn had gotten the death penalty.

No conviction, no dismissal, no mistrial. This was the ultimate resolution.

It was over.

Yuki had not lost her case—and the sociopath Stacey Glenn was dead.

Part Four

DOC

Chapter 76

CINDY AND I were at Susie's early in the evening, and even at six p.m., the Caribbean-style eatery was jammed.

Crazy jammed.

The steel band was in midset; Susie was drumming up a limbo competition; rowdies, sloshed on tequila, were falling all over the pool table; and Lorraine, who is usually prescient when it comes to timing, had lost her touch.

She took our drink order, came back to read us the specials, came back again to show us her engagement ring, then returned to ask if we had everything we needed.

That was in the first five minutes.

I glared at her until she recoiled and scurried away. Claire and Yuki would be arriving at any moment, and I still hadn't had it out with Cindy.

"Stop beating around the bush, will you?" said Cindy, my dear friend. She put a little burn on it so that it sounded like a dare.

"Fine. Are you and Conklin dating?"

"He *told* you? Look, it didn't start that way, but—"

"Are you *sleeping* with him?"

"Excuse me, but who are you? Sister Mary Margaret of the Little Sisters of the Chastity Belt?"

"Yes, damn it. I am."

"Why? What is your problem?"

I held up my empty beer mug so that Lorraine would bring me a refill.

"Corona coming up."

"Lorraine," I said, "listen to this. Cindy is sleeping with my *partner,* and she didn't tell me."

"Uh-huh."

"Well, don't you think that as my *friend,* she should have told me?"

"Oh, no you don't, Lindsay," said Lorraine. "Don't you drag me into this. I'm a very happy girl right now and I don't want a beef with either one of you."

"Fine," I said. "Hit me again."

"Be right back."

"You're kidding, aren't you, Lindsay? You think I should've told you that I was going out with Rich when I knew all along you were going to make us both feel bad about it—and I don't even know why!" Cindy sat back in her seat and did, in fact, look confused.

"You don't know why?" I said. I was getting a swooping feeling in my stomach, telling me that I was wrong and she was right, that I had been uncool. And that whatever Cindy and Rich were doing together, it was their business.

8th Confession

Cindy didn't know much about my history with Rich, and I wasn't going to tell her—but maybe *he* would tell her.

Maybe he *had*.

Some hesitancy must have passed over my face because Cindy smelled blood. She leaned forward, stuck out her chin, and said, "*I get it*. Are you two doing it, Lindsay? Is that it? You tell me right now, because if you're sleeping with him, I will kick that dog to the curb."

"No. *No*. We're not. Don't want to and never have."

"Good," Cindy said. "That's really great. So tell me again: what's the problem?"

"It's a chain-of-command thing, Cindy—"

"Are you ca-razy? I don't work for you."

"Conklin does! And he and I talk about stuff that you shouldn't know—for all our sakes. And I would have liked a chance to remind him."

"Even if that made sense—which it *doesn't*—we don't talk about you. We don't talk about your cases. We just have great sex and watch movies in bed."

My face heated up, and I dropped my eyes to the table. Cindy had just given me way too much information, and I'd completely brought it down on myself.

My beer was climbing into my throat when I heard, "Hey there, girlfriends."

I looked up to see Claire clearing the aisles as she came toward our table. She had her baby in her arms, my goddaughter, Ruby Rose. And Yuki and Doc were bringing up the rear.

"I'm not finished talking yet," I growled at Cindy.

"Fine," Cindy said. "Don't make me wait too long for your apology."

Chapter 77

YUKI WAS ALMOST giddy with delight.

They were all jammed together in the booth at Susie's, and her friends liked Doc. Correction. She could tell by their faces that all of them *loved* him. He was telling them about his day in the ER, saying, "A female patient comes in, says she's been doing unaccountable stuff at night since she started taking sleep meds. Apparently she unwittingly went to her medicine chest and swallowed down a whole bottle of pills.

"She shows me the empty bottle," Doc said.

Claire leaned forward, Yuki getting this great feeling that Claire was glad to have another doctor to talk to. She asked Doc what the pills were.

"Dramamine."

"For seasickness?" Claire said. "Those can't kill her."

Doc grinned, said, "She wanted to have her stomach

pumped, but I just told her it wasn't necessary. I said, 'Helen, you're all set. Book a cruise!'"

Claire started laughing, and the baby reached out, knocked a bottle of beer into Cindy's lap, and Lindsay broke up, laughing until tears came out of her eyes.

"I'm sorry for laughing," Lindsay said to Cindy. "No, I mean it. It's not funny."

Claire handed the baby to Doc so she could wipe Cindy down, and the baby pulled on Doc's nose and called him "Boog-ah." And he laughed at her, and she gave him a gummy chortle.

And the evening just kept coming on that way, one laugh leading to another even bigger one, Yuki feeling like it was her birthday, maybe the best birthday she'd ever had.

She told her friends about the Stacey Glenn case being over, and Lindsay launched into the story of the "snake who would not die," Claire expanding her arms to show how long the animal was, coming dangerously close to knocking a beer into Cindy's lap *again*.

Doc had said, "But seriously, folks, it's good to know what kind of snake it was. There's an antivenin, you know."

"Antivenom?" Cindy asked.

"Same thing, but 'antivenin' is the actual term," Claire said. "Anyway, it's not that easy to get, though *my* patients are past needing it, Doc. Came in handy that Sergeant Boxer can swing an *ax*."

The beer kept coming for all but Doc, who inevitably had to go to the hospital. Then came the best part of all. As Yuki stood to say good-bye, he put his arms around her and kissed her, dipping her down until she cracked up and everyone cheered, *everyone,* even people who weren't at their table.

"See you this weekend?" he said.

She nodded, thinking about what lingerie she would wear. And then he was gone.

Right after that, Cindy said she had a date and had to go home and change, and Claire left, too: "Got to get this baby girl into bed." And Lindsay said, "Yuki, you're not just the designated driver, you're the *only* driver."

Yuki didn't want the night to end.

"What if I drive you to my place? Why don't you spend the night?"

"Done," said Lindsay, knocking back her beer.

Yuki grinned. Having Lindsay all to herself, getting a chance to relive the evening and talk about Doc—well, that just put the icing on the cake.

Chapter 78

I STARTED YAPPING as soon as I got in the car with Yuki.

"Doc is fantastic."

"You really think so? I mean, *thanks,* and *yeah,* isn't he *great?*"

"Amazingly great. And he really likes you."

"How can you tell?"

"You just can. And then there was the Hollywood kiss in front of God and everyone."

Yuki laughed. It's one of Yuki's most priceless gifts, a laugh that can make the sun come out at night. Meanwhile, my mind was on fast-forward, and I couldn't wait any longer. Had Yuki known? Had everyone known but me?

As soon as the car was in gear and we were moving, I blurted, "Yuki, did you know about Rich and Cindy dating?"

"Noooo. Really? I can't believe she didn't tell me!"

"Exactly," I said. "How'm I supposed to feel, my partner having sex with one of my best friends?"

"It's kind of a good match, though," Yuki was saying, taking a left, the car speeding downhill, causing my stomach contents to slosh.

"She's always liked him," Yuki said, "but who doesn't? Wait a minute, Linds. Have I missed the obvious here?"

I rolled down the window, and the wind hit my face. Yuki was asking me, "Do you want me to pull over? Are you sick?"

"I'm fine," I belched.

"Okay, so what's this about? Your partner's dating your friend. Why is that a problem?"

I rolled up the window, just left it cracked about an inch. "Rich and I. We've had a couple of *moments*," I heard myself say.

Yuki's mouth dropped open as she headed the car across a straightaway, stopping at a light, then swiveling her head so she could look at me.

"Define '*moments*.'"

Suddenly I was telling Yuki everything: about the near miss Conklin and I'd had when a case took us to Los Angeles. I told her how we'd stopped before things went too far, and how the chemistry just wouldn't let up. That it had been sparking even when my apartment burned down, when I'd moved in with Joe. Even a week ago when Conklin had planted a steamy kiss on my lips by the car.

I was still talking when we pulled into the underground garage beneath Yuki's apartment building. She shut off the engine and turned to face me.

"Are you in love with him?"

8th Confession

"In love? I don't know what to call it, but we have *something* special..."

"So this isn't about Cindy. This is about Conklin."

I shrugged.

"You have something pretty special with Conklin that you have turned down repeatedly and have no intention of acting on, isn't that right?"

I was drunk and I was being interrogated by my friend the prosecutor. I had no defense.

"We've talked about it," I said. "It was my choice, and I'm glad that we've never done anything that would destroy Joe."

"So how do you feel about Joe? Tell me the truth."

"I love him."

"Prove it to me, because right now, I don't get it."

I excused myself, got out of the car, walked over to the huge trash can by the elevator, and threw my guts up. Yuki was there with a Wet-Nap, an arm around my waist, a packet of gum.

But she didn't let me off the hook.

We went back to the car and resumed our places, and she said, "Tell me the whole truth and nothing but."

I told her that when I'd met Joe it had been that thunderbolt right between the eyes, and it had been mutual. And since that day, Joe had never let me down. That he'd changed his whole life to be with me. That he was not only my lover but my best friend, too, the person I could be real with. That the only fear I ever had about my love for Joe was taking the next step with him, because it would be for good.

"If we get married, I can never leave him," I said.

"And that's a bad thing?" Yuki asked me.

"It's a scary thing."

"I'm no expert, but isn't 'scary' appropriate when you've been traumatized? When someone you love has died?"

I nodded. She was talking about Chris, my former partner and boyfriend who'd been gunned down on the job.

Yuki reached out, took my hand.

"Lindsay, it's okay to have chemistry with Rich. You can't help that. It's fun, maybe, and cool to have someone with you all the time who has a big crush on you. You've already decided he's not for you, but he's your back door, your escape hatch, because you're afraid to get married. Do I have that right?"

Tears were coming now. Yuki tightened her grip on my hand.

"Let him go," she said. "Let *yourself* go."

Yuki held out her arms and folded me in. She's a tiny thing and I'm an Amazon, but somehow that awkward hug was just what I needed. I was crying in earnest and Yuki was stroking my hair.

"You know what I want with Doc?" she said. "Exactly what you have with Joe."

Chapter 79

CINDY WAS AT her desk in the bull pen the next morning, scrolling through her notes in order to double-check her memory. Then she found it, the note she'd made of her impromptu interview with the girl who called herself Sammy, the strung out teen who'd mentioned that "people" had killed Rodney Booker, not one person but at least two.

Cindy had felt haunted by that word—"people"—sorry that Sammy had bolted before she'd followed up on what might have been a significant lead to finding out who killed Rodney Booker.

Cindy called Lindsay again, this time leaving her a message thanking her for the sweetheart roses. Then she grabbed her handbag and left the Chronicle Building, taking the short walk to From the Heart.

A homeless guy about her age, name of Angel, flashed his

gold-capped smile and opened the door to the soup kitchen while giving Cindy a sweeping bow.

"Hey there, Ms. Cindy Thomas. We named you the sweetheart of From the Heart. By popular vote."

Cindy grinned, asked Angel if he knew a girl named Sammy, and Angel said, "Sure, I know Sammy. She's inside now."

Cindy searched the large room, finally seeing Sammy working behind the steam table, serving up lunch to the long line of street people. Sammy was wearing nice slacks, expensive layered tops in bright colors, her pale yellow hair neatly braided down her back.

And although Sammy's pupils were large enough to see from across the room, the teenager was clearly a volunteer, not a client.

Cindy crossed to the steam table, said, "Hi, Sammy. Do you have any time for me?"

Sammy looked not just nervous but jumpy. "No," she said. "I just can't."

"Please."

"I can't talk to you in here," Sammy sputtered. "I'll meet you at Moe's in a half hour if you'll leave now."

Cindy waited for Sammy at Moe's, and after an hour went by, she ordered a grilled cheese on rye. As soon as it came, Sammy dropped into the seat across from her.

"You're too much, Cindy," the girl said, shaking her head. "I warned you to watch out, but you just can't leave things alone."

"I can keep a secret," Cindy said, "but I can't just drop this story."

"No? Well, my father has me under house arrest. He doesn't want me talking to anyone, especially you." The girl crunched Life Savers, ordered a Coke. "Classic," she said to the waitress.

"Why not me?"

"Because you are looking to get yourself killed."

Cindy stirred her coffee, said, "See, this has me confused, Sammy. Why am I in danger? What's so special about Rodney Booker that makes writing about him life-threatening?"

"Because his killers aren't street people, Cindy. His killers don't want to be exposed, arrested, charged with *murder.*"

Cindy said, "I need your help."

Sammy sat back in her seat, her eyes wide with fear. She said, "I need your help, too. I want to get away from here. Move out of town. But I have no money. I'll make you a deal. Can you get me some kind of advance on that reward? Like ten grand?"

"No *way,*" Cindy said. "That money is there until Bagman's killers are convicted. I can get you a couple hundred bucks if that'll help."

"Forget it. Thanks, but no thanks. I said I needed *help,* and by the way, screw you," said Sammy.

As soon as Sammy left the diner, Cindy paid the check and walked back to work. Sammy had finally gotten to her. The teenager's fear could be druggie paranoia to the max, but Cindy was getting a different feeling—that Rodney Booker's murder was tied to something bigger, something *organized.*

Which meant that she was out of her league.

She called a number she knew by heart. "Rich," she said, "we've got to talk."

Chapter 80

CONKLIN FOUND SKIP WILKINSON at MacBain's, one hand in a bowl of peanuts, the other around a mug of freshly drawn brew. Wilkinson was a skinny kid with a buzz cut, went to the academy with Conklin. He was now in Narcotics and Vice, or as he called it, "Drugs and Whores."

"So you want to talk about Bagman?" Wilkinson said.

"Anything you can tell me. He's a homicide that's going cold."

"Yeah, well, I can't tell you too much. We had a few brushes with him. He was strictly a small-time drug dealer."

"What kind of drugs?"

"Crack. I brought you his file."

Wilkinson lifted a dog-eared folder out of his battered briefcase, passed it to Conklin. "We never had enough probable cause to arrest him. Sickening, what he was doing."

"What was that?" Conklin asked. There was no arrest sheet,

no mug shot, just handwritten notes stapled to the back of the folder marked BAGMAN JESUS. They hadn't known his name.

"He was turning teenage girls into pushers. He had a network of them. Sent them out on the street to sell. I'm not sure he wasn't having sex with them all.

"This is all from street talk, not reliable sources. So we planted a couple of female cops on the street, waited for him to take the bait, but he didn't do it."

"And you gave up? Look, I'm not being critical. We haven't had time to work his murder more than a handful of hours—"

"We didn't quit," Wilkinson said. "But as I said, Conklin, he was small-time. Crack is bad, but we're being overrun by *meth,* which is far worse. Kids were making it in their basements. It was easy and cheap, but since the crackdown on ephedrine, meth has become big business.

"It's huge, going out of control. Organized crime is getting involved. The stuff is streaming in from Mexico. I don't mean to chew your ear off, but it's getting away from us. And it's killing good kids. One hit, and they don't stand a chance."

Conklin said, "So Rodney Booker was a crack dealer. We didn't have that."

"We would've landed Bagman eventually, but we had bigger dogs to worry about. And then someone got to that bastard first. And I say great. Glad they took that fucker down and made sure he was down for good."

Chapter 81

AT JUST BEFORE EIGHT on a gray morning, Cindy stood between me and Conklin, pointing her finger in the direction of a young woman striding up Fifth Street.

"That's *her*. Red shirt, blond braid. That's *Sammy*."

Sammy heard her name, turned her head, saw Conklin sprinting toward her, and took off like she had jets on the heels of her shoes. She flew off the sidewalk and into the street, ducked in front of a fish truck that was accelerating as the light turned green.

I thought the truck might have clipped her—but the gears ground into third and the truck sped up as Conklin rounded the tailgate. I was running, too, slipping through openings in the clogged street and sidewalks, barking out, "Police! Step aside!" as I ran.

I could hear Conklin huffing, that's how close I was, when

a crack in the sidewalk grabbed the toe of my shoe and I went down. My breath left me.

I staggered to my feet, and then a citizen pointed the way. By the time I caught up with them, Conklin had boxed Sammy into an alcove between two buildings, was yelling to the wide-eyed and panting kid, "Stop running and *listen*."

A cluster of homeless people rose up from the sidewalk outside the soup kitchen, some sidling away, others circling around Conklin and Sammy. It was a menacing crew, and there were a lot of them. I flashed my badge, and the grumbling crowd backed off, gave us room.

"We want to talk to you at the station," Conklin was saying to the girl. "You'll come in, be a good citizen. Understand? Cooperate, and we won't book you."

"No. I *don't* understand. I haven't done anything."

"See, I want to believe you," said Inspector Conklin of the melting brown eyes. "But I *don't*."

Chapter 82

TWENTY MINUTES LATER, Sammy, last name still unknown, sat across from us in Interview Room Number One, the video camera peering from its spider perch in the corner of the ceiling.

Sammy had no ID, but she admitted to being eighteen. She was legal, and we could question her. I'd done my best to befriend her, tell her I understood why she was frightened and offer her assurances, but the kid wasn't buying it.

Her answers were evasive, and Sammy's crappy attitude told me that she was hiding something big. And as pissed off as I was, I had a growing sense that whatever she knew could help us clear the Bagman Jesus case — maybe *today.*

The sullen teenager had dark circles under her eyes and the hollow cheeks of a meth addict going through withdrawal. She tore open a roll of Life Savers and ground the candy between her molars. I smelled Wild Cherry, and for the first time, I could swear I smelled her fear.

Was Sammy afraid that Bagman's killer would come after her if she talked? Or was she implicated in his death?

I tried again, nicely. "Sammy, what's bothering you?"

"Being here."

"Look, we're not trying to scare you. We're trying to find out who killed Bagman. Help us, and we'll make sure nothing happens to you."

"Oh, like that's the problem."

"Help me understand. What *is* the problem?"

The tough-girl mask dropped.

Sammy shouted, "I'm just a kid! I'm just a *kid!*"

That got to me and made me want to back off.

Instead, I bore down. I took off my jacket so that Sammy could see my gun.

I said, "Cut the crap. Tell me what you know, or you'll be spending the best years of your life in prison as an accessory after the fact in Rodney Booker's murder."

Conklin went along. He deferred to me, called me "Sergeant," made his eyes hard whenever Sammy looked to him for help.

We never gave the kid in her a chance.

Chapter 83

CONKLIN HAD TOLD ME that Bagman had a network of girl crack dealers, but I hadn't envisioned a girl like Sammy: still pretty, well-dressed, a white girl who spoke as though she'd had a family-values upbringing and a good education.

How had Bagman gotten his hooks into her?

When I leaned on Sammy, she teared up, so Conklin pushed a box of tissues across the table. Sammy dried her eyes, blew her nose, gulped some air.

And then she started to talk.

"We sold crack, okay? Bagman paid us with crystal, and we used it with him. Spent days and days blowing clouds, not eating or sleeping, just having out-of-control *sex!*" she shouted into my face. "These outrageous orgasms, ten, twenty times, one on top of the other—"

"Sounds *great*," I said.

"Yeah," Sammy said, missing the sarcasm. "Un*real*. Then

he'd drive us to work, and when we'd made our numbers, we'd come home to Bagman Jesus."

"How many girls are 'we'?"

Sammy shrugged. "Three or four. No more than five living in the house at any one time."

"Write down their names," Conklin said, bringing the girl a pad and pen. Sammy came back to earth, gave Conklin a look meaning *Are you crazy?*

I asked her, "What do you mean, 'drive us to work'? Drive what?"

"Bagman had a van, of course."

Sammy's voice was starting to crack. Conklin went out of the room, returned with a high-octane cola, and handed it to the girl, who drained the can in one long swallow.

I thought about Rodney Booker, the handsome man who'd gone to Stanford and joined the peace corps, then taken a hard turn into the drug business, giving it an original and especially cruel twist.

Sammy had described the horror, seemingly without understanding what was making me sick. Booker had kept a willing harem of teenage crack dealers, and he'd addicted them to a drug that delivered mind-blowing sex — until they burned out and *died.*

Booker was a modern-day devil.

Of course someone had killed him.

I asked Sammy where Booker's van was, and she shrugged again. "I have no idea. Have I done my civic duty? May I go, please?"

Conklin pushed on. "So let me get this straight. Booker was cooking meth in his house?"

"He was for a while, but it was dangerous."

Sammy sighed long and loud, remained silent for a few seconds, then resumed.

"My whole life dried up when Bagman died. Now my freaking parents are 'cleaning me up.' You know what it's like to drop down a well? That's my life. I'm going out of my mind."

"Uh-huh," Conklin said. I admired his tenacity. "You told Cindy Thomas that you know who killed Bagman—"

"I never said that."

"Sergeant?" Conklin said.

"We have enough," I said, standing up, putting on my jacket.

"You have the right to remain silent," Conklin said to Sammy. "Anything you say can and will be used against you—"

"You're *arresting* me?"

Sammy stiffened as Conklin got her to her feet, clamped the cuffs around her wrists.

"I want my phone call," she said. "I want my *father.*"

Chapter 84

SAMMY'S FULL NAME was Samantha Pincus, as we found out when her father blew into the squad room like a winter squall.

Neil Pincus was a lawyer who worked pro bono for the down-and-out habitués of the Mission District, where he and his brother had a two-man law practice in the same building that housed From the Heart.

I sized Pincus up as he stood over me at my desk and demanded to see his daughter. He was five ten, a taut 160, late forties, balding, and his scalp was sweating from the steam that was shooting out of his ears.

"You're holding my daughter for something she said without counsel present? I'm going to sue you each individually and I'm going to sue the city, do you understand? You didn't read her her rights until she indicted herself."

"True," I said. "But this wasn't a custodial interrogation, Mr. Pincus. Her rights weren't violated."

"Sam didn't know that. You terrified her. What you did was tantamount to torture. I'm a heck of a victims' rights lawyer, and I'm going to send the two of you to *hell*."

Jacobi was watching from behind the glass walls of his office, and twelve other pairs of eyes in the squad room were cast down, sneaking peeks.

I rose to my full five-foot-ten, plus two inches for my shoes, and said, "Take it down a few notches, Mr. Pincus. Right now this is just between the four of us. Help your daughter. Get her to cooperate, and we won't book her."

Pincus grunted in disgust, nodded, then followed us to the interrogation room where his daughter was waiting, hands cuffed in front of her. Her father squeezed her shoulder, then wrenched a chair out from the table and sat down.

"I'm listening."

"Mr. Pincus, by her own admission, your daughter is a junkie and a dealer," I said. "She was involved with Rodney Booker, also known as Bagman Jesus, now violently deceased. Samantha was not only selling crank for Booker but she told a very credible source that she knows who killed him. She's a material witness, that's why we're holding her, and we need her to tell us who Booker's killer is."

"I'm not admitting she was dealing," Pincus told us, "but if she was, she's not doing it now and she's not using either."

"Well, everything's fine, then," I snapped.

"Listen, her mother and I are on her. Early curfew. No cell phone. No computer. She volunteers in a soup kitchen so she can see how bad life can get—and she works underneath my office."

Pincus lifted his daughter's cuffed wrists so I could see her watch. "It's a GPS. She can't go anywhere without me knowing. Sam has become a model of sobriety. I give you my word."

"Is that all, Mr. Pincus?"

Samantha wailed.

"Where's your decency?" Pincus spat. "Booker was scum. He was dealing to kids who sold to kids. Not just to my daughter but to other girls. Many good girls. We reported him."

"Who's 'we'?" I demanded.

"The Fifth Street Association. Look it up. I filed a complaint on behalf of the association in February, and again in March. Again in April. The cops did nothing. We were told, 'If you don't have proof, fill out a form.'"

"You own a gun, Mr. Pincus?"

"No. And I'm asking you for a break. Release Samantha into my custody. Jail, even for a night, could destroy this child."

We agreed to let the girl go, gave Pincus a warning not to let her leave town.

As soon as the two had left the squad room, Conklin and I went to our desks and called up Pincus's name in the database. He didn't have a sheet, but Conklin found something else.

"Neil Pincus has a license to carry, and he's got a registered Rohm twenty-two," Conklin said over the top of his monitor. "A cheap dirty little pistol for a cheap dirty little lawyer. That son of a bitch lied."

Chapter 85

CONKLIN AND I were at the door to Pincus and Pincus, Attorneys-at-Law, by noon, and we had four other cops with us. When the door opened, we pushed past the reception area, and I handed Neil Pincus a warrant.

I said, "Keep your hands where I can see them."

Pincus blinked stupidly. "What?"

"Did you think we wouldn't find out about the gun?"

"That . . . *thing* was stolen," Pincus said. "I reported it." The lawyer pushed back his chair, said, "I kept it in here."

I opened a desk drawer, bottom right, saw the metal gun box. I lifted the lid, stared at a cardboard box for a Rohm .22. The box was empty.

"You kept this gun box locked?"

"No."

"Where'd you keep the ammo?"

8th Confession

"Same drawer. Look. I know that's a violation, but if I was going to need the gun, I was going to need it *fast*. Sergeant, I rarely opened the box," said Pincus. "It could have been stolen any time in the last six months. You turn your back for a second around here, take a phone call or take a piss—"

I stepped in front of Pincus, jerked open the rest of his desk drawers as Conklin did the same to brother Al's matching desk in the next room.

Then the six of us jacked open the file cabinets, tossed the supply room, looked under the cushions on the cracked leather sofa. After a short while, the Pincus brothers settled down, talked over us to their clients, acted normally and entirely as though we weren't there.

When we came up empty, Conklin and I visited both of the Pincus homes, one in Forest Hill and the other on Monterey Boulevard. Good neighborhoods, places where bad kids didn't happen. We met the two nice wives, Claudia and Reva, both of whom had been asked by their husbands to cooperate.

We acquainted ourselves with the insides of the Pincus family closets, cupboards, hope chests, and tool chests, and the Pincus wives voluntarily let us search their cars.

Their places were as brilliantly clean as white sheets hanging from the line on a sunshiny day.

Executing those warrants had been physically and emotionally draining. I was wrung out and depressed, and we had nothing to show for our work.

Had Neil Pincus's gun been used to kill Bagman?

Chapter 86

CONKLIN AND I got into the squad car we'd parked outside Alan Pincus's house.

I owed Jacobi a call and an explanation, and knew he'd go bug-nuts when I told him we'd spent our day chasing Bagman's hit man when a psycho was dropping the mayor's friends with a poisonous reptile.

I was about to say so to Conklin, but now that we were alone, the elephant in the car could not be ignored.

Conklin turned down the radio, jumbled the car keys in his hand for a moment, and said, "Cindy talked to you about...uh...us."

"Yep. It was quite a surprise," I said, holding his gaze until he looked away.

"She said you were upset."

I shrugged.

"I'm sorry I didn't tell you, Linds—"

"Hey. I'm fine. *Fine*," I lied. "Once I thought about it, I realized you two are a natural."

"It's only been, like, a *week*."

"Whatever. As Jacobi says, 'I love you guys.'"

Conklin laughed, and that laugh told all. He was having a wonderful time with my bodacious, cheeky, bighearted friend, and he didn't want to stop.

The guy who'd kissed me last week—that guy was gone. Sure, I'd rejected him, and sure, I didn't own him. But even so, it hurt. I missed the Richie who'd mooned over me.

I wondered if his sleeping with Cindy was a roundabout way of sleeping with *me*. It was a crummy thought, hardly worthy of me, but—*ha!*—I thought it anyway.

And I remembered Yuki's advice: "Let him go. Let *yourself* go."

Conklin was watching my face for a sign, perhaps my blessing, so I was glad when knuckles rapped on my window. It was Alan Pincus, home early from work.

He was bigger than his older brother, had more hair. Otherwise, they were clones.

I buzzed down the glass.

"Sergeant Boxer? Are you people done? Because I want to get my family life back to normal."

"We're done for now, but we're not going away."

"I understand."

"Anything comes up we should know about, call us."

"Boy Scout honor."

Pincus held up three fingers, then turned and marched up the walk to his front door. Was he sticking it to us? I couldn't tell. When he was inside, I said to Conklin, "Let's call Cindy."

Chapter 87

LATER THAT DAY, Conklin, Cindy, and I had MacBain's Beers O' the World Pub practically to ourselves. We had a table in the back, a bowl of freeze-dried peanuts, and diet colas all around.

Cindy's face was flushed, and it had nothing to do with her proximity to my partner.

"You let them go? You didn't hold them, squeeze them—"

"Sounds like a pop song," Conklin cracked, and he was so high on Cindy, he actually sang a few lines: "Hold me, squeeze me, never let me go. . . ." But Cindy was not in the mood.

"How can you make fun of me?"

Conklin's smile dropped. "Cin, we would've if we could've—but we can't make an indictable charge. Not yet."

"But you're working the case? Swear to God?"

Conklin and I both nodded, Conklin adding, "We are *seriously* working the case."

Cindy dropped her head into her hands and groaned. "I put this guy on the front page of the *San Francisco Chronicle.* 'Bagman Jesus, Street Saint.' And he's what? Turning teens into drug dealers? And you think that's why someone killed him? God Almighty. What do I do now?"

"Do what you always do," I said to my friend. "Run with the truth. And hey, Cindy, this is a better story, right?"

Her eyes got bigger as she saw the size of the headline in her mind. "I can cite reliable sources close to the SFPD?"

"Yes. Sure."

Conklin paid the tab, and we three left the bar together. Cindy headed back to the *Chronicle* and an emergency meeting with her boss, and Conklin and I walked over to the Hall.

Back in the gloom of the bull pen, Conklin booted up his Dell. I sorted through the messages that had come in while we were out, found one from St. Jude that Brenda had marked URGENT. I had punched in half of McCorkle's number when Conklin said, "Unbelievable."

I stopped dialing. "Whatcha got?"

"Rodney Booker's van is in impound, Lindsay. The day after he was killed, it was towed from a no-parking zone."

I called impound, located the car, and put in a rush order to have it brought to the crime lab.

Our dead end had sprung wide open.

And that's what I shouted over my shoulder to Jacobi, who was advancing on us, breathing fire, as Conklin and I fled the squad room.

Chapter 88

BY SEVEN THAT NIGHT, CSIs were making the most of our warrant to search Booker's van. The brainiac Brett Feller and his muscular cohort, Ray Bates, had disassembled the blue van into piles of assorted parts. And they'd found Bagman's bag strapped to the underside of a backseat with a bungee cord.

The two young men weren't done yet. They unscrewed nuts and bolts and tire rims, hoping for a hidden dope cache or a weapon, but when Conklin and I opened the brown leather mailbag-style pouch and looked inside, I said, "Stand down, guys. This is it."

I lifted items out of the bag. Conklin laid them out on the light table, and Feller, an intense twenty-four-year-old with a touch of obsessive-compulsive disorder and an eye toward being the next Gil Grissom—for real—lined everything up squarely and took photographs.

My heart was banging *ta-dum, ta-dum* throughout this process, and frankly I was surprised at my own excitement.

In the past weeks, I had gone in and out of caring about Bagman Jesus. At first I'd written him off as one of the dozens of street people who were killed every year in a dispute over a choice sleeping location or a finger of booze.

By the time Cindy said, "Nobody gives a *damn*," I did.

When Bagman Jesus turned out to be a drug dealer, I lost interest again. Now he'd morphed into a predator without conscience, and I was going through Bagman Jesus whiplash.

Who capped this guy?

What will we learn from his stuff?

Opening Bagman's bag felt like waking up on Christmas morning to find that Santa had left his entire carryall under the tree.

I took out my notebook, kept track of our findings.

Items one through fourteen were miscellany: a moldy sandwich in a Ziploc bag, several bundles of bills rubber-banded according to denomination—looked to be no more than two thousand dollars.

There was a worn Bible inscribed with Rodney Booker's name in the flyleaf, and what seemed to be the biggest score: a half dozen bags of sparkling white powder—maybe six ounces of crystal meth.

But of real interest was item number fifteen: a leather folder about five inches by eight inches, what travelers use to hold their plane tickets and passports.

Conklin opened the folder, removed the contents, and unfolded the papers, handling them as if they were the Dead

8th Confession

Sea Scrolls. As my partner put papers down on the table, Feller took photos and I named the documents out loud.

"Service record for the van. Oil change and lube, one hundred seventy-two thousand, three hundred thirty-four miles. Looks like a winning lottery ticket, five out of eight numbers, dated the day before Booker's body was found."

I noted some deposit slips, a little more than three thousand in cash over a three-day period, and there were receipts from fast-food restaurants.

But when CSI Bates found Bagman's wallet deep inside a door panel, the contents nearly blew down the walls of the crime lab.

Chapter 89

THE WALLET WAS SLIM, a good-quality goatskin with the initials RB stamped in gold on the corner. I took out Booker's driver's license and found a sheet of yellow paper in the bill compartment.

I unfolded it, my eyes taking in the data, my brain, a few beats behind, trying to make sense of it.

I said, "This is a bill of sale. Rodney Booker bought a bus from a used-car lot in Tijuana on May second, just days before he died.

"It was an old school bus, says here, nineteen eighty-three."

I stared at the yellow paper, but my inner eye was on Market and Fourth right after an old school bus had blown up, filling the air with bloody mist, littering the street with body parts.

Ten innocent people had died.

Others had been injured, scarred for life.

8th Confession

I remembered hunkering down on shattered glass, talking with the arson investigator Chuck Hanni as he pointed out the broken parts and melted pieces in what was left of the rear of the bus, showing me that the vehicle had been a mobile meth lab.

The owner of the bus had never been identified.

"What did Sammy say?" I asked my partner. "Bagman used to cook meth in the house—but it was too dangerous?"

"Right."

I took a second piece of paper from the wallet. It was plain white, six by four inches with a glue-strip edge, obviously torn from a notepad, folded in half. Handwritten on the paper was a tally converting pesos to dollars. A scribbled word jumped out at me: "ephedrine," the main ingredient in methamphetamine.

Conklin was breathing over my shoulder. "That's a signature, isn't it? J something Gomez."

"Juan."

The name Juan Gomez was as common as John Smith. That might not mean much, but it was the name on the ID of the meth cook who'd been blown across the intersection at Fourth and Market, dead from the blast before his head had been bashed in against a lamppost.

I could hardly believe the treasure I held in my hands.

Rodney Booker had been branching out from small-time crack sales to big-time meth. He'd bought the ingredients, hired a cook, bought a bus, and turned it into a meth lab.

And on its first drug run, Booker's lab had sent ten people to God. Bagman's motto had never seemed as ironic to me as it did right now: Jesus Saves.

Chapter 90

YUKI WAS WORKING OUT with her video trainer when the intercom buzzed and her doorman's voice crackled over the box on the wall, saying, "Dr. Chesney is here to see you."

Elation shot through her.

Doc was early! The doorbell rang, and Yuki opened the door wide—and Doc kissed her. And Yuki made the most of it, putting her hands all through Doc's blond Ricky Schroder hair, wriggling and moaning in the doorway.

He grinned at her, said, "Glad to see me?"

She nodded, smiled, said, "Uh-huh," and they kissed again, Doc kicking the door shut behind him.

This was the thing that was priceless: how *these* kisses were even *theirs*.

Only she and Doc kissed this way.

"Hi, honey. How was your day?" Yuki said, coming up for air, laughing at the idea of making a "couple" joke.

8th Confession

When was the last time she'd done that?

Ever?

"Not too bad, sweetie," Doc said, scooping her up and walking her backward to the couch, where he dropped her gently into the overstuffed cushions, but she said "oof" anyway, and he settled down beside her.

"Bee sting, broken collarbone, and a baby halfway delivered in the waiting area," Doc said, touching her hair, stroking the half-inch-high stand-up buzz cut that he'd started with his clippers weeks ago and liked so much.

She was starting to like it, too.

"Any day I don't get stabbed by a syringe from an HIV-positive patient is a good day for me," he said.

"I second that," said Yuki. "So are you gassed up, packed up, ready to go?"

Because she was. As soon as she zipped up her bag, they'd be off for their Memorial Day weekend in Napa, the long, romantic drive, the beautiful hotel, the huge bed with a view.

"I am. But there's something I have to tell you first."

Yuki searched his eyes. Thinking back a couple of minutes, she remembered that Doc had looked a little *jittery* when she'd first opened the door, and since she'd been feeling a little nervy herself, she'd chalked it up to their upcoming big weekend. That soon they'd be making love for the first time.

Now his smile was tentative, and that alarmed her.

Was their weekend going to be cut short?

Or was it worse than that?

"John, what's wrong? Are you okay?"

"Depends on how you look at it," he said. "This is going to be rough, Yuki." He was holding her hand, but he kept lowering his eyes.

"The problem is, you tell someone too soon, and it's presumptuous. You tell them too late, and you've messed with their minds. In our case it's both: too early *and* too late—"

"You're scaring me, John. Spit it out."

"A few days ago when you said that you hadn't had sex in a couple of years—"

"That was stupid of me. It's *true,* but I was nervous. My brain...just overflowed."

Doc fixed his slate-blue eyes on her. "I haven't had sex in a couple of years either."

"You? Come *on.* I don't believe you."

Yuki's brain was on rewind, thinking how *she'd* gone to the hospital to see Doc after the car accident. *She'd* agreed to show him the city. After their first soft kiss, *she'd* dived in for a longer, sexier one—like she'd done just now.

She'd been driving the whole fantasy.

He'd been following her lead.

Yuki was mortified. Why hadn't she listened to her mother?

"Be like swan, Yuki-eh. Hold head high. Swim strong and silent." She had no patience. Instead she'd taken after her father. The tank driver.

"Please, just say it," Yuki said.

And then he did tell her, his voice halting, the story coming out in bits and pieces on a jagged time line. And although Yuki could hardly grasp what he was saying, her vision narrowed. There was a loud humming in her head.

And then everything went black.

Chapter 91

I SAT IN a wobbly chair across from Yuki and Cindy at Casa Loco, a Mexican joint near Cindy's apartment specializing in two-star chicken fajitas. It was dark outside, and the windows reflected our colorless images, making us look like ghosts.

Especially Yuki.

Cindy was both propping Yuki up and pumping her for more information when Claire arrived, dropped down in the chair next to me.

"You were right not to go away with him," Cindy was saying to Yuki. "You can't make decisions when your head's been through a blender."

The teenage waitress removed our plates, and Claire ordered coffee all around. Yuki said, "I keep thinking maybe I should have toughed it out. Just gotten into the car—"

"And if you hadn't felt better?" Cindy asked her. "What a

bloody awful weekend this would've been if you'd been stranded in Napa with someone who might have repulsed you."

"I hate it when you sugarcoat things, Cindy."

"Well, I'm not wrong, am I?"

"So let me get this straight," Claire said, bringing herself up to date since talking to Yuki on the phone. "Doc was born with ambiguous genitalia? The doctors didn't know for sure if he was a boy or a girl?"

Yuki nodded, used a forefinger to wick the tears out from under her eyes.

"They told his parents that if they conditioned him as a girl, he'd never know."

"They got *that* wrong," I said.

Claire said, "It's a damned tragedy, Yuki. I'm sure the parents were under a lot of pressure to tell people the baby's sex. Anyway, it was a theory based on practicality. Even if the chromosomes read XY, if the parts looked messed up, they did the surgery. 'Easier to make a hole than a pole,' they used to say. Then, they'd advise, treat the kid like a girl. Give her estrogen at adolescence, and by God, she'll be a girl."

"They named him Flora Jean," Yuki sputtered. "Like you said, Claire, they took a baby boy and made him a girl! But he never felt like one, ever—because he *wasn't* a girl. Oh my God. It's so sick!"

"So he reversed the process when he was how old?" Claire asked.

"Started when he was twenty-six. After that, he went through about four or five years of hell."

"Oh man. That poor guy," I said.

8th Confession

Yuki lifted her teary eyes to mine. "I'm crazy about Doc, Lindsay. He's sweet. He's funny. He's seen me as a real bitch and as a total wimp. He *gets* me—but how am I going to stop thinking of him as a guy who used to be a girl?"

"Aw, Yuki. Where did you leave things with him?"

"He said he'd call me over the weekend. That we'd go out to dinner next week and talk."

"Doc cares about you," I said. "He's showing you how much he cares by telling you what happened. Giving you time."

"I don't know what to do," Yuki choked out.

Cindy held Yuki and let her cry until Claire reached across the table and took Yuki's hand.

"Sugar, take it easy on yourself. It seems complicated, but maybe it's not. And nothing has to be decided right now."

Yuki nodded, and then she started to cry again.

Chapter 92

I GOT TO the squad room before eight on Monday morning and found a thick padded envelope on my desk. The routing slip showed that St. Jude had messengered it over from the Cold Case Division and had stamped the envelope URGENT, URGENT, URGENT.

I remembered now — McCorkle had called me, and I hadn't called him back. I ripped open the envelope, dumped out a tattered detective's notebook, found a note from McCorkle clipped to the front cover.

"Boxer — check this out. This subject knew the last of the nineteen eighty-two snake victims and a few of the new ones. She's expecting your call."

I hoped "she" was a hot lead that hadn't gone cold over the weekend, because right now, all we had on the "snake killer" was ugly press coverage and five dead bodies twiddling their thumbs in their graves.

8th Confession

Conklin wasn't in, so I killed a few minutes in the coffee room, putting milk and sugar in the last inch of coffee sludge left over from the night shift.

When I returned to my desk, my partner was still absent, and I couldn't wait for him any longer.

I opened the notebook to where a neon-green Post-it Note stuck between the pages pointed to a twenty-three-year-old interview with a socialite, Ginny Howsam Friedman.

I knew a few things about Ginny Friedman.

She was once married to a deputy mayor in the '80s, now deceased, and was currently married to a top cardiologist. She was a patron of the arts and a gifted painter in her own right.

I scanned the cop's scribbled notes and saw where McCorkle had underscored her phone number, which I dialed.

Friedman answered on the third ring and surprised me by saying, "I'm free if you come over now."

I left a note on Conklin's chair, then took my Explorer for a spin out to Friedman's address in Pacific Heights.

Ginny Friedman's pretty blue-and-white gingerbread-decked house was on Franklin Street, one of the blocks of fully restored Victorian houses that make San Francisco a visual wonder.

I walked up the steps and pressed the bell, and a lovely-looking gray-haired woman in her early seventies opened the door.

"Come in, Sergeant," she said. "I'm so glad to meet you. What can I get you? Coffee or tea?"

Chapter 93

MRS. FRIEDMAN AND I settled into a pair of wicker chairs on her back porch, and she began to tell me about the snake killings that had terrorized San Francisco's high society in 1982.

Friedman stirred her coffee, said, "There's got to be a connection between those old killings and the recent ones."

"We think so, too."

"I hope I can help you," Friedman said. "I told Lieutenant McCorkle that it was stinking horrible when those prominent people kept dying in eighty-two. Scary as hell. Keep in mind, we didn't know why they died until Christopher Ross was found with that snake coiled up in his armpit."

"And you knew Christopher Ross?"

"Very well. My first husband and I went out with him and his wife often. He was a very handsome guy. A thrill-seeker with an outgoing personality, and he was wealthy, of course.

8th Confession

His gobs of money had gobs of money. Chris Ross had it all. And then he died.

"Some said it was poetic justice," Friedman told me. "That he was a snake who was killed with one—but I'm getting ahead of myself."

"Take your time," I said. "I want to hear it all."

Friedman nodded, said, "In nineteen eighty-two, I was teaching fifth-grade girls at the Katherine Delmar Burke School in Sea Cliff. You know it, I'm sure."

I did. Sea Cliff was an A+ oceanside community, uncommonly beautiful, populated by the uncommonly wealthy.

"The young girls wore green plaid uniforms and did a maypole dance every year. Streamers and all.

"Sara Needleman and Isa Booth were both in my class in eighty-two. I still can't believe that they're dead! They had charmed lives. And when I knew them, they were both darling children. Look at this."

Friedman handed me a small leather book with glassine pages filled with snapshots. She turned to the back page and pointed to stepped rows of ten-year-old girls in a class photo.

"There's Isa. This is Sara. And this girl, poor thing, with the sad eyes. She was always the odd girl out," Friedman said of a young girl with shoulder-length dark hair. The child looked familiar, but although my mind was on search, I couldn't place her.

Friedman said, "She was Christopher Ross's illegitimate daughter. Her mother was the Ross's housekeeper, and Ross paid for his daughter's schooling at Burke's. I helped to get her admitted.

"The other girls all knew her circumstances, of course, and some of them were unkind. I said to her once, 'Honey, what doesn't kill you makes you stronger,' and she seemed to take courage from that.

"And then Chris died, and his wife, Becky—who had previously looked the other way—fired Norma's mother, cut her and the child off without a penny. Chris must've thought he'd live forever, and he hadn't provided for them in his will. Anyway, poor Norma was dropped from the school.

"And you know, I was right. It didn't kill her, and I think it did make her stronger."

I stared at the picture of the sad-eyed little girl—and suddenly the pieces locked into place with such force I could almost hear them clang. When I met Norma Johnson, her hair was caramel-blond and she was thirty-three years old.

Friedman said, "Last time I spoke with Norma was about ten years ago. She had created a little gofer business for herself, used her old contacts to get work.

"She let down her hair with me over a nice lunch in Fort Mason, and I'll tell you, Sergeant, and it gives me no pleasure to say it, Norma was very bitter.

"You know what those rich girls called their old school chum? They called her 'Pet Girl.'"

Chapter 94

CONKLIN TOOK A CHAIR in Jacobi's office, but I was so revved up, I couldn't sit. I was also freaking out. We'd interviewed Norma Johnson twice, written her off as a suspect both times and kicked her.

"Am I missing the obvious?" Jacobi asked me. "Or are you?" His meaty hands were clasped together on his trash heap of a desktop.

"Maybe it's me. What's the obvious?"

"Did you consider that Ginny Friedman might be the *doer*? She not only admits to knowing one of the original victims, she knew half the current ones, too."

"She has a solid alibi, Jacobi. Didn't I say that?"

"You said she had an alibi, Boxer. I'm asking for details."

There were times when reporting to Jacobi was like having bamboo slivers pushed under my fingernails. Had he forgotten we'd worked together for more than ten years?

Had he forgotten he used to report to *me?*

"When the killings happened, Ginny Friedman was cruising the Mediterranean on a sailing ship," I told him. "She learned about the killings when the ship docked last week in Cannes. France."

"I know where Cannes is," Jacobi said, pronouncing it in the plural.

"I have Friedman's round-trip airplane receipts and her travel documents from the *Royal Clipper* on my desk. The ship left port before the Baileys were killed, and it didn't return until Brian Caine and Jordan Priestly were dead."

"You're sure?"

"I examined her passport," I said. "The photo was current, and the book was properly stamped. She wasn't in San Francisco over the last month, Jacobi, no chance. But McCorkle is checking her out anyway."

Jacobi picked up the receiver on his phone, punched all five of his lines so no calls could come through. Then he fastened his eyes on me.

"Tell me more about this Pet Girl."

I told Jacobi that Johnson's father, Christopher Ross, wasn't married to Norma's mother, that the mother just changed the bed linens and vacuumed the floors in his Nob Hill manse.

"Ross was so rich, he was beyond scandal," I said, "at least, while he was *alive*. After he died, Norma's mother was canned and little Norma was officially an outcast.

"Her daddy left her nothing. Her friends treated her like dirt. And then she started working for them."

"She had keys to their houses," Conklin added, "and passwords to their security systems. She also had plenty of opportunity. What did she say, Lindsay? That nobody even knew she'd been there. That her clients liked it that way."

"She was just ten when her father was killed?" Jacobi asked.

"Right. She couldn't have killed those highfliers from the eighties. But the fact that her father was a victim might have inspired her."

"Copycat," said Jacobi.

"So we think," I said.

Jacobi slapped his desk, and dust flew up.

"Pick her up," he said. "Go get her."

Chapter 95

I SAT BESIDE Conklin at the table in the interrogation room, ready to jump in if needed, but he had the interview under control. Norma Johnson liked him, and Conklin was showing her what a good person he was, a guy you could trust — even if you were a freaking psycho.

"I don't understand why you didn't tell us that your father had been killed by a snake, Norma," Conklin said.

"Yeah. Well, I would have told you if you'd asked me, but you know, I didn't connect my father's death to any of this until you said that the Baileys and Sara had been killed by a snake."

"Brian Caine and Jordan Priestly? Did you know them?"

"Not well. I work for Molly Caldwell-Davis occasionally, and I've met Brian at her place once or twice. Jordan was there all the time, but we weren't friends."

"Did you work for Molly on the night of May twenty-fourth?"

"I'd have to look at my book, but no, wait. Didn't Molly have a party on the twenty-fourth? Because I was *invited*. I dropped by, didn't know anyone, so I said 'hey' to Molly and left after about ten minutes. She didn't need me to walk Mischa."

"And so your relationship with Molly was what? How would you describe it?"

"Um, business-casual. I met her through an ex-boyfriend of mine. You may have heard of him. McKenzie Oliver?"

"The rock star who died from a drug overdose?"

Norma Johnson played with the ends of her hair. "Yeah, that's the one. We weren't dating at the time."

Conklin made a note in his book, asked, "Do you have any thoughts on this, Norma? Anybody jump into your mind who could've killed your dad and then, like, twenty-three years later, maybe killed a bunch of people you know?"

Johnson said, "No, but this is a very small town, Inspector. Everyone knows everyone. Grudges can last for generations, but even so, I don't know any killers. I'm pretty sure of *that*."

Johnson's demeanor was low-key, bordering on snotty — and that was crazy. For the third time, she was in a small room with cops. She had to know she was a suspect. She had reason to be nervous, even if she was innocent.

She should have been asking if she needed a lawyer. Instead she was flipping her hair around and flirting with Conklin.

I made a mental note: *Tell Claire to review McKenzie Oliver's autopsy report.*

And another: *Find out if Norma Johnson had access to or owned a poisonous snake.*

I excused myself, stepped outside the interview room, and stood with Jacobi behind the glass. Together we watched and listened as Norma Johnson told Conklin about her pedigree.

"I don't know if you know this, but my father was the great-great-great-grandson of John C. Frémont."

"The Pathfinder? The explorer who mapped out the route to California just ahead of the gold rush?"

"That's the one. My bloodline is royal blue, Inspector. I've got nothing against the wannabes I work for, in case that's what you're thinking. John C. Frémont went down in history—and he started out life just like me. He was a bastard. Literally."

"I'm very *impressed*, Norma. So please, help me out here. You know San Francisco like nobody else. Upstairs, downstairs, every way, and I'm on the outside. I wasn't even born here."

"You want to know who killed all those people? I already told you. I have no idea."

Conklin smiled, showed his dimples. "Actually, I was going to ask you who you think might be the snake killer's next victim."

Johnson sat back in her chair, then cocked her head and smiled at Conklin. "The next to die? You know, my circle is getting kind of small. I'm thinking the next victim could be *me*."

"Holy crap," I said to Jacobi. "I don't like the sound of that. What's she planning to do?"

"Pin a tail on that donkey," Jacobi said. "Don't let her out of your sight."

Chapter 96

WE LOST PET GIRL literally right out of the box. Whether she'd gotten swept up in the foot traffic on Bryant or jumped into a cab, I didn't know, but Conklin and I stood stupidly out on the street, blinking in the sunlight, looking for a honey-blonde in black—and seeing everything but.

"Try her phone," I said to Conklin. "Tell her you have another question. Make a date to meet her."

"I get it," Conklin said. "Find out where she is."

I grunted, "Sorry," for my Jacobi-like behavior and watched Conklin dial and listen to Johnson's outgoing message.

"Hi, Norma. It's Inspector Conklin. Give me a call, okay? Got a quick question for you."

He left his number and hung up.

"Let's—"

"Check out her house," he said.

I muttered, "Wiseass," and he laughed, and we made for the car. Thirty minutes of traffic later, we parked close to the Twenty-fifth Avenue gate to the Presidio.

The Presidio has a long history, first as a Spanish fort right on San Francisco Bay, then as army housing when it was seized by the U.S. military in 1846. Nearly a hundred fifty years later, it went private, becoming a mixed-use assortment of business and residential buildings.

The renovation produced some beautiful Mission Revival–style redbrick buildings with white porches. Other housing was condemned and was gradually crumbling into the bay.

Pet Girl's address indicated that her apartment was in the picturesque and cheapest part of the former barracks, a long walk from where we stood. And what got to me instantly was that Norma Johnson's home was within viewing distance of Sea Cliff, where she'd gone to the Burke School—and where she'd been disgraced.

I'd thought status was important to her. So why had she put herself on that particular burner and turned up the jets?

Conklin and I walked quickly through the parklike Presidio surrounds, crowded on that workday with windsurfers changing in the parking lot, enjoying the breeze coming off Baker Beach.

And then Norma's apartment was in sight, one of two attached units with a small yard in front. The trim needed a paint job, and there was a bike lying on the long grass in front of Norma's door as though it had been dropped there in a hurry.

I knocked, called Norma's name, knocked again, harder— and still no answer. I thought of Pet Girl saying to Conklin, "The next victim could be *me*."

8th Confession

"Exigent circumstances, Rich. She could have hurt herself. She could be dying."

I told him to kick the door in, but Conklin put his hand on the knob and turned it, and the door swung open. My gun was in my hand when we stepped inside Pet Girl's apartment. It was clean and small, with what looked like cast-off furnishings, except for a picture of Christopher Ross in an elaborate frame over the console table in the hallway.

I heard muffled footsteps and a rumbling sound but couldn't identify the noise or the direction it was coming from.

Conklin was behind me as I moved toward the back of the small duplex apartment, calling out, "Norma, it's Sergeant Boxer. Your door was open. Could you please come out? We have to talk."

All was silent.

I indicated to Conklin that he should stay on the ground floor, and I took the stairs. The upstairs rooms were so small, I could see into every corner, but still I turned over beds, tossed closets, looked for loose wall panels, the works.

Where the hell was Pet Girl?

I went through both small rooms, the bathroom, and the closets once more, but Norma Johnson wasn't there.

The invisible Pet Girl had gone invisible again.

Chapter 97

I WAS STARTLED by the sharp crash of heavy objects falling to the floor below, and then I heard that rumble again, a sound like muted thunder, maybe a heavy rolling door—and I heard voices.

Conklin is talking to Norma Johnson.

By the time he called out to me, I was halfway down the stairs.

My partner was in the kitchen, staring into an opening between a counter and the fridge through a doorway I'd thought too narrow to lead to anything but a broom closet. Apparently a pocket door had been rolled into an opening in the wall—and there was a room behind it, looked like a pantry.

"Lindsay," Conklin said in a measured tone, "Norma has a weapon."

I edged into the eight-by-ten kitchen until I could see

Johnson. Her back was to the pantry. Conklin was standing only four feet in front of her, barring her exit.

I did a double take when I realized that Norma Johnson's weapon was the snake she gripped in her right hand. It was slim, banded, gray and white, a deadly krait, its tail lashing, its head swaying only inches from Johnson's neck.

"Get out of my way, Inspector Conklin," Johnson hissed. "I'm leaving by the front door, and you're going to let me go. And I'm going to lock the door behind me. The snakes won't bother you as long as you are very quiet and move very slowly."

As Johnson inched toward Conklin, I could see behind her to the pantry. Metal shelving along the wall held a number of twenty-gallon aquariums, and the floor of the room was covered with broken glass.

My hands went ice cold as I understood the crashing sound. Pet Girl had pulled some of the snake tanks over, and they had smashed on the floor. Snakes were loose in the apartment, looking for hidey-holes, probably winding around corners into the small kitchen where Conklin and I were standing.

"I want you to open the oven and put that snake inside!" I shouted to Pet Girl. "Do it now, or I'm going to shoot."

Pet Girl laughed.

"Nope, not going to do that," she said, showing me a pretty smile I'd not seen on her face before. "So what's it going to be, Sergeant? Let me go? Because if not, it doesn't matter to me if Kali bites me or if you shoot me. There's no difference to me at all."

A clock ticked on the wall above the stove. I heard Norma

Johnson's breath quicken, and I saw that Conklin's face was blanched. He was afraid of snakes, deathly afraid, but he stood like a rock within striking distance of Pet Girl's lunatic idea of a pet. I couldn't get a clean shot.

"Move aside, Inspector," Johnson said to Conklin. "Save yourself and let me go."

"I can't do that," said Conklin. And then he snapped out his hand like he was grabbing a fly from the air. He was going for her wrist, but before he could grab her, she launched the snake at Conklin.

Conklin jumped back, but the snake was airborne. My partner raised his hand as it came toward him, wriggling sinuously, batting against his palm. It clung to his hand for an instant, hanging over his wrist—until Conklin shook it off and it fell to the floor.

He stepped back, holding his wrist, then turned his ashen face to me.

"I've been bitten," he said, standing stock-still. "The bastard got me."

Chapter 98

NORMA JOHNSON BOLTED.

She tried to bulldoze her way past me, but I came out of my horrified trance, grabbed her arm, and wrenched her around.

Her shoulder popped and she screamed, but the pain didn't stop her. She picked up a coffee mug with her free hand and, gripping it as if it were a rock, hauled back and aimed a ceramic punch to my jaw.

I ducked, kicked at her knee with all I had. She screamed again and dropped to the floor. I rolled the yowling woman onto her stomach and bent her arms back, cuffed her as I yelled to Conklin, "Rich! Lie down on the couch. Lower your arm to the floor so that it's below your heart. *Do it now.*"

Conklin walked unsteadily into the next room as if he were already dying. I noted the time, grabbed my cell phone, and called Dispatch, told Kam that Conklin was down.

"We need an ambulance *forthwith*," I said, giving the address. "Call the hospital, say that the victim has been bitten by a snake. It's a krait. K-R-A-I-T. We need antivenin *now*."

"Antivenom?"

"Yes. *No*. It's called *antivenin*. And send uniforms to take our collar into custody."

I walked over to Johnson, who was writhing, squeaking out little yelping cries.

I stooped down and said, "Do you have any antivenin here?"

She mewled, "If I did, I wouldn't tell *you*."

I kicked her in the ribs, and she howled. I asked her again.

"No! I don't have any."

I didn't believe her. I opened her refrigerator and took inventory. Three cups of yogurt, box of eggs. Six-pack of Coors. Wilted radishes. No vials that looked like something that could save Conklin's life.

I can't lie. It felt like dozens of eyes were staring at me. I was creeped-out to the ends of my hair, and even though I was terrified for my partner, I still had a little terror left over for myself.

I watched the floor as I made my way to the living room, where Conklin was lying on a blue plaid sofa, his arm lowered to keep the poison from traveling to his heart.

Only a minute or two had passed since he'd been bitten, but I had no idea how long it would take for that bite to paralyze his central nervous system. How long it would be until Conklin couldn't breathe.

8th Confession

Was it already too late?

I whipped off Conklin's belt and placed it just below his elbow as a constricting band. "I've got you, buddy. The ambulance is on the way."

Panic welled up inside me like a tsunami, and the tears were working hard to bust down the dam. But I couldn't let my partner see that. I just wanted to be 10 percent as brave as he was.

I forced my mind off the odds.

And I focused on the distance between us and the closest hospital. I thought about the *Amazing Race*–style run the paramedics would have to make carrying stretchers from the Twenty-fifth Avenue gate all the way out to the end.

And then there was the antivenin.

How would the hospital get antivenin in time?

The souls of every dead person I'd ever loved visited me as I held Richie's good hand and listened for sirens: Jill and Chris and my mom—I couldn't bear it if Conklin died.

I heard the sirens blare and stop.

To my overwhelming relief, twelve minutes after Conklin was bitten, paramedics bearing stretchers bombed through the door.

Chapter 99

I YELLED OUT to the paramedics and the cops. "Poisonous snakes are loose all over the freakin' floor. They're *lethal*."

"You said a cop is *down*?" asked a uniform.

I knew him. Tim Hettrich. Twenty years on the force and one of our best. But he and Conklin had a feud going, started when Conklin moved up to Homicide. I thought maybe they hated each other.

"Poisonous snake bit Conklin."

"A cop is *down*, Sergeant. We're going in."

As Conklin was strapped onto the gurney, I walked to where Norma Johnson lay cuffed on the floor. Her face was puffy and her nose was bleeding, but I had a sense that if a snake crawled out of the pantry and bit her, she'd be ecstatic.

Maybe she wanted to die as her father had died.

8th Confession

I halfway hoped she'd get her wish, but my more rational mind wanted to hear the story.

I wanted to know what Norma Johnson had done, to whom, and why. And *then* I wanted the State to try her, convict her, and kill her.

I stood over Norma Johnson, and I read her her rights.

"You have the right to remain silent, you disgusting coward," I said. "Anything you say can and damned well *will* be used against you in a court of law. You have the right to an attorney, if you can find one slimy enough to defend you. If you can't afford an attorney, the State of California will provide one for you. We do that even for scum like you. Do you understand your rights, Pet Girl?"

She smiled at me.

I grabbed her arms by the cuffs and jounced her, putting the strain on her popped shoulder, making her scream.

"I asked you, do you understand your rights?"

"Yes, yes!"

Hettrich said, "I've got her, Sergeant." He brought her to her feet and hustled her out the door. I wanted to leave, too. But I had to see what was inside that pantry.

I had to know.

I walked over to the opening and stared at the metal shelves filling the narrow room. I could see the kraits slithering through the remnants of most of the tanks, every one of those snakes loaded with venom.

It was stunning to think what Norma Johnson's intentions were in owning so many snakes. How many more people had she hoped to kill before she was caught?

What was in this sick woman's mind?

I told a uniform to seal and lock the place, and then I left Pet Girl's snake house. I ran toward the ambulance, got in just as the EMTs loaded my partner inside.

I sat next to Richie, took his good hand, and squeezed it.

"I'm not leaving you until you're doing push-ups. Shooting hoops," I said to my partner, my voice finally cracking into little pieces. "You're going to be fine, Richie. You're going to be perfect."

"Okay," he said, his voice just above a whisper. "But do me a favor, Linds. Pray for me anyway."

Chapter 100

WHEN THE AMBULANCE DRIVER took a left, I knew we were going to a place I never wanted to see again.

Yuki's mother had died at San Francisco Municipal Hospital.

I'd stalked those halls for days on end, hoping to trap a deranged "angel of death," learning in the process that Municipal was geared toward high profits, not patient care.

I called up front to the driver, "General is closer than Municipal."

"We're busing the snakebite victim, aren't we, Sergeant? Municipal's got the antivenin coming in."

I shut up and did what Conklin had asked. I prayed to God as I held his hand, and thought about what a fine person Richard Conklin was, how much we'd been through together, how lucky I'd been to have him as a friend and partner.

Traffic parted in front of us as the ambulance screamed up Pine, then jerked into the lot and jolted to a stop outside the emergency-room entrance.

Doors flew open and medics scrambled.

I ran beside Conklin's gurney as he was rolled through the automatic doors. That awful hospital disinfectant smell smacked me in the face, and I felt a wave of panic.

Why here?

Of all places, why did we have to bring Richie here?

Then I saw Doc coming toward us.

"The medevac chopper is on the way," he told me and Conklin. "Rich? How do you feel?"

"Scared out of my freakin' mind," my partner said. I thought he was slurring his speech. I put my hand over my mouth. I was so afraid of losing it. Of losing *him*.

"Any numbness?" Doc asked Conklin.

"Yeah. In my hand."

"Try to relax," Doc said. "It takes some time for the venom to have an effect. If you were in a jungle, that would be one thing. But we've got you, Rich. You're going to be okay."

I wanted to believe Doc, but I wouldn't be comforted until Rich was back on his feet. As my partner was wheeled away, I told him that I'd be standing by in the waiting room, and I grabbed Doc's sleeve.

"John, you're sure the antivenin you got is the right stuff?"

"I've had the Aquarium of the Pacific on standby since Claire told me about the folks who died from krait bites. I fig-ured there was a chance we could need antivenin."

"Thanks, Doc," I said, gratitude washing through me. "Thanks for being so damned smart."

"Don't mention it," he said. Then, "I'm going to look in on Rich."

I found a dark corner of the waiting room and called Cindy. I repeated to her what Doc had told me. And then I made a call to a hotel in Amman.

It was one in the morning there, but after a verbal tussle, the desk put me through. He sounded groggy with sleep, but he brightened when he heard my voice. It was some kind of miracle that I could find him when I needed him most.

"I was just dreaming about you," he said.

"Good dream?"

"I think it was a circus dream."

"What's that?"

"Tightrope. I'm wearing this spandex thing. Bodysuit. With sparkles."

"You?"

"Chest hair coming out the top."

"Joe!" I laughed.

"I'm way up there on this platform, size of a dinar."

"And that's . . . ?"

"A Jordanian coin. And you're on the tightrope coming toward me."

"What am I wearing?"

"You're naked."

"No!"

"Yeah! Carrying a lot of stuff in your arms, balancing on this rope. And I'm supposed to catch you when you get to my dinar."

"What happens?"

"Phone rings."

"Joe, I miss you, honey. When are you coming home?"

Chapter 101

NORMA JOHNSON'S SHOULDER had been popped back into place, and she was on a few hundred milligrams of Motrin. She sat across from me in the interrogation room, twiddling a business card, her "whatever" expression back on her face.

If Conklin had been here, he would have smooth-talked her. I wanted to backhand that smirk right off her face.

Pet Girl snapped the card down on the table, pushed it toward me so I could read, FENN AND TARBOX, ATTORNEYS-AT-LAW.

George Fenn and Bill Tarbox were two triple A–rated criminal-defense attorneys who catered to the top 2 percent of the upper crust. Fenn was steady and thorough. Tarbox was volatile and charming. Together, they'd flipped more probable slam-dunk guilty verdicts into dismissals than I wanted to remember.

"Mrs. Friedman is paying," Pet Girl said.

She was toying with me, making me wonder if she'd

lawyer up, or more likely she just thought she was smarter than me.

"Call your lawyers," I said, unhooking my Nextel from my belt, slapping it down on the table. "Use my phone. But since this is all new to you, let me explain how the system works."

"Uh-huh. And I'm going to believe everything you say."

"Shut up, stupid. Just listen. Once you ask for a lawyer, I can't make a deal with you. This is how we see it on this side of the table: you assaulted a police officer with a deadly weapon. Conklin dies, you're dead meat walking.

"Setting that aside, we've got you cold on five counts of murder. You had access to every one of the victims, and they were killed by the same rare, illegally imported snake you kept by the dozen in your apartment.

"A law-school intern could get you convicted.

"But we won't be using a law-school intern. You'll be going up against Leonard Parisi, our top gun, because you killed VIPs and because this is what's known as a high-profile case.

"We can't lose, and we won't."

"That must be some crystal ball you have, Sergeant."

"Better believe it. 'Cause here's what else I see in there: while your lawyers are getting great press on Mrs. Friedman's dime, your old school chums are going to testify for the prosecution.

"They're going to *trash* you in court, Norma. And then they're going to tell the press all about you, how *sick* you make them, how *pathetic* you are.

"And after you've been exposed as the godless, heartless psychopath you are, the jury is going to convict you five times over. You understand? You're going to be *disgraced*—and then you're going to *die*."

I saw a flash of panic in the woman's eyes. Had I gotten to her? Was Norma Johnson actually afraid?

"So if it's such a dead cert, why are you even talking to me?"

"Because the DA is willing to make you a deal."

"Oh, this should be good. Like I haven't seen this ploy a hundred times on *Law and Order*."

"There's a wrinkle, Norma. A smidgen of wiggle room on that death penalty. So listen up. The chief medical examiner reviewed your old boyfriend's autopsy report, and she says it doesn't pass the sniff test."

"McKenzie Oliver? He died of a drug overdose."

"His blood test was borderline for an OD. But he was in his thirties, otherwise healthy. So the ME who did his autopsy didn't look any further.

"But this is a new day, Norma. We think you killed him because he dumped you. His coffin is being hoisted out of the ground this minute. And this time, the ME is going to be searching for fang marks."

Johnson looked down at the business card Ginny Friedman had given her, looked at my phone, looked up at me.

"What's the deal?"

"Tell me about the murders, all of them, including what you did to McKenzie Oliver, and we'll spare you the humiliation of a trial and take the death penalty off the table. This offer expires when I get out of this chair."

There was a long pause, a full two minutes.

Then Norma Johnson said, "That's not good enough."

"That's all we're offering."

I gathered my papers and buttoned my jacket, pushed away from the table.

Pet Girl piped up, "What will you take off my sentence if I give you the person who killed those richies in nineteen eighty-two?"

I choked down my surprise—and my excitement.

I turned to the one-way mirror, and a second later, Jacobi opened the door, poked his head into the interrogation room.

"Hang on," he said to me. "I'm getting Parisi on the phone."

Chapter 102

THE INTERROGATION ROOM got smaller as the combined four hundred fifty pounds of Red Dog and Jacobi came in.

Parisi is six two, has coarse red hair, pockmarked skin, a size-50 waist, and a smoker's baritone. He *could* be funny, but if he wanted to, he could scare his own mother into a heart attack.

Jacobi is another unique terror if you don't know and love him as I do. His unreadable gray eyes are like drill bits. And his large hands are restless. Like he's looking for a reason to ball them up and strike.

The two hulking men dragged up chairs, and I saw Pet Girl's snotty demeanor waver.

"Now I think I should have a lawyer," she said.

"That's your right," Parisi grumbled. He said to me, "Boxer, take her back to her cell."

As I got to my feet, Norma Johnson shouted, *"Wait!"*

8th Confession

"I'm not here to entertain myself," Parisi warned her. "So don't waste my time." He flapped open a file, fanned the morgue shots out on the table, asked Pet Girl, "Did you kill these people?"

As Johnson's eyes slowly panned the photos left to right and back again, I realized that *she'd never seen her victims dead.*

Was she repentant?

Or was she freaking impressed with herself?

Her eyes still on the photos, Johnson asked Parisi for his promise that she'd be exempt from the death penalty if she told him about her part in McKenzie Oliver's death, and when he agreed, she let out a deep sigh.

"I killed them all," she said, her voice breaking on her own self-pity, a couple of tears trickling down her cheeks. "But I caused them less pain in their deaths than they caused me in one day of my life."

Didn't Pet Girl know that tears were unnecessary? That all we cared about was her confession? That all we wanted were the *words?*

She wiped away her tears with the backs of her hands, and then she asked if the videotape was rolling. I told her it was, and she said she was glad.

"I want there to be a record of my statement," she said. "I want people to understand my *reasons.*"

More than an hour passed as Norma Johnson fleshed out her motives, detailing the victims' lives as only an obsessive voyeur could, describing their "unspeakably insulting behavior" toward her, none of which she deserved, and she told us how she'd painlessly put her victims down.

After she described stalking McKenzie Oliver, getting him into bed for a good-bye tryst, then stabbing him with the fangs of a krait, Parisi had what he wanted. No frills required.

He cut off her narcissistic rant midsentence, saying, "I have to be in court, Ms. Johnson. Tell me about the nineteen eighty-two murders if you want us to consider a reduction in your sentence."

"What are you offering me?"

"Right now, you're looking at six consecutive life sentences without possibility of parole," he told her. "Give us the nineteen eighty-two society killer, and you'll get to tell a parole board how sorry you are after you've served some time."

"That's all?"

"That's *hope*. That's a chance that maybe you'll walk free before you die."

Johnson covered her mouth. She was thinking long and hard, and as the silence did a few laps around the room, I couldn't even guess what she would do.

Parisi looked at his watch and pushed back from the table, his chair legs screeching like the brakes of an 18-wheeler.

"I've had enough, Lieutenant," Parisi said to Jacobi. "Wrap it up."

"My father," Norma said softly.

"Christopher Ross was one of the victims," I said. "He knew the killer?"

"He *was* the killer," said Pet Girl. "Daddy told me. He did them all."

Chapter 103

PET GIRL HAD just ratted out her dead father as the 1982 high-society killer. If the story was true, then her father had been a serial killer.

She'd followed his example by becoming one, too.

Was that really the truth?

Or was it all a desperate fiction to help herself?

I wanted to hear her say it *again* — and then she did.

"He told me who he killed and why. Daddy hated those phonies who sucked up to him because he was rich. He loved my mother because she was *real*."

Pet Girl reached into her blouse and pulled out a locket, opened it with shaking hands, and held it out to show Parisi the photo of Christopher Ross.

Parisi never shifted his eyes. He simply torched Johnson with his fearsome Red-Dog-will-rip-your-throat-out stare and said, "An allegation is worth nothing. You want the deal? I need proof."

Pet Girl twisted her head toward me for the first time since Jacobi and Parisi entered the room.

"My keys are in my handbag," she told me. "It's red ostrich skin, and I think I left it on the console table in the foyer."

I nodded, said, "Red bag. I'll find it."

"Look for a brass key with a round top, goes to a padlock on my storage unit," she said. "Bay Storage, unit number twenty-two. I've got all of my father's papers stored there. Inside one of the boxes is a file marked 'Natajara.'"

"Is the box numbered? Labeled?"

"Should be right in front. I think second or third tier on the right-hand side—"

I was inside my head, thinking about how I would run upstairs to get a search warrant for Johnson's apartment, when my cell phone rang—Brenda, our squad assistant, shouting into the mouthpiece, "Lindsay, two old guys—"

The interview-room door flew open, and two distinguished-looking gentlemen burst in.

Bill Tarbox was in blue seersucker and a red-and-white polka-dot bow tie, looking as if he'd left his Panama hat out in the Rolls. Fenn's haircut was so sharp, you could cut yourself on his sideburns.

Fenn glared around the room, identified his client, and said, "Norma, stop talking. We're your lawyers, and this interview is over."

Chapter 104

I WAS WITH CONKLIN in his private hospital room with its view of the parking lot. He looked pale, his hair lying damp across his forehead, but his smile was strong and he was cracking jokes, all very good signs.

I angled the reclining chair toward his bed.

"You're not *mad,* are you, Rich?"

"Why? Because you cracked Pet Girl while I lay here like a sack of sand? Why would that make me mad? I mean, come on, Lindsay," he said, turning his brown eyes on me. "Nailing that psycho, even if I wasn't *there* at the triumphal moment—that's what's *important.* Nurse! I need a cyanide drip, *stat.*"

I laughed. Rich had stood up to frickin' Pet Girl's snake attack, and for that alone, he was a hero. He was *alive*—and both our shields, McCorkle's, too, had been buffed to gleaming for teeing up Norma Johnson for the DA.

This was what we liked to call "a great day to be a cop."

A nurse's aide brought in an early-bird blue plate special for Conklin, and as he moved the mush around his dish, I told him about my return to Pet Girl's apartment.

"Animal Rescue said that the place was clean, but seriously, how did they know they'd gotten every last snake? I walked on *tiptoes,* Rich, and I'm not even sure my tiptoes touched the ground."

He grinned, said, "Yer a brave lass, Lindsay."

"I grabbed that handbag, slammed the door behind me, found the keys. Fifty of the sixty-two were brass with a round top."

"Did one of them fit the lock?"

"You in a hurry?" I asked him.

"No, no. Take your time."

I laughed again, glad that Conklin would be out of this house of horrors as soon as Doc gave him the thumbs-up.

"I met McCorkle at Pet Girl's storage unit," I said. "He brought this big kid along with him from the lab.

"So we get the door open, and we're staring at maybe *ten yards* of cardboard cartons. Big Kid starts taking the boxes down, and McCorkle and I flip through files for five hours looking for 'Natajara,'" I said.

"Turns out Natajara is the name of an Indian god, wears a cobra around his shoulders. Natajara *Exports* sells poisonous reptiles."

"Lindsay, you *rock.*"

"Yes, I do. I found the correspondence between a Mr. Radhakrishnan of Natajara Exports and Christopher Ross, CEO of

Pacific Cargo Lines. And I found an invoice for a crate of kraits. Dated January nineteen eighty-two."

"Asshole kept a record of his snake buy? But how do you figure he was the killer and also a victim?"

"McCorkle thinks his death was an accident, possibly a suicide. We'll never know, but this is for sure: Norma Johnson is going away for six consecutive lifetimes—and McCorkle has stamped his cold case *closed*."

I was high-fiving my partner when a curly-haired blond tornado blew into Conklin's room with a gift-wrapped box and a bouquet of helium balloons.

"Hey, you," Conklin said, clearly delighted.

"Hey, you, too."

Grinning, Cindy said hi to me, kissed Conklin, hugged him, put the box on his stomach, and demanded he open it. "It's a bathrobe," she said. "I don't want anyone seeing your buns but me."

Conklin laughed, his face coloring. As he worked on the ribbon, I said, "Sounds like my cue to leave. Hope to see you at the Hall tomorrow, bud."

I kissed Conklin on the cheek and hugged my irrepressible friend Cindy, and as I left the room, I had a thought: *Cindy and Rich are good together.*

They really are.

Chapter 105

THAT NIGHT, just as Claire, Yuki, and I came through the door to Susie's, the power went out, instantly plunging the place into a dusky giddiness. Strangers bumped into one another, ordering beer while it was still cold, and the steel drummer carried on without a microphone, ramping up his mellow voice and singing out, "Salt, tea, rice, smoked fish, are nice and the rum is fine any time of year...."

We three pressed on toward the back room, took our usual table, saving Cindy's seat until she finished taking Conklin home with his new bathrobe.

"She is coming, though?" Yuki asked.

Claire and I shrugged dramatically in unison. Yuki laughed, and Lorraine put candles on the table. She brought us a pitcher of draft, a big basket of chips, and a bowl of salsa, saying, "This is dinner until the power goes back on."

I hijacked Cindy's time, used it to tell Claire and Yuki

about Pet Girl's confession and the wrap-up of McCorkle's old cold case.

Claire jumped in to report on her newly revised autopsy of McKenzie Oliver's body, purring, "The bite mark was just above his shoulder blade. No one would have found those pinpricks unless they were purely looking for them."

Just then, Cindy breezed in and found our table. She was out of breath but glowing as she slid in beside Yuki. Lorraine brought over another sweating pitcher of beer, saying, "We're closing up, ladies. This is the last, and it's on Susie."

I filled Cindy's glass, and she lifted it to all of us.

"To you guys, for saving Richie's life."

"What?" Claire sputtered.

"You, Claire, for telling Doc about the kraits. Otherwise he wouldn't have put the aquarium on standby. And you, Linds, for getting that belt around his arm, telling him what to do."

"Are you planning to thank the Academy now? What I did for Conklin, he'd do for me. That's what it means to be *partners*."

"True, but you did it."

"Don't mind her. She's full of L-U-V," Claire told me.

"She's full of *something*."

"And *you*," Cindy said to Yuki.

"I'm innocent. I had nothing to do with saving Conklin's life."

"You found Doc."

"Well," Claire said, "I guess we should all be thanking you, too, Cindy."

"Come on."

"Conklin's been pining for Lindsay for so long, and since she didn't tumble, I guess it's good of you to give that boy something to live for."

Cindy lowered her lashes, put a hilarious spin on it when she said, "The *pleasure* is all mine."

We all laughed, even me, even Cindy. And when we'd wiped away our tears, Yuki said she had something to tell us.

"I'm going away for a couple of weeks. My uncle Jack invited me, and I have vacation coming."

"You're going to Kyoto?" I asked.

"It'll do me good to get away."

"Are you going to see Doc again?"

"We're going to, you know, 'play it by ear.' But my heart's not in it, Lindsay. Or more accurately, my head's not in it."

Claire said, "You can't fake it, sweetheart."

"Can't, couldn't, won't," said Yuki.

Chapter 106

MORNING CAME, and Conklin was at his desk when I got there. He was scrubbed and shaven and looked like he'd won a million dollars. The day crew gathered around our desks wanting to shake Conklin's hand and tell him how great it was to have him back.

Brenda had baked and was saying, "Nobody doesn't like peanut-butter-chocolate cake," and she was right, but we hadn't gotten more than two bites into it when Conklin took a call from Skip Wilkinson, one of his buddies in Narcotics and Vice.

After Conklin announced his name, all he said was "Uh-huh. Uh-huh. No *kidding*. Yeah. Yeah. We'll be right there."

He hung up, said to me, "Narcs busted a crack whore last night. She was carrying a twenty-two registered to Neil Pincus. They're holding her for us."

We drove to the nondescript station house, a former

Roto-Rooter plant taking up a quarter of a block on Potrero at Eighteenth. We took the stairs to the third floor at a run.

Skip Wilkinson met us at the gate.

He walked us back to the observation room, where we could see the suspect through the one-way mirror. She was a young black female, bony, dressed in threadbare jeans and a filthy pink baby-doll top. Her blond weave was coming loose, and judging from her fidgety stare and her shakes, I figured she'd had a bad night in lockup and was in need of a fix.

Wilkinson said, "That's Lawanda Lewis, age seventeen. Here's her sheet."

I read, "Two arrests for prostitution. This is her first drug arrest. You're looking at her for homicide?"

Anything was possible, but I didn't see it.

"Did you catch her address?" Wilkinson asked me, stabbing the rap sheet with his finger. "It's on Cole Street. That's Bagman's house.

"She lived there. Maybe she still does. Anyway, she was one of his girls. She could be your doer. Take your shot," said Wilkinson.

It was one of those can't-believe-it moments.

That do-gooder attorney Neil Pincus lied when he said he didn't own a gun. Then he said it was stolen. I thought that was a lie, too, but I never expected his gun to turn up.

I was wrong.

Chapter 107

CONKLIN AND I walked into the interrogation room, Conklin pulling out a chair for me, showing what a gentleman he was. I sat and so did he, and the girl tried to get small in her chair as Conklin told her our names.

"Lawanda," he said nicely, "is this right? You used to sell drugs for Bagman?"

The girl stared down at the table, picked polish off her nails, didn't look up at all.

Conklin said, "Look, we don't care about the drugs. We know what kind of life you were living with him. We know how he used you."

"Bagman treated me fine."

"Is that right? So you had no reason to kill him?"

"Kill him? Me? I didn't kill him. No, no, no. Not me."

We had no proof that Lawanda Lewis had used the gun or even that Neil Pincus's weapon had killed Rodney Booker.

The slugs lodged inside Bagman's head were so soft and so fragmented, they could never be matched to anything. But I was sure Lawanda Lewis couldn't know that.

"I have to tell you, Lawanda," I said, "you're in very serious trouble. Your gun was used to kill Bagman. Unless you give us reason to think otherwise, you're going down for his murder."

Lawanda Lewis sprang up from the chair, squatted against the wall in the corner of the room, and covered her head with her hands. She was in withdrawal to the max. In a minute, she'd be screaming, foaming at the mouth.

"I didn't do it! I didn't kill anyone!"

"That gun says different," Conklin said.

"I need something. *I'm dying.*"

"Talk first, then we'll get you fixed up."

As Lawanda crouched in the corner, rocking and wailing, I was running the crime in my head, trying to put it together.

Say the girl had needed a fix. Booker had told her to go out and work. She had Pincus's gun. So she followed Bagman and held him up on the street, and when he didn't give her the drugs, she shot and robbed him. But how could she have also beaten him? She was small. Certainly no match for Booker.

"You'll get me a fix?" she asked Conklin.

"We'll get you help," Conklin said.

Lawanda was scratching at her skin, ripping at her hair. I was sure we'd lost her, that she'd fallen down a black hole of misery and didn't know we were still there.

But she hung on. Still rocking, still staring at the floor, she shouted as if possessed, "Sammy Pincus gave me the gun so I could protect myself on the street!"

I got out of my chair, walked over to Lawanda, stooped down so I could look in her eyes. I asked her, "How did Sammy Pincus get that gun?"

The girl stared at me as if I were as dumb as a brick. "She took it from her father. Mr. Neil? *He's* the one who killed Bagman Jesus."

Chapter 108

MY HEART WAS banging against my chest like a hammer on a steel drum. Conklin was behind me as we pounded up the narrow stairs leading to the law offices above the soup kitchen called From the Heart.

A gaggle of girls from the nail salon tried to pass us, saw the determination on our faces, and backed right up and flattened themselves against the wall at the landing, one of them saying loudly to the rest of them, "Those are *cops!*"

I banged on the door to "Pincus and Pincus," and when a voice said, "Who is it?" I said, "Mr. Pincus, this is the police."

Al Pincus, the bigger, younger brother, came to the door.

"How can I help you?" he asked, barring our entrance with his body.

"For starters, you can let us in," I said.

He sighed, opened the door wide, called over his shoulder, "Neil, the police."

Neil Pincus stepped out of his office. He was dressed as he was the last time I saw him: gray pants, white shirt, cuffs rolled up, no tie.

I took the warrant out of my inside jacket pocket and showed it to "Mr. Neil."

"You're under arrest."

He snatched the warrant out of my hand, unfolded it, scanned it fast, said, "Are you crazy? I didn't murder anyone."

"We have your gun, Mr. Pincus. Showed up in the hands of a witness who will testify that you shot and killed Rodney Booker."

"That's nuts," said Neil Pincus, wandering back toward his office. "I'm calling my lawyer."

"Stop right where you are!" Conklin shouted. "Hands up where we can see them. *Do it now.*"

I hadn't expected resistance, but I was prepared for it. As Conklin held his Glock on Neil Pincus, I shoved him to the wall and cuffed his hands behind his back.

"You have the right to remain silent," I said as I frisked him.

"Hey!" Al Pincus shouted. "Let my brother go. You've got it all wrong. I'm the one who killed Rodney Booker."

"Al, no! Listen," Neil Pincus said to me, "Al had nothing to do with it. *I* did it. I killed the bastard because of what he did to my daughter."

"It was me, and I'm not sorry," Alan Pincus insisted.

"Booker was an evil bastard. What he did to Sammy—that kid once had all the promise in the world.

"Neil wanted to get him legally, but Booker was too slick. So I took my brother's gun. I found that shit on the street corner, and I shot him in the head over and over and over."

"Thanks," I said. "There were enough bullets in Booker and he took enough of a beating that both of you could have killed him. In fact, that's my theory. You two took him down together."

I read Alan Pincus his rights and Conklin cuffed him, but a niggle of worry was starting at the back of my brain.

Neil Pincus said he did it.

Al Pincus said *he* did it.

What kind of case could be made based on the hearsay testimony of Lawanda Lewis, a drugged-out crack whore who might be dead before any of this came to trial?

I answered my own question. If each of the Pincus brothers took credit for killing Bagman, if each said he did it alone, that could give a juror reasonable doubt. One juror was all it took for a mistrial—and I doubted the city would stomach more than one trial for a lawless freak like Rodney Booker.

And then I got it.

The Pincus brothers had planned it this way.

Conklin and I marched the two men down the stairs, my mind racing ahead to separating them, interrogating them, trying to get one to flip the other. But when we got to the bottom of the stairs, my train of thought was derailed.

A crowd was waiting at the open doorway—and that's when things got really *crazy*.

Chapter 109

A MOB OF PEOPLE had poured out of From the Heart onto the street. There were homeless people and there were volunteers, and in the thickening crowd I saw people who didn't look like they belonged: businessmen and -women from the surrounding area.

I shouted, *"Stand back! Let us through!"* But instead the crowd tightened around us, jostling us, threatening to turn ugly. I fumbled for my phone, pressed numbers without looking, and somehow managed to get the desk sergeant on the line.

I gave him my badge number and location, said we needed crowd control. *Forthwith.*

A man wearing a good suit pushed toward us, calling out to me, "Sergeant, Sergeant, I'm Franklin Morris, a member of the Fifth Street Association. I can't let you arrest these men because *I* shot Rodney Booker—and I can prove it. Neil tried to stop me from doing it, but I had to do what was right. *Tell her, Neil.*"

It was the beginning of a chain reaction, the likes of which I'd never seen before—and could have never imagined.

"I'm Luvie Jump," said a black woman wearing purple frames and a dashiki over her tights, turning her thin body sideways, edging toward me as she talked. "Don't listen to Mr. Morris, Sergeant. He's Neil Pincus's best friend. Listen to *me.*

"We called the police *repeatedly,* and they did nothing. Rodney Booker was a one-man plague. He sold drugs. He turned nice girls into druggies and whores. I shot him because he was the devil. Ask anyone. I did it with Neil Pincus's dirty little gun and I'm ready to come in."

I was getting dizzy and a little sick.

The car was only twenty yards away, but the crowd was so deep, I couldn't see it. I listened for sirens, but I heard nothing save the uproar around me.

And yet another man confessed, grabbing at my sleeve, saying his name was Harry Bainbridge. He was black, with Rasta hair and gold teeth, looked homeless, said he beat Booker with a two-by-four after he blew the man's brains out with Pincus's Saturday night special.

"Those newspaper stories saying what a good man Bagman Jesus was? He was dog shit. Where was you people when we called you? Why I have to be the one to get blood on *my* hands? But I did it, lady cop. I stole Mr. Pincus's gun, and I shot that mother. He was begging for his life, and I didn't care because of what he did to my girl, Flora."

A woman stepped forward, or maybe it was a man dressed as a woman, I couldn't be sure. Said her name was Mercy.

"That bastard turned my little sister into a whore. He pumped her full of meth and she died on the street. Right over there. I had to kill that fucker, you see? I'm already certified as crazy—so I wasn't worried about no jury."

"Mercy! Shut up. Don't admit to nothing. I did it," said a man who looked like a young prizefighter.

His nose was smashed to one side, and he had the look of a person whose brain had been rattled against his skull too many times.

"I shot Bagman six times with the lawyer's gun. *Bam-bam, bam-bam, bam-bam,* and when Bagman dropped, I kicked him. I hit him with these," he said, shaking his fists. "I terminated that piece of crap for what he did to our neighborhood."

A familiar blond-haired girl, gaunt-faced, pretty as a cheerleader on meth, came forward.

"My father, my uncle Al, they're not guilty of anything but trying to save me," said Sammy. "I said I loved Bagman, but that was a lie. After I killed him, we *all* lied so the police wouldn't suspect any of us. But he was a tyrant. He enslaved me. That's why I took my father's gun—"

It was clear to me now, clear as glass. This chaos had been *organized.* Had the Pincus brothers planned this since the day they—or someone—killed Bagman Jesus?

Cruisers and police vans, all with sirens whooping, flew up Fifth Street and braked on the sidewalk, scattering the crowd. Cops jumped out, swinging their bats, shoving the crowd back.

"Take these two in," I said to the cops standing closest to me. I handed the Pincus brothers over, and as they were escorted to the van, the crowd surged forward again.

Neil Pincus turned his head as the officer was folding him into the back of the van. He said, "One second, Officer. Sergeant Boxer?" he shouted. "Don't you see? Either *all* of us did it or none of us did.

"And even if you get anyone to trial, you'll never get a conviction. Rodney Booker's killer is a frickin' *hero*."

Chapter 110

WITH THE HELP of the mob squad, Conklin and I flattened six people against the wall and frisked them. We made sure we had their names, then we had them loaded into cars and vans so they could come to the Hall for questioning.

I wanted to hear all eight of them tell us the story of killing Bagman, how they did it, and why.

I was behind the wheel, still sweating as Conklin and I drove back to the Hall of Justice. That mob scene had shot my heart rate into the stratosphere, and it was still well above my normal sixty-eight beats per minute. But I was happy. Make that *exhilarated*.

I glanced into the rearview mirror and saw Franklin Morris and "Mercy" behind the grille at my back, chatting as if we were driving them to lunch.

Why should they worry?

The Pincus brothers might be disbarred for confessing to

homicide, but someone else would step in to defend this group of conspirators, one or all of whom were guilty of Rodney Booker's murder. But I thought Neil Pincus's prediction was right.

If these people stuck to their stories, no jury would convict. Eight confessions were eight times worse than one, each contradicting the other, so reasonable doubt would rule. I wondered if there'd even be a trial.

I said to Conklin, "Cindy's going to get a movie deal out of this one. 'From folk hero to mass killer, a drug dealer is brought down by a conspiracy of street vigilantes.' You should call her."

"No, you do it. I don't want to mess with the chain of command."

I smiled, said, "Okay. After we take care of business, I'll give her the exclusive."

I was quiet after that.

As I turned the car onto Bryant Street, I thought about Bagman Jesus, a charming and handsome lowlife who'd sold crack to kids, turned girls into meth addicts, a man who had commissioned a mobile meth lab that had blown up, killing ten people, most of them ordinary citizens on their way to work.

I don't condone street justice.

If we could nail Booker's killer, we would. But maybe this time, law enforcement would bow to a different kind of law. Bagman Jesus, the street saint who wasn't, had been taken out faster and smarter than we could have done it—and without giving him the possibility of parole.

8th Confession

It was indisputable that our city was better off now that he was gone.

"Whatcha thinking, Lindsay?" Conklin asked me.

I turned to look at him, saw that he, too, was feeling fine. I said, "I was thinking that in a funny way, this is a good day to be a cop."

Epilogue

HAPPY AT LAST

Chapter 111

AS JOE PILOTED his nice black Mercedes S-Class, I relaxed in the seat beside him. It was great to look to my left and see his gorgeous face, his strong hands on the wheel. Every time he caught me looking at him, he turned to look at *me.*

We grinned at each other like high-school kids with a first crush. "Keep your eyes on the road, buster," I said to him.

"I want to take that dress off you," he said.

"I just put it on!"

"I remember," he said, leering. "Now what was it you were telling me?"

"Yuki."

"Right. Yuki's going away for a few weeks."

"She *was* going away for a few weeks, then Parisi called her into his office and said, 'I've got a case for you, Ms. Castellano. I think there could be a promotion in it. And a raise.'"

Joe turned the wheel, and we swept into the drive leading to the Convent of the Sacred Heart in Pacific Heights, an insanely beautiful and kind of creepy old mansion where Joe's friend the mayor was holding a big fund-raiser for inner-city children.

It was an A-list event, and Joe was high on that list because he was a government contractor, the former deputy director of Homeland Security, and a specialist in Middle Eastern affairs.

Valet parkers in Flying Dutchman outfits stepped out of the shadows, and spotlights out front transformed the school into an elegant nightspot. Guests wearing Prada-everything emerged from their expensive cars, and Joe got out of ours.

He handed the keys to a valet, then came around and opened the door for me. I took his arm.

"I want to hear the rest of the story," he said.

We headed toward the arched stone entrance. I was conscious of being dressed up for a change: wearing high-heeled shoes, putting my hair up, zipping into a long, tight red dress, and it felt good knowing that if ever a gown was made for a five-foot-ten-inch blonde, I was wearing it. And if ever there was a good-looking man in a tuxedo, I was on his arm.

"Oh. So Parisi says to Yuki, 'I'm giving you the Rodney Booker case. Congratulations.' He handed her a *bomb*, Joe. Eight defendants, no witnesses, an unmatchable possible murder weapon, and an unsympathetic victim. She's going to work on this for a year, and then she's going to get killed in court."

"Poor frickin' Yuki."

"One day she's going to catch a break. Maybe. I hope."

8th Confession

We stepped over the threshold into a cocktail party in high gear. Beautiful people were engaged in avid conversation, laughing, their voices echoing in the magnificent Reception Room with its high, coffered ceilings designed to look like the Vatican—sixteenth-century Italian High Renaissance.

A waiter came by with a tray of champagne flutes, and Joe and I each took one.

After a sip, Joe set his glass down on a nearby table, reached inside his pocket, and took out a black velvet box I'd seen many times before. He had presented it to me twice, and although I'd never fully accepted it, I'd kept it safe through fire and through moving to Joe's, and every once in a while I'd opened the box, just to see where I stood in my own mind.

And now Joe was opening that black clamshell case again and holding it so that the five diamonds in the platinum setting twinkled like a crystal chandelier.

I looked up at him, thinking he didn't need the trappings. I would love him in a spangled spandex bodysuit. I smiled.

"I have this sense of déjà vu," he said.

My butterflies did cartwheels, but I stood still, holding the gaze of my blue-eyed hunka man.

"Do I have to go back to Queens and live with my mother? Or will you marry me, Lindsay? Will you be my wife?"

As people swirled around us, a band started to play a kind of corny but very sentimental big-band tune from the '40s. It was utterly perfect.

I put down my glass and held out my hand.

"Is that a yes?" Joe said. "Or are you asking me to dance?"

"Both. It's a definite double yes."

Joe's face buckled with emotion. He said, "I love you, Blondie." He wiggled the ring onto my finger and kissed me. I felt the power of our kiss, the way it sealed this perfect moment and blessed our future together.

I put my arms around Joe's neck, and he held me tight. As we swayed to Glenn Miller's "Moonlight Serenade," Joe's voice was soft in my ear: "You're not changing your mind. We're getting married."

"Yes, Joe, we will. I love you completely. I truly do."

Chapter 112

NORMA JOHNSON WAS resting in her maximum-security cell in the Central California Women's Facility. The cell was eight by eight feet of beige-painted metal containing two narrow pallets, one bunk over the other, a sink, a stainless-steel toilet, and unless you counted the cell mate snoring overhead, that was all.

Her cell mate was Bernadette Radke, old enough to be her mother, a murderer like she was but nowhere near as smart or as cool. Bernie had killed her husband by running him down with a pickup truck, and then, as she was "bookin' outta there," she ran a red light and killed three more people. One of them was an eight-year-old kid.

Despite her body count, Bernadette was a lightweight.

She had done no planning, had no finesse. She was just a borderline mentally challenged rage freak, but that was fine with Pet Girl because Bernie was her virtual slave.

Everyone was.

Norma Johnson wasn't Pet Girl anymore.

She had no duties, no responsibilities, and every guard in the place, every trustee, had to take care of *her.* Her food was prepared. Her blue uniform was washed. Her sheets were folded. Her mail was delivered, and guess what? There was a lot of mail. From fans. From magazines. From Hollywood.

She was a celebrity now.

Everyone wanted to know her, to talk to her. They were both afraid of and in awe of her.

And she felt like the homecoming queen in this place. For the first time in her life, she thought she was where she belonged.

Norma lay on her pallet, looked up at the underside of the bunk above her, projected her whole life onto that blank screen. She turned over the many moments that had made her who she was, examined the greatest ones, and told her own story to herself.

She especially reviewed the one story she'd never told anyone: about the time her daddy had brought her to his house on Nob Hill when no one was there. He'd shown her the snakes he kept in his private room, shown her how he handled them, and told her how they could be used to kill.

She remembered how much she loved him then. How she worshipped him. But there was something else, too. *The question.* Why couldn't he fully acknowledge her?

Her mom was usually right downstairs, running the vacuum in the living room. Why couldn't Daddy kick out his wife? Why couldn't he make Norma and her mom his real family, since he loved them both so much?

8th Confession

And then something happened.

His wife came in and saw Norma and her father together, and she'd gotten enraged.

"No, Chris. Not *here*. I told you. *Never* bring that girl into my house."

And her daddy had said, "Yes, dear. Sorry, dear."

And Norma had been holding the snake in her hand, its jaws held open at the hinge by her thumb and forefinger, just like Daddy had taught her.

But at that moment, there was panic in his face. He said, "I've got to get you out of here." Like she was trash. Not flesh and blood. Not his daughter. Not the descendant of a senator's daughter and the first citizen of California.

She'd ducked under his arm, run past "the witch" and down the hallway to the master-bedroom suite. And there, where they slept together, she'd slipped the krait under the covers of the bed where it was dark and snug, just what that snake would love. And she thought she was leaving the krait so that his *wife* would die—but she knew that her daddy slept in that bed, too.

He found her in the master bathroom. He banged on the door.

"Hurry up!" he'd shouted.

It was the last thing he'd said to her. She came out of the bathroom and ran out of the house and sat for hours on the curb.

She'd cried when he died.

And everything changed after that. But she wasn't sorry. She'd stood up for herself, and now life was good again. All of her needs were being met. And she was the baddest, most important citizen in this place. She was respected here. She was respected.

"You okay in there, Norma?" the guard asked, coming to let Norma and Bernie out for their hour in the yard, keys clanging, making that comforting sound.

"I'm just fine," said Norma Johnson, giving the guard a rare smile. "Never better."

For a sneak preview of James Patterson's terrifying new thriller, *Swimsuit*, available from Century June 2009, read on . . .

Chapter 1

KIM MCDANIELS WAS barefooted, wearing a blue-and-white striped Juicy Couture mini-dress when she was awoken by a thump against her hip, a *bruising* thump. She opened her eyes in the blackness, questions breaking the surface of her mind.

Where was she? What the hell was going on?

She wrestled with the blanket draped over her head, finally got her face free, realized a couple of new things. Her hands and feet were *bound*. And she was in some kind of cramped compartment.

Another thump jolted her and Kim yelled this time, *'Hey!'*

Her shout went nowhere, muffled by the confined space, the vibration of an engine. She realized she was inside the trunk of a car. But that made no freaking sense! She told herself to *wake up*!

But she *was* awake, feeling the bumps for real and so she fought, twisting her wrists against a knotted nylon rope that didn't give. She rolled onto her back, tucking her knees to her chest, then *bam*! She kicked up at the lid of the trunk, not budging the lid a fraction of an inch.

She did it again, again, *again*, and now pain was shooting from her soles to her hips but she was still locked up and now she was hurting. Panic seized her and shook her hard.

She was *caught*. She was *trapped*. She didn't know how this had happened or why, but she wasn't dead and she wasn't injured. So, she *would* get away.

Using her bound hands as a claw, Kim felt around the compartment for a tool box, a jack or a crowbar, but she found nothing and the air was getting thin and foul as she panted alone in the dark.

Why was she here?

Kim searched for her last memory, but her mind was sluggish, as if a blanket had been thrown over her brain, too. She could only guess that she'd been drugged. Someone had slipped her a roofie, but who? When?

'*Hellllllpppp! Let me out!*' she yelled, kicking out at the trunk lid, banging her head against a hard metal ridge, her eyes filling with tears, getting mad now on top of being scared out of her mind.

Through her tears, Kim saw a glowing five-inch long bar just above her. It had to be the interior trunk release lever, and she whispered, '*Thank you, God.*'

Chapter 2

KIM'S CLAW-HANDS trembled as she reached up, hooked her fingertips over the lever and pulled down. The bar moved – too easily – and it didn't pop the lid.

She tried again, pulling repeatedly, frantically working against her certain knowledge that the release bar had been disabled, that the cable had been cut – when Kim felt the car wheels leave the asphalt. The ride smoothed out, and that made her think the car was maybe rolling over sand.

Was it going into the ocean?

Was she going to drown in this trunk?

She screamed again, a loud wordless shriek of terror that turned into a gibbering prayer, *Dear God let me out of this alive and I promise you* – and when her scream ran out, she heard music coming from behind her head. It was a female vocalist, something bluesy, a song she didn't know.

Who was driving the car? Who had done this to her? For what possible reason?

And now her mind was clearing, running back, flipping through the images of the past hours. She started to remember. She'd been up at three. Make-up at four. On the beach at five. She and Julia and Darla and Monique and that other gorgeous, but weird, girl Ayla. Gils, the photographer, had been drinking coffee with the crew, and men had been hanging around the edges of the shoot, towel boys and early morning joggers agog at the girls in the little bikinis, at the wonder of stumbling on a Sporting Life Swimsuit shoot right *there*.

Kim pictured the moments, posing with Julia, Gils saying, '*Less smile, Julia. That's great. Beautiful, Kim, beautiful, that's the girl. Eyes to me. That's perfect.*'

She remembered that the phone calls had come after that, during breakfast and throughout the whole day.

Ten freaking calls until she turned off her phone.

Douglas had been calling her, paging her, stalking her, driving her crazy. It was Doug!

And she thought about earlier that night, after dinner, how she'd been in the hotel bar with the art director, Del Swann, his job to oversee the shoot, be her chaperone afterwards and Del had gone to the men's room and somehow he and Gils, both of them gay as birds, disappeared.

And she remembered that Julia was talking with a guy at the bar and she'd *tried* to get Julia's attention but she wouldn't make eye contact – so, Kim had gone for a walk on the beach . . . *And that was all she remembered.*

Going out to the beach, her cell phone clipped to her belt in the 'off' position. And now she was thinking that Doug had flipped out. Rage-aholic that he was. Stalker that he'd become. Maybe he'd paid someone to put something into her drink.

She was getting it together now. Brain working fine.

She shouted, *'Douglas? Dougie?'*

And then, as though God Himself had finally heard her calling, *a cell phone rang inside the trunk.*

Chapter 3

KIM HELD HER breath and listened.

A phone rang, *but it wasn't her ringtone*. This was a low-pitched burr, not four bars of Weezer's 'Beverly Hills', but, anyway, if it was like most phones, it was programmed to send calls to voicemail after three rings.

She couldn't let that happen!

Where was the damned phone?

She fumbled with the blanket, ropes chafing her wrists. She reached down, pawed at the flooring, felt the lump under a flap of carpet near the edge, bumped it farther away with her clumsy . . . *oh no!*

The second ring ended, the third ring was starting and her frenzy was sending her heart rate out of control when she grasped the phone, a thick, old-fashioned thing, clutched it with her shaking fingers, sweat slicking her wrists.

Swimsuit

She saw the caller ID number, but there was no name, and she didn't recognize the number.

But, it didn't matter *who* it was. Anyone would do.

Kim pushed the "send" button, pressed the earpiece to her ear, called out, hoarsely, 'Hello? *Hello? Who's there?*'

But instead of an answer, Kim heard singing, this time Whitney Houston, 'I'll al-ways love you-ou-ou' coming from the car stereo only louder and more clearly.

He was calling her from the front seat of the car! She shouted over Whitney's voice, 'Dougie? Dougie, what the hell? *Answer me.*'

But he didn't answer and Kim was quaking there in the cramped trunk, tied up like a chicken, sweating like a pig, Whitney's voice seeming to taunt her.

'Doug! What do you think you're doing?'

And then she knew. He was showing her what it was like to be ignored, teaching her a lesson, but *he wouldn't win.* They were on an island, right? How far could they go?

So, Kim used her anger to fuel the brain that had gotten her into Columbia pre-med, thinking now about how to turn Doug around. She'd have to play him, say how sorry she was, and explain sweetly that he had to understand *it wasn't her fault.* She tried it out in her mind.

See, Dougie, I'm not allowed to take calls. My contract strictly forbids me to tell anyone where we're shooting. I could get fired. You understand, don't you?

She'd make him see that even though they'd broken up, that even though he was *crazy* for what he was doing to her, *criminal* for God's sake, she was still his darling.

But – and this was her plan, once he gave her an opportunity, she'd knee him in the balls or kick in his knee caps. She knew enough judo to disable him – as big as he was. Then, she'd run for her life. And then the cops would bury him!

'Dougie?' she yelled into the phone. 'Will you please answer me? Please. This really isn't funny.'

Suddenly the music volume went down.

Once again, she held her breath in the dark and listened over the pulse booming in her ears. And this time, a voice spoke to her, a *man's voice* and it was warm, almost loving.

'Actually, Kim, it *is* kind of funny, and it's kind of wonderfully romantic, too.'

Kim didn't recognize the voice.

Because, it wasn't Doug.

We support

I'm proud to support the National Literacy Trust, an independent charity that changes lives through literacy.

Did you know that millions of people in the UK struggle to read and write? This means children are less likely to succeed at school and less likely to develop into confident and happy teenagers. Literacy difficulties will limit their opportunities throughout adult life.

The National Literacy Trust passionately believes that everyone has a right to the reading, writing, speaking and listening skills they need to fulfil their own and, ultimately, the nation's potential.

My own son didn't used to enjoy reading which was why I started writing children's books – reading for pleasure is an essential way to encourage children to pick up a book. The National Literacy Trust is dedicated to delivering exciting initiatives to encourage people to read and to help raise literacy levels. To find out more about the great work that they do visit their website at www.literacytrust.org.uk.

James Patterson